To Hal
with best
wishes

TIANANMEN FLIGHT
a novel

TIANANMEN FLIGHT
a novel

PATRICK S. NICHOLSON

mosaic press

Canadian Cataloguing in Publication Data

Nicholson, Patrick S.
Tiananmen Flight

A Novel
ISBN 0-88962-760-6

1. China - History - Tiananmen Square Incident, 1989 - Fiction. I. Title.

PS8577.I245T52 2000   C813'.6   C00-932966-8
PR9199.3.N495T52 2000

No part of this book may be reproduced or transmitted in any form, by any means, electronic or mechanical, including photocopying and recording, information storage and retrieval systems, without permission in writing from the publisher, except by a reviewer who may quote brief passages in a review.

Published by Mosaic Press, offices and warehouse at 1252 Speers Road, Units 1 and 2, Oakville, Ontario, L6L 5N9, Canada and Mosaic Press, PMB 145, 4500 Witmer Industrial Estates, Niagara Falls, NY, 14305-1386, U.S.A.

Mosaic Press acknowledges the assistance of the Canada Council and the Department of Canadian Heritage, Government of Canada, for their support of our publishing programme.

Copyright © 2001 Patrick S. Nicholson
ISBN 0-88962-760-6

MOSAIC PRESS, in Canada:
1252 Speers Road, Units 1 & 2,
Oakville, Ontario
L6L 5N9
Phone/Fax: 905-825-2130
mosaicpress@on.aibn.com

MOSAIC PRESS, in U.S.A.:
4500 Witmer Industrial Estates
PMB 145, Niagara Falls, NY
14305-1386
Phone/Fax: 1-800-387-8992
mosaicpress@on.aibn.com

Le Conseil des Arts   The Canada Council
du Canada   for the Arts

Dedication

To Ena
My life's love.

Acknowledgements

I must acknowledge those friends who struggled with earlier versions of this book; George and Teller Weatherly, Brian Ives and my daughter Natasha. Also Francis Hanna who read it twice and suggested significant "tightening", Howard Aster who skewered cliches and adverbs, and Keith Garebian who streamlined it for speed. Thank you all!

Then there is my wife, Ena, whom I owe a special debt of gratitude. She read it uncountable times until it finally passed muster. Gramercy!

MUCH DESCRIBED, HAPPENED.

Names have been changed ...

Prologue

Saturday 3 June 1989.
At dawn this morning, Beijing looked like a war zone...
-CBC News Report

Saturday 3 June 1989, 12:30 p.m.

The tank track churned, the blue tent crumpled. Metal squealed, people screamed, bloody fists beat–impotent, tight in terror. Explosions shook, bullets zinged, yellow tongued black smoke billowed; but the girl ran straight, leaping, stumbling, arms forward, hands shaking, muttering, praying, panting, sliding on slippy crimson, running–running to the place, to the place she had left him, the place now ploughed flat, the place of death, blow-flies spinning, settling, arguing.

She crumples to the soggy, red-toothed track of blue tatters and, fist in mouth, knuckling eyes, reaches for the severed hand. The thumb twitches! She pulls back with a choke as though scalded, then, trembling and sniveling she reaches again, picks it up as though fragile, squeezing the tight fingers gripping her gold Celtic-cross, necklace dripping a slow ooze of blood. She holds it gently to her, rocking, sobbing, shirt sticky, hair wild, face smudged.

"I will make you famous," he had told her. "Singular among Chinese women, revered, *the* symbol, *the* symbol of the movement, always recognized, immortal."

Head back, eyes tight, heart-welling to breaking, she is dragged, hands tearing his hand from her hands, cross chain ripping her thumb but staying. The tanks are returning, they are saying. You must not stay; they are looking for *you*–especially you. You must leave Beijing. You must change, change so even he would not recognize you.

I
HONG-KONG TO BEIJING

MONDAY 23 OCTOBER 1989

The lights of the Hong Kong flight came on. On their way to Tiananmen China. The rush in Peter Daley's stomach dissolved to unease. Something with faint menace. Was it, as Ane thought, too soon to visit China? "Daley-Double" she called him: the objective scientist blinkered when he didn't want to see. No, after all the massacre was three months ago. Plenty of time.

The engines hummed. Funny how one checks, he mused, as if anything could be done.

He ran his fingers round his too-tight ascot.

Blankets draped the aisles and pillows pushed from underseats. Windows streamed red sun.

While Ane was dozing, he riffled the arrangements, replaying the conversation with colleague, Choi, and the correspondence with Ny, his Research Associate who had returned to Beijing.

Choi was in charge of the World Bank program of student exchange between Minster University and the Beijing University of Arts and Sciences. Two months ago Daley had run into him in the corridor – a happy, rotund Chinaman, who claimed he was not fat, just six inches too short.

Choi had invited him to his office and he had followed. Choi's black hair was salt sprinkled but his happy face unwrinkled. His office was chaotic. Daley had moved a pile of envelopes, wondering how Choi ever found anything. Rumour had it, he'd decided to clean up and discovered an unopened letter from the sixties! Daley had never forgotten Choi's immediate visit when Lisa, their little one, had died.

As he sat down, Choi had said: "Understand you go Japan, ya."

"Hakone...October. Seventh International SSI...er...Solid State Ionics Conference, batteries, probes and things."

"I need a favour. Supposed go Beijing to interview graduate students for Minster, ya, but since Tiananamen, I not welcome."

He had located a pack of cigarettes and lit one, blowing a cloud of smoke above him. "You could go on diplomatic visa. Easy for you. You have no connection with Chinese demonstrators. You, 'round eyes,' they pleased you visit. Need goodwill. Not stop you travel anywhere. Anywhere."

"Round eyes?"

"Ya. Westerners, 'round eyes,' - *kwailo*."

"Suppose I could visit Ny. Been at me ever since he went back."

"How well you know him?"

"He was my Postdoc."

"Important to see *good* students, ya. Spend too much time with poor ones. Never be anything but B-students. Ya!"

"We *are* doctors Choi. Look after the sick!"

Choi had laughed, ash missing the ashtray. "Money no problem...ya. There are funds to pay fare to Beijing. Chinese then take expenses ya."

"Sounds reasonable."

"We lose money if not use. Ya ."

"Diplomatic visas.I'm no diplomat."

Choi had leaned forward and touched Daley's sleeve. "Very important. All roads out of Beijing, 'Red Roads.' Search everything for 'democrats.' You talk to *no* strangers, no people not know. They are clever - have to be - I sorry but too dangerous for you without diplomatic visas."

"How can I recognize them?"

"Your host, Ny. You trust him?"

"Suppose so."

"Good! Then no problem. You distinguished scientist, they like you visit - distinguished foreigners welcome, very welcome. All people in your party protected, ya. Be careful you know them. Car will be flagged."

"Say again?"

"University car with special flag."

Choi had combed his whole hand through his hair. "Must warn you. University President I knew, Dong Lin, injured in demonstrations, leg broken. Demoted...ya. Hates new President. He arsehole, new President. 'Party man'. Don't like. Hundred percent politician, know nothing of academia. Not like predecessor. Watch for new President."

There had been a little silence. The clatter of autumn rain washing Choi's windows had filled their space.

"Protocol require he treat you well. He will be genial host but be wary. Grapevine say Dong Lin now Vice President, try discredit him. Steer clear, ya!"

"How much does the President have to do with the program?"

"Prestige! Backfire since troubles. Students in Canada not return China. Don't think he bother you though, don't worry."

He had decided to go, as much for Choi as for the opportunity to see China. Ane would be thrilled but wouldn't believe it – him going somewhere dangerous! He'd surprise her.

He remembered Choi's intensity. Odd, he never showed emotion, not even at their loss of Lisa.

So he had agreed to go, but nothing so far! He had contacted Ny who was surprised but pleased and arranged the interviews and a series of visits and lectures. He would meet them in Beijing.

The lecture slides were prepared. He was to visit a titanium factory in the mountains. Knew nothing about titanium. He was a ceramist, not a metallurgist.

Ane broke in, elbowing him. "You still got that coin, the looney?"

"Bit ahead aren't you? Landing back in Toronto and getting a luggage cart."

"Best be prepared. We may have to leave quickly. Do you really think it's safe, China? It's only a few months since they killed those students in that square."

"Tiananmen. Don't worry. Choi said it's okay as long as we have dipo visas. Besides I'm sure they will have caught most of 'em. I mean, fancy flaunting a big 'Statue of Liberty.'"

"Wasn't called that was it, that statue?"

"Don't remember but she certainly looked like the one in New York. Bloody red rag to a bull."

She shook her head. "I have a bad feeling."

"A professor visiting a few students, giving a few talks? Totally non-political. No worries. Besides, you know I'd run a mile from danger. Promise you, we're out if things go queer."

He studied her as she leafed through the flight magazine. Looks good: suede suits her. Even with sleep and yesterday's makeup, her complexion is fresh, clear, English at its best. As she tucked in her chin to straighten her blouse bib, there was no sign of doubling.

The smell of fresh coffee filled the cabin.

"See if you can get some coffee love," he asked, pulling himself up and standing into the aisle.

The tiny toilet smelled of disinfectant and cologne. He held the handle with one hand and aimed with the other.

The face in the mirror was tired. Age lines were deep but it was still handsome. His hair was full and wavy though its dark brown was helped these days by Ane's color conditioner. Funny it doesn't work on my beard.

Blue eyes still young, but the pouches are getting larger. Age made his face more interesting–like detailing a smooth statue. He hated getting old. Was he really the "snap-crackle-pop" daughter Claire had christened him for unsociable flatulence – all mouth and trousers?

He undid the ascot, smirking as he felt the pantyliner conscripted to hold the silk stretched on his neck. Had worn ascots since his neck thickened beyond his shirt collars. Problem was it thinned to a string on his neck. One night watching a serious woman on TV explaining "Always," a penny had dropped. Bloody made for it.

He grinned at the mirror.

He sipped the welcome coffee. Children were running the aisles again and piling the toilets. A middle-aged woman splashed on too much cologne and the cabin filled with the scent of flowers. In the aisle an old Japanese stood, hands on opposite seats, swinging one leg forward then back, then the other and back, slowly, purposefully, as he'd probably done every day since these skies were empty.

Ane studied the man she'd lived with for twenty-four years, softly laying a hand on his arm, giving it a squeeze then looking back at the clouds smudging the wings.

Like rolling in sheepskin, she sighed. She loved clouds, could see so many things in them: mountains bathed with distance, criss-crossed ski hills, wisps of fine gray hair.

Her Peter had an abhorrence for bad news.

He was born in Kingston-on-Thames, London, 1936 and moved to Ireland for the war. His father, a tactless cockney with a heart of gold, had stayed in Yorkshire at Thorpe Arch, to design armaments. They lived in County Tipperary, five miles from Tipperary town, in the small gate-house lodge of Kingswell House. On a clear day the church steeples and houses of Tipperary could be seen against the Tipperary hills and Galtee mountains.

A childhood of imagination in Grandad Jerry's labyrinths of hedges, arches and mazes – endless hideaways for cowboys, crusaders and musketeers. Above the gardens in the sand and pebbles, he had constructed a lilliputian town of cottages, shops and churches. He tracked cars of wood pieces Jerry had carved with scarred fingers and Mick McQuaid-plug knife. No toys in wartime, just make-do's and imagination.

Sometimes he talked of the burning turf, kerosene lamps, water bucketted from the well, milk twice daily from a farm, Sambo the cat sleeping under his chin, and Vicky the terrier whose discipline he'd ruined by play. No radio, only books, thoughts, and wild Irish stories.

Trouble is, sometimes he can't see now for then.

The family left Ireland in 1946 for Boston Spa near Thorpe Arch, Yorkshire. School had been nuns at St Edwards, Clifford, a small village a mile walk away and Jesuits at St. Michaels College, Leeds, a daily bus ride of fifteen miles.

He obtained a respectable degree in Ceramics from Leeds University in 1963, then a Fulbright Scholarship took him away from her to the sunshine of the University of California, Berkeley, across the bay from San Francisco. She joined him a year later and they married early 1965 in the Sierra mountains at Placerville, one hundred and twenty miles from the Bay Area.

Doctorate studies finished, he was advised by a friend: "Be a big fish in a little pond!"

So they came to Canada in 1969 to live on Hamilton Drive with their children, Edward, Beth, and Claire.

Clouds now enveloped the aircraft like smoke. They were losing height.

She dipped a biscuit in her coffee. "Shame about Beth."

He laughed. "Don't think I've ever seen her so mad."

"Suppose we did rush her. But fancy coming home after a year in England with a *boyfriend* in tow."

"Yes, but there was no need to throw a tantrum. All you wanted was the brown bag you'd lent her. Turned it out on the kitchen floor, then threw it at you. Still can't control her temper, can she?"

"I'd hoped London would cure her but she did relented when you agreed to bring her a Chinese seal set. "

The bag traveled everywhere with them. It had zipped pockets and was bottomless.

There was a small silence, then she remembered something. "Ny's daughter's coming to Bojai with us."

"Never knew he had a daughter. All that time in Canada and he never mentioned her."

"Chinese seem to have families they've not seen for years. Accept it as part of life."

"Perhaps he's secretive for good reason! Look what happened in June and it's only October." He stopped but it was too late.

"Look, I'm sorry to go on, but I still think it's too early, to visit China, I mean. We can see Hong Kong, then go home."

The floor rumbled and the wing pushed flaps into the skeins of cloud. The Captain drawled the local time and weather. Daley looked at his watch–7 a.m.– to 7 p.m. local time, same day, no need to adjust.

He squeezed her arm. "Look we'll be okay, really. Always makes me nervous that. Doesn't it you?" He nodded at the outside. "Seeing light through."

"Stop changing the subject. What?"

"The wings."

She looked but ignored the wings. "Suppose you're right. We do have visas. Can I see them? I mean they are so very important."

He passed them to her. "Stamp. Hell - isn't it?" she giggled, "specially this big pink one. See." She held the big pink circle with Chinese written round a sort of altar with stars above.

"Impressive. Maybe something special that one. Done second, anyway. See, it covers the edge of the blue one."

"Has subtitles. 'Good for one entry.' 'Valid until November fifth'."

She mumbled the rhyme about days in the month. "All the rest have thirty- one. That's only fourteen days, Peter. Bit fine, isn't it?"

"It's enough. Greg says we'll be glad to get out by then."

She gave him back the passports and he pocketed them, definitely less comfortable than his mien suggested.

The Hong Kong landing was alarming. Mountains appeared suddenly at equal elevation, skyscrapers littering their base as the wings whipped over ships so low Daley could read their numbers. Towers closed in giving way to dingy concrete apartments covered in washing and muddled antenna as the airplane slipped to the right and the flight-path canyon narrowed. The undercarriage groaned down as they slipped along sloping roofs.

Suddenly gantries grew like corn on either side. Now the plane was hurtling a freeway like a giant insect pursuing fleeing cars. Kerosene filled the air as the wheels touched down. Daley took Ane's hand and grinned.

"Welcome to Hong Kong," said the tannoy.

The taxi stopped and started through the evening traffic.

They passed clusters of glistening glass towers bathed orange in the tired sun, muddled among wartime-gray buildings with small iron-rail balconies hung with everything from creepers to overalls like an erupting rash.

"Peter, the luggage, it's heavy, 'specially the green suitcase. We ought to give the driver a tip."

"You insisted on bringing that bloody Indian dress of Beth's. Hell, we've got enough clothes to visit for a month!"

"Don't forget, Choi said there'd be a banquet. Well, that dress is Canadian."

"So?"

"So I want to wear a Canadian dress. Besides, I like it!" There was an irritable pause. "Anyway, it doesn't weigh anything like your transparencies and stuff. That's what's heavy, not my clothes. Why d'you need such a big magnifier anyway?"

"To see the slides. It's why we're invited to China in the first place."

He linked his arm through hers. "It's a long way round, I suppose, flying through Hong Kong but I'm looking forward to seeing the place, aren't you?"

"We're only seeing it because Greg recommended it. He insisted we stay at the Regent on the way home and that's why we're making the round trip."

The Ramada facade was narrow and tiled. Daley struggled up it with the green case wobbling on tiny wheels. He shivered.

The chill of oncoming night was canceling the warmth of the taxi.

As swishing doors hushed the evening traffic, they clicked to reception.

"Got your Gestapo boots on haven't you?"

She hated them for being too exhibitionistic.

The clock above the desk said his watch was ten minutes fast: 8:15. He leaned on the counter, relieved. Good night's sleep then.

He watched the busy receptionist, full blouse and smile that closed her eyes. She confirmed their reservations and passed him the key.

The room was furnished in red mahogany with lights that worked when the key tab was inserted in a slot. There were two single beds – Japanese style. Daley opened the curtains to admit the waning sun, as Ane put clothes in drawers and hangers.

He was watching a rickshaw full of sailors struggling in the street when she yelped.

"God! Look what we've done! We've got Beth's stuff, driving license, credit cards. Everything!"

"Serves her right! Threw the bag at us, remember. She'll just have to do without them."

He thumbed through his daughter's life: a photograph of a blond boyfriend, a book of meal tickets for Ryerson College, a card offering ten percent off photographic supplies. "Don't worry. Most of this she can do without, temporarily anyway, even her passport." He waved the slim blue book at her. "Shame about her other ID's though. She was looking forward to goin' to the Gown and Gavel, now she's nineteen."

"Passport's important though, isn't it? She can't replace that, can she?"

"Doesn't need it. We'll be back before she goes anywhere."

"I worry about these." She held up the book of meal tickets. "She won't eat, you know."

He laughed. "Don't worry about Beth, she'll not starve." He linked his arm through hers. "Remember how she eats us out of house and home after saying she's not hungry. Just put them back and forget 'em."

"The passport too? Don't you think you should put it with ours?"

"No. Don't want to pull out three passports, do I, 'specially where we are going."

"Well, put it in your other pocket."

"Don't have one. Harris tweed's old, only one inside pocket. Hey, let's celebrate. Go out to eat. Hell, we've not been in Hong Kong before."

She did not look up. "I'm so tired. Don't think I could stay awake."

"Lets see. There may be somewhere nice, close."

He went to the bedside table, slid open the small drawer and lifted out the telephone directory. A magazine fell to the floor. *Time*.

He leafed the directory. "No yellow pages."

"Don't worry. Look what I've found." She passed him the small bottle of dinner-wine secreted on the aircraft. "We have two, so let's have them with some cheese and crackers. It's been such a tiring day."

Beaumes de Venise, Cote de Rhone Villages, 1986. He decanted the red liquid into the tooth glasses she brought from the bathroom. "Good. Couldn't face it early morning, could you?"

She shook her head and they sat on the edge of the bed crunching crackers and sipping wine.

"Hard to find him these days, isn't it." They were lying in bed, showered, warm with weariness.

She chuckled. "That's trouble - 'hardness.' Well, lack of it, anyway."

He laughed and instructed the tiny head: "Wake up, Jim. It's yer birthday!" He slapped the limp appendage on his stomach with a hollow pop. She started to giggle. The more he slapped, the more she shook until her pleas to stop, please stop, broke them both down.

"He's downsized, like everything else these days!" she squeaked, stomach aching.

They hugged, giggles dying, then kissed, feeling each other's tears.

The sun through the curtain turned him to his more comfortable side. The city was waking. He lay listening to pigeons murmuring, occasional cars rumbling and tram cars rattling in the distance. Half sleeps punctuated by shooting pains finally flung him up with a jolt – Hong Kong, they were in Hong Kong!

Tuesday 24 October

He padded to the window and tipped his watch to the morning light, 6.30...6.30, Tuesday.

It had rained. The earthy smell of the washed tarmac of Chatham Road swept in as he opened the window.

He turned and considered Ane's bed-head. The comfortable warmth of thirty years suffused well-being. He enjoyed these moments before the day started–time when idle thought was not guiltily stolen. He sat in the wicker chair facing her, an unknown smile playing his lips.

Friends had persuaded him to attend the Leeds University Nurses Halloween Ball, 1962. Arriving early at the Downs' Nurses Home, he had seen her standing on a chair, hanging bunting in the ceiling of the Hall, laughing like champagne. She was slim, medium height, maybe one hundred twenty pounds. A full bosom and auburn hair back-combed to a chocolate ice cream swirl, emphasized her long neck. Her face, fresh and oval, was lit by cheeks curving like peach halves to large brown eyes and a small nose that wrinkled when she laughed. Her voice, as they danced, was as soft as a chanteuse whispering a strange song.

He looked out the window.

She had worn a full skirt of large green flowers, wide red belt, and a Scottish blouse with a lace bib.

He stirred and crossed his legs against the early chill.

Time had pendulated her bum, filled her waist and settled her bosom, but her neck was still delicate, and her eyes young. Thick hair to her shoulders.

He searched for a word. "Phlegmatic," he decided. Like all nurses, sensible and empathetic. A village girl given to wandering woods and sitting for hours watching animals, unnoticed. More familiar with flowers than people, she was full of the inner peace such beings enjoy.

He plugged in the Ramada hot water canteen and opened an envelope of Earl Grey – her favorite tea.

The day held great promise. The sun was chasing the morning clouds, as a jogging Chinese, punching this way and that, passed a yawning silk lady awaiting the first bus.

"Here's your tea," he said in her ear so as not to startle her.

"How about joining me?" she invited in a husky morning voice, fingers creeping towards his fly.

"Careful, I'll spill this on you."

"You don't play anymore. Used to like it when we played."

"It's a lovely day."

"Don't change the subject. Why don't we play?"

"We will. Just let me get this Chinese thing done. Besides I've got a funny feeling about the whole thing."

"I'll give you a funny feeling and you will know why."

He laughed, pulled back the full cup to save it spilling and kissed her.

"That was nice," she said wistfully. "We could at least do that more often."

He sat on the bed tying his shoes. She was in the bathroom singing through the shower. As he pulled tight, the lace broke – Damn! Now he'd have to carefully nip-hold one elusive end whilst easing the other back through the eyes. He eventually won, realizing his tongue had been out helping. He tied a keeper knot on each end as Ane emerged, toweling her hair, still singing.

"Can we find a market?" she bubbled. "There's sure to be one in a city that's all Chinatown!"

The clouds lined the backdrop of robin's egg blue behind the clutter of roofs. They walked under bamboo scaffolding .

"Does Beth know you've got this?" he asked, linking his arm through the long, black and white wool, square-check coat.

"She gave it to me. It's out of fashion now."

"God! These young girls. They spend all that money and in a month they don't care."

"They enjoy swapping clothes! We used to! You men've never understood."

The sea sachet of fresh fish mixed with pungent manure hit as they rounded a corner – Cross Street market, was waking up. Stalls of cardboard, wire, wood, and binder twine were being erected like unstable card houses. Everywhere was smell and everything was noise. A dog on a short lead, barked interminably at nothing.

As they threaded their way through the confusion, Ane grabbed Daley's arm. "Look at that!" she said, incredulous and horrified at the same time. He followed her outstretched arm to a line of whole pigs hanging bright crimson, upside down from a rail. Beside was a stall covered with an explosion of flowers like a grotesque wreath. A man was pruning thorns off long-stemmed roses.

"Let me buy you some flowers."

"I'd love some. Trouble is we'll have to leave 'em behind. Better you buy me some when we get to Beijing."

He chuckled – flowers in October, Beijing – following her down a *cul-de-sac*, past an old man, grey hair nearly gone, leather face creased around closed contented eyes, feet in a pail, unconcerned hens clucking around.

Shouts made them turn. A sneakered youth, trailing a bag like a relay baton, was fleeing a startled old lady who was slowly giving chase. A crowd joined her as if attached by invisible thread, and the youth, glancing over his shoulder, knocked into a smartly dressed Chinese examining a piece of red silk, then lost balance stepping in a basket of eggs. The hue and cry engulfed him.

"Let's not get involved." Ane said.

"Did you see that?"

"Stupid! Fancy trying to steal a bag in broad daylight."

"No, not that. The man in the dark suit."

"What about him?"

"Strange. Totally ignored the fracas. Not one of the crowd, too well dressed – shiny shoes, tie, suit."

"Look at yourself before you say that! Maybe like us he's looking for a bargain."

Daley shrugged. Everywhere the smell of food muddled with fish and barbeque smoke. Down a side-alley, mothers with children were picking and sorting piles of old clothes. A gush of water surged the gutter from an upended bucket, splashing his shoe. A pile of people milled around a window covered in lottery tickets.

The cacophony was increasing; the market was coming to life. A clock tower announced 7.30 through the warming air. They walked past live crabs being grabbed and sorted into tanks with no thought for the pinch of the audibly snapping claws. A sleepy cat emerged from a corrugated roof, stretched and blinked.

They strolled along Kimberly Road, quiet after the raucous market. Incense wisped from tiny shrines between shops, gentle reverence amid the closed nightclubs. An old man was collecting Coke cans in the dusty gutter.

As they turned onto Chatham, the Ramada in the distance, she linked her arm through and, swinging playfully, said quietly: "Peter, that man in a suit. Don't turn! The one you noticed. I think he's looking in a shop window across the street!"

"So what? I'm starvin'. Give my right arm for bacon and eggs."

"Blue suit, blue and red tie, dapper, carrying a piece of red cloth."

"So?"

"Saw him stop when we stopped. He just came round the corner and stopped dead. Think he's following us!"

"Don't be daft – us!"

"He is!" she said irritably.

As he held the Ramada door for her, the aroma of hot bread hit him and his hand slipped. The heavy door swung, catching her as she came through.

"That wasn't very nice!" She cut off suddenly as she was spun the other way by a tall Chinese, rushing, arm out to stiff the door. The impact dislodged a crunch of paper in his hand but he hurried on, long hair and coat flying, too-sweet aftershave billowing.

"How rude! What am I, a punching bag?"

He took her arm but she wrenched it away. "What you doin'? That hurts!"

"Sorry, love, letting go the door. I smelled bread and am so bloody hungry."

He nodded after the wild figure. "Forget him. Ignorant sod. Dropped this." He bent and picked up the paper.

She stamped her foot. "You don't seem to care! Almost knocked me flying and you don't care. All you can say is you smelled bread! Serves him bloody right too. Hope it's important!"

"Look, love, let's have some breakfast. You'll feel better."

They were shown to a two-seat table in the window. In the next booth, two schoolgirls, gray and blue hats on the table, gray and blue skirts pulled tight over knees, black hair braided with gray and blue ribbons, were helping each other over-apply crimson lipstick. One gave a tarty smile as he sat down.

Muffled traffic noises reached through the translucent window, blurring the Mozart muzak.

"Excuse me, Peter, must pay a visit. All that walking."

He followed her walk. Good for me, she is. Thank God I'd the sense to marry her.

A quiet voice over the divider. "Don't like Sis' Mary Bernard, do you? She hits too hard."

"Don't like her either. My favorite is Sis' Mary Patrick. Gives me sweets. Helps me write home."

Daley rolled the words round his memory. Uniforms. Convent girls, Sister Mary. That's it – nuns. Starch and Pears soap.

The sun briefly sprinkled the table with lights like a dance hall mirror-ball.

Write home. I should write home. So hard to find time. She once gave me all her time. He took a deep breath and, to deflect guilt, flattened the paper ball on the table. Chinese interrupted in three places by numbers.

12.15 10/24...510...114.

Meaningless.

Maybe important. Bad-mannered bugger – let him bloody well do without it!

Not knowing where to throw it, he rolled it back and forth on the table between finger and thumb.

"S.M. Winifred's bad, isn't she?" Cautious words, words denied said.

"I keep out of the Sick Room. Don't tell anyone if I'm sick. Rather go to class ill than go there."

"Fruit juice, sir?"

"Eh?"

"Fruit juice?" An all-smiles waiter with an acned nose.

"Oh, er. Yes, grapefruit please."

"And the lady?"

"Oh. Orange. Yes, orange, please."

Whispers. He strained to hear.

"She touches you, you know, there! When you're sick in bed and she helps you wash, she uses a cloth everywhere, well, except there. Always rubs there with her fingers gently. Nice really."

Daley craned, motionless.

"But I get ever so, well, you know...uncomfortable."

"Hot. You get hot." Giggles and poking sounds.

"Jennifer Knowles! You are awful! How could you say things like that?"

"Well, do you?"

There was a small silence.

Shifting cloth on leather, clinks of cutlery.

Nuns. Human after all. Always knew they were. He'd served altar at nun's weddings. Always good money. Ten shillings – a lot in those days. Some of the novices had been beautiful, long hair flowing the altar carpet, cropped by Father Gaston, singing sonorous Gallic, breath full of stale cigarettes and garlic. He had seen their glazed eyes as the priest lifted the white veils and slipped on the silver rings. Not really there – somewhere else – wedding a wraith, cleaving to a mirage. No wonder they stray.

"Not been the same, though, has she, since Pavlova left? Irish poetry in English class, gone hasn't it?"

"She was my House Sister, Pavlova. Fetched and carried for her for two years. Do anything for sweets she would."

"What House?"

"Theresa. It's a wonder her teeth weren't rotten. She ate so many. Something funny about her teeth. Never did figure it. Smiled too carefully."

"I'm in Bernadette, so never knew her."

Quiet. Buttons slid the tabletop.

"I think she loved her. You know...funny love."

"'Queer' you think," said the other girl in a loud voice.

"Shh! Keep your voice down." Stifled giggles.

"Could be. Seemed to spend a lot of time in the Sick Room, Pavlova."

"Maybe she liked it, you know." More giggles. "Rubbing."

Daley adjusted his seat, careful not to lose the smoky words.

"Never did like her though. Too stuck up. She was old, must have been at least eighteen! Not missed her since she left."

Their breakfast arrived.

He idly bounced the paper ball. Wish I'd known Pavlova. Would have shown her the real thing – gently, of course.

The bouncing ball escaped and he bent to retrieve it. Numbers. Numbers spinning his head. First's obviously a time...and a date.

He drew a surprised breath. Today. Twelve-fifteen.

He hummed to himself. "I'd like to get you on a slow boat to China."

He grinned at the proposition but froze mid-next line.

That's *our* flight time?

His pulse quickened, then he relaxed. Seeing somebody off.

Bacon wafted the divider and he glanced at the kitchen door.

Bet 510 is the flight number.

He pulled the tickets from his inside pocket.

Toronto-Tokyo. Tokyo-Hong Kong. Hong Kong-Beijing. CAC 510.

Right! He flattened the crumpled ball to recheck the numbers.

Right on!

114? No idea. Landing time with the point missing? Nah, takes longer than an hour to get to Beijing.

He looked up as Ane sat down.

Best bacon an' eggs I've ever had. Better for the wait, he thought, tonguing traces from his teeth as they walked the first-floor corridor.

He carded the slot and pushed the door. It was impeded.

He shouldered it. It gave. Muffled road noises filled the black. The robe had fallen behind the door so he bent and pulled it out. The disembodied clock radio clicked red – 9.00. Gone two hours.

He fumbled the card into the power slot and, as light flooded the room, his jaw dropped.

The bed was littered with the brown bag; the suitcase spread on the floor. Socks, underclothes, hung drawers like dog tongues. Suits protruded from closet doors like an overfull Japanese train.

Ane gasped, pushed roughly by and, picking up her underclothes, pushed them into a hanging drawer and shut it with a slam.

He stood in shock – always hyper about her underclothes – as if ripped off by the perpetrators.

She pushed up her sleeves, pegged her hair behind her ears and started to pick up the bed. The pillows were littered with panty-liners, ripped box gaping like a skull.

"You brought *those*!" she accused.

"Sorry, you weren't supposed to know."

"Imagine what they thought!"

"Who, the thieves? Who gives a shit! Probably thought they were yours."

"Bet it was *him*," she said slowly.

"Who?"

"That man. The one who knocked into me. He was in such a hurry!"

"Don't be daft." His voice caught. 114.

He was looking at "114" on the door behind her!

The room number.

"Nah, not possible. Must be an inside job. The door wasn't forced, so they must have used a card. Better tell the desk."

"Wait, Peter. Think we should see what's been taken. Bound to ask, aren't they?"

Couldn't tell her. No way. Nervous enough as it was. This'd put bloody tin-hat on it.

"Everything seems to be here," she announced finally. "Even our emergency dollars. Don't understand. Why do all this and take nothing?"

He shrugged. "Who knows? Maybe something that wasn't there."

"You mean drugs?"

"Possibly."

There was a small silence. "Good job I keep the passports, isn't it? Should imagine they're valuable in Hong Kong."

They glanced at each other and, without a word, she picked up the brown bag and systematically checked each pocket.

"Driving licence's here. Can't find her passport, though. Swear it was with it!"

"Probably fell under the bed."

She stretched an arm into the dark.

"Try this." He passed her the emergency flashlight.

"Nothing! Suppose we'd better report it missing!"

"Okay. But we'll tell the desk and *let them* tell the police. We'll miss the flight otherwise."

She glanced at the clock. "Oh, God! That's right. Better move."

So they'd taken Beth's passport. Maybe they finger western visitors as a source of passports. After all Hong Kong will soon be part of China and passports must be at a premium.

"Should I take this?" She waved the *Time* magazine at him. He nodded. "Maybe we'll be stuck for something to read." She wriggled it into the brown bag.

She wore the kilt skirt to cheer herself up. It swished, long slit opening to its silver safety pin.

"Looks nice, Ane. Keep your Scottish blouse on. You'll wow 'em in Beijing."

"I'm too messy on aeroplanes. The space is so small, I spill food, especially on these." She boosted her breasts.

"You're not supposed to do *that*. S'*my* job." He jiggled her generous front.

She circled his wrists, threw off his hands and pulled away quickly. "You're a bad sod. Don't handle the goods if you're not going to buy."

He hoisted on the Harris Tweed. She got mad at him for wearing the same jacket every day, but he knew she would never understand – the pockets carried a man's life – things were always there, dependable.

He unslotted the key tab and plunged the room into darkness. A tiny flash in the mirror, the telephone message light.

"FAX for you, sir. You can pick it up at the desk."

"Who knows we're here?" Ane wondered. "How'd anyone find out?"

"Jackie's Travel'd know. Anyway, let's see what it's about."

The desk clerk passed the rolled-up sheet and he gave it to Ane as he signed for it. Then he remembered.

"Oh, by the way. We've mislaid a passport."

"Yours, sir?"

"No, actually my daughter's. Had it by accident. Seems to have disappeared."

"Do you have the number, sir?"

"'fraid not. Never thought to get it."

"That's all right. Canadian, sir?"

Daley nodded.

"We will report it for you, sir. Please write out the full name and address of your daughter."

"It's from Louisa, Peter. Choi's out of town. Says thank you but it's not necessary to interview the students. The Chinese insisted on a deadline so they've been selected already."

"Let me see. What the hell's Choi about? All this way then he changes his mind!"

"It's not his fault. Seems the *Chinese* insisted."

"Makes no difference. The tour's set up so lets go. Look at it this way –one less job to do!"

He stuffed the roll of paper into his pocket.

"Peter, do you think this means they won't meet us?"

"Taxi's waiting. Let's discuss it on the way. If we miss the plane the whole thing's academic."

A Jaguar angled to the curb, wheel turned like a pointing ballerina.

He needed time. Must be an explanation. Not at all like Choi. In all the time he had known him, he'd never been capricious.

They subsided into the rear seat, the smell of leather round them. The console clock said 10:30.

Ane was shaking. "Look. I'd better warn you, I'm *not* getting on that plane if nobody's going to meet us. You can go if you like, but I'm not!"

She looked away to hide brimming eyes. God, this always happens. Looks like I'm upset when really I'm angry.

He tried to calm her. "Look, the interviews were only secondary – a favour for Choi. So he cancels them. What's important is that Ny has set up visits, lectures, dinners, meetings. Don't want to let *him* down. Besides, Choi's paid for the tickets and Ny's lot are going to pay for the tour. It's a free ride, so let's enjoy it."

"But what if they don't meet us?"

"Let's cross that bridge when we come to it. I think they will. Ny knew we were staying at the Ramada. Could have canceled. He didn't, so I'm for risking it."

There was a silence.

"Suppose you're right," she sighed eventually, rolling her fingers nervously in her lap. "But I wish it hadn't got *so* complicated."

They gathered speed on the freeway.

"Sometime I'll have to bring my wife on one of these trips. Feel sorry for her, don't you? Alus bring me girlfriend. Not fair really, is it?"

She giggled and poked him playfully. "All I know is, whoever she is, I'd rather be your girlfriend."

The aircraft turned and gained speed. Take-off was not as dramatic as landing. Ane loved this part of the journey – the raw power of the engines clawing for air, the bumping becoming smoothness. She shivered. Headed for God knows what. Probably not be met. Why wouldn't he face facts?

Once the plane was level, a slight, pale woman with tight grey curls and large wire glasses sitting opposite, pulled a long wool garment with two needles through it from her bag. She smiled at Ane, unwound yarn and began to click loops from one needle to the other. An English spinster. Teacher. Won't need the sweater where she's going: Choi'd said Beijing in October could be warm. The frayed arms flopped like dead things over her knee.

"Penny for 'em, Ane!"

"Nan always wanted to see China. Wonder what it'll be like."

"Shame she passed on before she'd a chance."

"Nobody expected her to die. Soldiering into her nineties, drinking more Teachers whisky in her tea than tea!"

This is good. Not spoken about her grandmother since she died. She was skipping to her with yesterday's wild flowers. Tears shone and her chin dimpled. He squeezed her fingers and she rested her head on his shoulder.

A smiling girl dangled a hot towel in his face. It was steaming lavender.

"Watch these. You're allergic, aren't you?"

She smiled at the stewardess and shook her head.

"Was always a problem for her, Peter, being born Christmas Eve."

"Hardly be her fault?"

"Used to say her mother blamed it on the duck plucking, though what that can have to do with it, escapes me."

He elbowed her. "Getting ready for Christmas. All that pulling and pushing. Must have brought her on."

"You're awful. Fancy thinking that."

"You're very like her, Ane. Have her tenacity, her down-to-earth common sense. She'll never dee whilst thar lives." He missed the "Missus".

Stewardesses circulated free headphones. Daley squeezed the cord between finger and thumb and pulled it to spin the wires straight.

The TV screen in the doorway snowed on. The fanfare dissolved into the sonorous riffs of "Saint Elmo's Fire."

A comfortable silence fell; he hummed a few bars under his breath.

"Peter. I'm sorry to keep bringing it up, but don't you think we should have a plan?" She lifted his earphone and repeated the question. She was pulling at her wedding ring - a sure sign.

"It's that FAX, isn't it?"

She nodded, looking down.

"Don't worry! Too much loss of face for Ny *not* to turn up. Important to be associated with a Westerner!"

"But he might think the tour's been canceled."

"So what! We have valid visas, money, and tickets. We'll just go to the Beijing Hotel and wait for Greg."

"But nobody speaks English and we have no Chinese money."

"It's an international airport. Somebody'll speak English. Hell, they *like* Western money."

He grinned. "It's an adventure. We'll have fun."

He was not as convinced as he sounded. Something still didn't add up. Couldn't put his finger on it.

The cabin quietened. He pulled out the crumpled FAX, smoothed it flat and perused it, nervously pulling his beard. "Ane, don't you find it surprising, Choi going out of town when his daughter's getting married? That's the reason he asked me to go to Beijing! He was so *relieved* I could go."

"I find it more surprising *Louisa* sent a FAX. There's no one more ungadgetty than she is. Kids had to program her answering machine."

"You're right. That VCR the bridge group bought her for winning - covered with a cloth and flowers last time I saw it!"

She chuckled. Liked Louisa - her kind of girl.

"Think they've postponed the wedding, or what?"

"You don't postpone weddings, Peter!"

"Where's area code 514?"

"Montreal."

"How'd you know that so quick?"

"It's Michel's code. Ecole Polytechnique."

"Well, this was sent from Montreal then."

"But what's she doing in Montreal? The wedding's Saturday. No way she'd leave Hamilton."

"Maybe that's it!"

"What?"

"Well, what if a friend sent it for her or even one of those professional places? Could come from anywhere then."

"I suppose. Louisa's certainly hopeless with gadgets."

He rolled the paper backwards to flatten it, then spread it out again.

"Here! Look at this."

"Looks like pencil."

He turned the page ninety degrees. There was a long line of narrow scrawl up the side. He had missed it in the edge crinkles.

"Pencil won't write on thermopaper."

"I don't understand what it says."

"'Watch for Boadicea in Long John's army.'" He read with his finger.

They looked at each other.

"Why'd Louisa write something like that?"

"She didn't. Wasn't *transmitted*. It was *written* in Hong Kong, in the hotel! Here, hold this, Ane, please." He uncovered the pencil eraser.

"See, it rubs out. FAX doesn't."

"Well, what's it mean?"

"Means I'm right. Don't know why, but it was written in Hong Kong. Before we picked it up."

"What on earth does the sentence mean, though?"

He shook his head. "Can't make any sense of it. "Bodicea" – an ancient English queen; "Long John"– a whiskey, a Bourbon."

"Well, we're not going to decipher it. Maybe written on the wrong FAX by mistake."

"Wish it hadn't been written at all. In fact, wish the bloody FAX hadn't been sent!"

It had not escaped him that both "messages" had appeared at the Ramada. He tried to force them together, the dropped note and the pencil on the FAX. Wouldn't fit, and obviously the FAX had arrived *after* they returned from the market, otherwise the desk would have given it to him when he reclaimed the key. So the rushing Chinaman could not have written on it – he was out of it! If not, then who did?

A smiling stewardess in China Airlines blue cloak pushed a meal at him. Bloody movie's still going he grumbled.

The spinster's wool got tangled in her tray much to the annoyance of the suddenly sullen stewardess.

Children ran through the aisles and peeped over seat tops. Aeroplanes seem to come replete with kids, screams, giggles, wheels, and wings.

"Coffee, sir?"

"Did you pack the Instant, Ane?"

She smiled like a cat with cream on its whiskers. "You'd be proud of me. Not only coffee but creamer and sugar too. Even All-Bran!"

"I *am* impressed!"

"Can I have extra sugar, please?" he asked a stewardess, who handed him a fistful. "We'll probably have to drink pots of awful green tea. Need sugar in me pocket."

"You goin' to buy Christmas presents this trip?" She loved to scour foreign markets for gifts for Word Processing at Minster.

"I know you laugh, but saves money! 'Specially if you don't *give 'em away* or insist *we* keep 'em! God, it frustrates me. I carefully plan Christmas and you blow it with largesse!"

"Promise me one thing, Ane. If you see anything you really like – *anything* - buy it! No procrastination. No going back later, no seeing it again somewhere else cheaper! Buy it!"

She smiled a little foolishly and nodded. He was right. She had missed treasures to save money, a Yorkshire trait, a grandmother trait.

Faintly piqued, she shot back, "Like Miss Muffet said to the spider: Piss off hairy legs!"

Ane opened her paperback. A folded note fell out. She unrolled it and smiled.

"My dad hates daddylions," she read out loud. "I hate spring. We pull them, with yellow hands. My knees hurt. Yellow head is inemy. I like them. They are pretty."

"Claire had your measure! Even in Grade Four!"

The winter sun was drowning in clouds off the left wing. The intercom sing-songed as they plunged, and thumps heralded deployment of the undercarriage. Then they were pellmelling winter fields of straw stubble. The movie was still playing.

Touch-down signaled a rush to open ceiling hatches and disgorge under-seats.

Daley looked out the window and saw a traffic light.

A traffic light!

He pushed in front of Ane to see behind. A horde of bicycles jostled at the light like the start of the Boston marathon.

The airport buildings were grey, with dirty windows and rusting iron. There were few planes. The concrete control tower rose from the main terminal like a dirty finger, stiff red flag on top. Its clock, hands once black now mottled, said it was 2.15...ten minutes late.

The aircraft route was now defined by disheveled soldiers. Not the smart guards of Moscow, but more menacing.

Daley was looking forward to seeing Ny's cheerful face again. It'd settle Ane down. He'd badgered him to visit, in spite of the Tiananmen tragedy. The wiry, always smiling Chinaman had a face like an old leather glove. He saw him shinning a pine on the annual Christmas-tree hunt; at the Pinery camp, turning complete somersaults without touching the ground.

"Do you remember his pup tent?"

"Who?"

"Ny. Hard to get him out of it, remember? Like a kid he was. Something he'd only read about I suppose. Then, suddenly, there it was in real life!"

"He'd just better be out there, that's all!"

Muzak strained on to the scent of flowers.

Ny had written two respectable papers and defended them with a determination innocent of acrimony, a philosophy probably birthed in the fields of the Cultural Revolution. What a mad shit idea that was to send professionals into fields, for the good of their souls. Ny had mucked out horses for ten years, seeing his family once a year. If they'd not wasted ten years, God knows how far ahead they'd be.

His overriding ambition was a faculty position at the prestigious Beijing School of Arts and Science. For this he spent two years in Canada without his family. He never broached bringing them to Canada, as did many Chinese. He learned English from Rosica, a vivacious, Italian co-worker, so his wiry words with Latin tails were propelled with hands and arms as if launching birds. He would be their host; an interpreter Daley knew would embroider explanations into scientific argument.

People continued to stream past as though entering the rear door, but eventually the rush thinned and Daley looked back down the aisle.

"Get ready. After this smart guy with the red scarf."

"Looks bundled up. Must be expecting cold," Ane muttered, feeling she had seen him before. Probably had. They all look the same.

As they walked though the fuselage door, a bottle-green soldier clicked them with a hidden hand-counter.

Luggage carts were welded like rutting dogs, but they

struggled a pair free, piled in the bags, and joined the line before the X-ray machine.

The crowd noise was deafening, the air heavy with wet earth.

As Daley shuffled past a soldier, he realized the source of the funeral malodor was wet uniforms. Must be raining. Clouds had certainly had that in mind.

Being head and shoulders above, he could see the cadre of boy soldiers narrowing the exit and hear their curt shouts. Each held a dull black weapon on a shoulder strap, poking people unfortunate enough to be close.

"Peter. Can you see a Ladies anywhere?"

"Sorry. Doesn't seem to be one. Don't know an airport with toilets in the immigration area."

The wine bottle clinked. "Did we bring a bottle opener?" she asked, looking round the hall. No side doors and no female stick figures!

"A Japanese giveaway in the bag." He tapped his shoulder luggage.

The crush funneled into irregular lines.

They reached the first soldiers. The light cotton uniforms needed ironing and there was mud on the boot laces. They smelled of wet leaves. A left breast pocket bulged with a packet of Marlboro. How primitive the gun looks – rivets sticking out, no wooden "handle"– like something an amateur made in a garage!

Just ahead was a German. He went in.

They could hear nothing of the interview but saw him take off his jacket, pass it to a standing soldier, then watch in Teutonic disbelief as the pockets were emptied over the table and the contents picked over by a seated officer. The sleeves were pulled inside out and the lining probed front and back. He was then motioned to take off his shoes and socks, roll down the cuffs of his trousers and open his shirt. A soldier frisked him.

Daley and Ane were horrified.

The officer finished with the jacket and waved the confused traveler through. Loose laced, open shirted, silk lining of his jacket glistening on his arm, he shuffled away.

They were in.

Put the best face on it, he told himself, like approaching a doctor. He slapped the passports into the outstretched hand and watched as the officer flicked to the pastel seal.

With a sudden scrape the man pushed his chair backwards, stood parade ground stiff, saluted and, arm straight, clapped the passports closed and shot them back.

Daley was astonished!

Ane did not care. *There* was the way out!

They went past the devastated German, luggage littering the floor.

Through swinging doors, into the melee. Speechless!

"Can you believe that?" Peter shouted at her but she was not there. He saw the back of her head disappearing through a door.

"Just like bloody Russia - those visas. Really work! Just imagine. Up, salute – magic! – pushing a blood button," he prattled on.

Didn't take Western publications either. He waved the rolled *Time* magazine at the disinterested crowd: "Maybe nobody reads English."

There was one English placard: "American Bible Society". Daley rolled the carts to a bench and sat to let the crowd disperse.

If Ny was there, he would stay till the crowd thinned. He studied the faces rushing by and wondered if he would still recognize Ny, or Ny him. Don't be daft! In only two years, he wouldn't have changed that much!

She was back, pale green, almost sick. She grasped his arm tightly. "Oh, God, Peter, you've no idea! No idea." She leaned forward, head in her hands, saying nothing. He put his arm across her shoulders.

"That place is an absolute midden! I was desperate. It was Chinese. Women squatted over holes, shit everywhere, attendants in rubber boots were hosing piles that missed – drenching shoes and skirts. And the stench!" She gagged. "Tampons and towels strewn like dog-ransacked garbage and wet cigarette butts floating in the mess. No toilet paper; has to be bought, sheet by sheet. When I went in...went quiet – obviously western women don't go."

She pulled her coat tight.

"I was mortified. I had to step over them, laughing up at me! I saw a wooden door and ran to it, shoes soaked."

That's the smell.

"Closet with no latch. I held it shut and went. Seen a lot, but really wiped me out!"

He took her cold, shaking hands, palmed her chin, and gave her a gentle kiss. "It's over now, love. S'over."

How the hell do I tell her Ny's not here?

"Ny didn't come, did he?"

"I'm sure he will. Remember what a stickler he was for punctuality. Bugger was embarrassingly on time."

"I told you! It's Moscow all over again!"

"Look. It isn't! Moscow was Greg's fault. Had to try that damn fish soup and got anaphylactic shock. Everybody was left to fend for themselves while the Russians were coddling their superstar."

There was a silence.

It was cold.

The milling mob thinned but the noise was undiminished, volume doubled in the cavernous hall. The clock on the wall said ten past three. An hour after their scheduled landing.

"Do you think we should confirm our flight out?"

"Moscow again."

"I'm only saying they canceled our return tickets. Well, they did, didn't they?"

"A Russian ploy to get us to spend hard currency. Chinese probably won't bother. Too few visiting foreigners, 'specially now."

She gripped his arm. "Money! We've got no Chinese money. I hate being without money. No hotel, no plans, no telephone num-

bers, no Chinese, no one to meet us, and no money!"
"Okay, okay. You stay here. I'll go get some money."

She watched him walk towards the permanently open doors through which the cold October wind was rustling the rubbish littering the entrance. Drawing the black and white coat closer round, she sank her chin into its generous collar. How could he be so calm, trusting Ny and his ego trip? She pursed her lips. Well, I think the whole thing's been called off and he just won't admit it!

Daley headed for the Tourist Information "shack" just inside the open door. The crowd of taxi drivers lounging there moved as he approached. He struggled out his wallet. One of the loungers, face like a skull, with a huge flat hat, smiled, cleared his throat, said something in Chinese, and pointed across the hall. Daley turned and another driver ran after him.
"Want money? I change money. Want money?"
He waved the Travelers Cheques. "These," he said sanguinely. The man who smelled of old shit, scowled, chopped at the cheques and slouched off.
A girl at an isolated desk sent Daley to a wicket on the next floor. It was ten degrees warmer. A broken chair and blackened sweeping brush stood beside the bright chrome escalator. He stepped off beside rickety, bric-a-brac counters that stretched, sparsely supplied, along the back wall of an open tea restaurant.
The "Change" wicket was a hole-in-the-wall. The girl perused the cheques and glanced nervously at him. He scanned the upside-down cheque in her hand. The date was okay. He had not filled out the payee line but they were sure to have a stamp. His signature – probably the trouble – had deteriorated to illegibility during the original bank multi-signing.
It was decided he sign each cheque twice, back and front. The Manager was searched out and emerged, bulging mouth leaking lunch.
After comparing the signatures, he authorised the transaction with a curt nod and disappeared.

Banknotes were counted from the highly-coloured piles on the right hand side of the table along the back wall. The notes on the left were ignored. They seemed faded and dog-eared. Must give visitors new currency.

"Got new money, Ane."
"I've reached a decision. Bet it was Louisa's FAX!"
"What? What you talking about?"
"Bet that's why he didn't come!"
"Excuse me, sir." It was the American Bible Society girl; big glasses, big teeth, big tits, all smile, pointing her placard at him. "Roberts. An English woman. She knits. Was she on your flight, please?"

He nodded. She smiled quickly and left. His stomach rumbled.

"Do you have anything to eat in that case, Ane?"
"You're not listening, are you?"
"What?"
"It's all you can think about – your belly! Here we are bloody nowhere and nobody knows, and you're hungry! Here, find something for yourself!" She threw her bag onto his knee.
"No way! There's things in there Kitchener were afraid of!"
She crabbily passed him a packet of Lifesavers.
"Now look, let's get something straight. We're not stuck. Can always go to a Western airline desk and get help, or take a taxi to the Beijing Hotel Greg talked about. No. We'll wait an hour, then we'll make a move."

There was a glum silence.

Going to be a long hour. The whole place smelled like a cave.

Women brushed dust piles from one end of the concourse to the other, then back. An incongruous black Mercedes circulated the cyclists on the grey concourse outside the open doors, a beetle in ants. It had darkened back windows and a prim army driver.

He smiled and dozed back to a summer's day of dogs, cats, grannies, fisherman and kids, all trying to help as he desperately to'ed and fro'ed the motorhome on a Newfoundland pier – an elephant with mice in its toes.

Ane was miserable, damp, and cold. They had money but could be gypped by anybody! Christ, he was exasperating! How could he sleep!

Her toes were beginning to hurt. She watched the thinning crowd. What a muddle. Jeans, shirts, suits with t-shirts, baggy pants with smart blouses...as if they'd been shaken inside a bag of Sally Ann seconds and released all over the floor.

If Ny does come – and I'm sure he won't – I'll give him a piece of my mind!

She sat, looking round, seething. What a dump! A thin mist, like smoke from the next room, drifted the draughty doors, mixing petrol fumes into the dust stirred by the busy brooms.

Time passed at the pace of a climbing cripple.

No Ny.

II
BEIJING

The motorhome was shaking. Silly sods think they can lift it like a Volkswagen. Daley watched the broadbacked fishermen in the mirrors, pushing at the sides.

"Peter, wake up. Wake up." Ane was shaking his shoulder. "Ny's here!"

He woke with a start, cringing at the crick in his neck. Newfoundland dissolved as leg-cramp threatened.

Cold, he looked at her blankly.

"Ny's here."

"I'ma so sorry, Doc! Thoughta plane come ata three! You are so welcoming in China!" He pumped Daley's limp hand as he spoke.

Daley shook his head like a wet dog. Flip-flop sandals and no socks. Crazy, in this cold!

"I knew you'd come," he said with a wide smile.

Ny was excited. The same smile, perhaps turning more wrinkles, but aglow in the grey afternoon. No coat, a jean shirt, and sleeveless sweater –as though he'd run from a warm room – always been a tough old bird.

"You can't believe what happened," Daley started but Ny hefted the bags and waved them to follow.

"Pleasea come."

Ane was glad to.

Outside the wind was cold, holding the threat of winter. As they crunched into the back seat of the university Nissan, Ny immediately turned round.

"We had it alla planned but thoughta next plane. So sorry."

"Well, you came, Ny. That's what matters." Daley looked at his wife but she just huffed breath through her fingers, and stared out the window. The Mercedes was gone.

Finally she turned. "Thing is, Ny, we FAX'd you the exact time and flight number, everything! Even got confirmation!"

"Ah, FAXes go Administration." He turned his palm up in a helpless gesture. "Sometimesa tell us, sometimesa not. Nota very efficient, China."

"Well, it's time you got your act together!" she said truculently, and realising it was futile, turned back to the window.

They were driving a concrete, four-lane highway – like Detroit, except for the cyclists. She had never seen so many. Like the start of a bicycle race with them in the middle – six thick on each side, weaving and wobbling, all ages, shapes and sizes.

There was an uncomfortable silence.

Daley glanced out the back window. The terminal was fast receding, its postage-stamp flag pointing at the threatening clouds. The tower clock showed 4.3o. Two bloody hours since they'd arrived.

The flag reminded him and he bent to look at the radio antenna. On the end, bending it like a loaded fishing rod, was a small flag – gold hieroglyphics on rippling red.

"The flag, Ny."

"University car. No stop at controls. Very good."

"Will we go through one now?"

"No. Going *into* Beijing, noa controls. Maybe tomorrow."

'Red-roads,' Choi called 'em. He was right about the flag anyway. At least one thing was as it should be.

The driver wore a black leather jacket and had a passion for Western cars. Cut-out Ferraris and Lamborgini's decorated the dash and tunnel console. Probably not one of either anywhere in China. Seemed the preserve of Mercedes and Japanese.

"How's the family, Ny?"

"Well. You'lla meet them soon. Mya wife looking forward seeing you. She cook alla week!"

"And your daughter? Never knew you had a daughter Ny, you sly old fox."

"Didn't you?" he replied vaguely. "He'sa OK. Howsa lab?"

The grand sweep of freeway became patched as conversation circled Ny's Canadian associates and their lives. Ane half listened, watching out the window in disbelief. People were everywhere! Women shepherds shouted along the roadside as sheep, cyclists, and traffic muddled towards Beijing. There was a puzzling smell of camphor in the car which reminded her of the wardrobes of her childhood. Clothes reminded her. "We were robbed in Hong Kong, Ny!"

He stopped mid sentence. "Rob-bed?"

"Yes, robbed!"

His face fell. "Honga Kong is a dangerous place. Whata was taken?"

"Our daughter's passport, is all. I mean, we had it by mistake. Fortunately I was carrying ours," Daley said, tapping his inside pocket.

"You always do that!"

"What?"

"Answer my questions? He asked *me*!"

"Sorry. You tell him if you like."

"Canadian passports ara valuble ina Hong Kong. 'Specially now soona rejoin China."

"We reported the loss to the hotel. Maybe we should have told the embassy."

Ny looked startled. "Don'ta go Embassy, Doc. It'sa watched, it'sa dangerous!"

Daley decided they should lighten up. "Must say, it's good to see you, Ny. Suppose you thought we'd never visit, 'specially after the Tiananmen troubles."

"Troubles gone now. You'lla have happy visit."

They bumped across a drainage pipe laid on top of the road with sand piled either side.

Potholes were deep, pipes extant, and there were no traffic signs.

"Ny, Ane'd like to shop while I lecture. S'that OK?"

"Gooda shops for Westerners near Beijing Hotel on Changan Avenue. She go. Tomorrow you lecture and see the students for Minster. She go then."

Ane poked her husband. "So much for Louisa's FAX!"

"I thought they were cancelled."

"Why cancelled?"

"Well, we received a Canadian FAX in Hong Kong"

Ny shook his head. "No cancelled. Wednesday. Tomorrow. Ten-thirty."

Daley looked at Ane and shrugged.

The car entered an intersection. Everything flowed, like a crowded mall, people never colliding. Most on bicycles, some on mules and single-cylinder motor carts, some walking; some in cars. All moving in a terrifying stream. Red brick was piled in the road – outside sheds, shops and gardens and on walkways to drab apartments.

"Save till enough to build house," explained Ny.

A three-mule cart entered the crossing without stopping or looking. It plodded, driver facing backwards against the cold, mules indifferent to the chaos. The traffic light changed, the muddle moved.

"You hava many Chinese students these days?"

"Ty and Ku are still with me. They're now Canadians, you know. They got refugee status after Tiananmen."

"Why they do that?" Ny murmured.

Daley wondered if Canadian association was causing problems. Maybe *us* he extrapolated. Ny had been a good friend, but much had happened since his halcyon days at Minster.

"Suppose they had to really. The Chinese in Canada demonstrated and were photographed, identified. What could we do? Dangerous for them to return, so we gave them asylum."

"Now impossible fora student to geta passport. Must repay all education. Or pay another way! Sucha people dangerous. Bea careful! May seeka for you."

Ane was miles away. Oh, for a long soak in a warm bath.

There had been no mention of accommodations, she realised. Usually hosts can't wait to tell of their wonderful arrangements.

"So, Ny, where you goin' to put us?"

"University Guesta House. Opened justa for you."

Feeling was returning to her feet and with it, her good humour. "Here's a little something for you, Ny." She held out a parcel. "Hope it reminds you of Canada."

"You're very kind. Thinka you enjoy China."

To protect cyclists, lorries, and buses had side grids like the hammock netting of old men-o-war. There was no lane discipline and for the most part no lanes.

A truck piled with coal and frozen people swerved to avoid an old lady scraping up horse droppings. Everywhere was dust. Not the dust of settled-down dining rooms, of dimmed polished surfaces wisked by feathers, but the dust of clinging dirt that defies dousing and scrubbing, a deep relieving dust whose bright ochre colour ingrained every crevice with the gentle touch of earth, ever present, everlasting, everywhere.

Ny led them up an impressive marble stair and proudly unlocked their room.

Dank and dark, breath ghosts proceeded their walk in. Through a dusty window, the sun of late afternoon – battle won with the rain – was losing at last to rising mist that seemed everywhere, even inside, as if the window was open. The walls were shiny as though wet and a lone drop, under the sill started, ran, stopped, started again, and then joined others to drip on the floor.

A large wood-covered radiator occupied the window wall. Ane strode to it with relief.

Cold! Well – tepid at one end.

A partially silvered mirror doubled the desolation. The stone floor was covered with faded Chinese carpet. There was a TV under a plum velvet cover. The paint was peeling from the shower walls, the toilet leaked, and the sink gurgled for ever. Hot water was for one hour in the morning and one at night, announced a wrinkled sign in six languages on the broken mirror.

The "closet" was two rough brackets, piece of pipe between and was lined with torn wallpaper with spring flower motif.

Ny left and Ane busied herself. Clothes were hung in the pipe closet or put on, but in spite of double-socks, longjohns, sweaters, coats and scarves, they were cold – the cold of English November bedrooms.

"If we push the beds together, Peter, we can double the covers."

He pushed with his knees but the bed didn't move. The frames had to be physically lifted in a series of head and foot heaves.

Never had he felt so cold: they should invent a damp index like the wind-chill factor. Ane donned Beth's long coat but she was approaching desperation. "We can't stay here, Peter. No, I'm *not* staying here! My back hurts and this is making it worse."

"We have to for now."

"Well, I'm not! If we have to, I'm off home."

"Don't be silly! How the hell they going to move us now?"

"I don't care. You tell 'em. I mean it!"

"Tell who for Chris's sakes? Ny's gone. Nobody's out there." He waved at the door.

"Go and see! Do something. Don't wait for me to do it."

"Listen. It's not the case. I'd be more than happy to do something. It's just not possible."

She glowered at him, then looked away in frustration.

He was worried. Since her fall from a horse, her back gave him concern. She'd insisted on not being moved, though her neck was broken, till the paramedic stumbled across the field. Two days later, in a sweltering hospital of broken down air-conditioners, she refused the morphine, and, determined to walk, was home in a week.

"Let me rub it."

"Stop trying to change the subject. I want out. Do you hear? Out!"

His heels clattered on the deserted stone stairs and in corridors. The telephone exchange was closed tight. Nobody. Nobody anywhere.

She was sitting on the bed as he had left her. "Look there really isn't anybody. The place is deserted, like it's closed. Ny's coming to take us to dinner, remember. Let's ask him then."

"You'd bloody better. I mean it! I'll go home!" She stomped off to the bathroom to try warm her feet.

He sat heavily on the bed. She was right. The place was like Tipperary in March. He recalled the sodden Sundays on damp, brocaded furniture in the lonely front parlour – mountains, hills and Tipperary town mantled in mist. He sighed. Youthful Ireland was a soggy ghost.

He was suspicious they'd not been expected. Place had been specially opened for them, Ny had said. Known for weeks they were coming, so why not open it?

Emerging with a teapot in her hand, Ane wagged it at him. "There's no hot water! Can't even have a cup of tea!"

"Here, try this." He passed her the room thermos and she poured its liquid into the pot.

She was near breaking, so cold her legs had lost feeling. "How can we possibly stay here? No water, heat, nothing. You got to move us!" She stamped her foot then sulked on the bed, pulling the borrowed coat round her .

He turned the old fridge to expose its coils and struggled the bulky plug into the wall socket. No hum, nothing. There was the sound of crackling paper. "What you doing?"

"Folding paper. Me dad used to wrap paper round his chest, before cycling to work. Kept him warm. I'm going to try it."

He pulled himself up. There was one more thing he could try. Four of the room lights were table-lamps, so he gathered them beside her. One cord was not long enough, so he shifted the bedside table to it. She shivered and watched in cynical silence but smiled wearily and shuffled up, careful not to break the woollen envelope.

He clicked on the bulbs with a triumphant smile. The last flashed out!

"Bugger!" he complained, going to the bathroom for another.

"Peter, wait!" she shouted after him. "Don't do what I think you're going to do. I couldn't stand it all dark as well!"

"What d'you mean?"

"That night in Moscow, the Academy Nauk. Remember?"

He sat down beside her.

The bulb beside the bed had blown and he'd taken one from bathroom. The element broke immediately he touched the bulb. Incredulous, he'd removed another, then another, and another, all round the room, every one breaking as he did. They sat in the dark all night, having tried unsuccessfully to make the old lady guarding the samovar of their floor, understand. She was more interested in the stukas bombing Leningrad as they did all night, every night, on Soviet TV. The tungsten was so impure, it embrittled once lit!

She was right though: better three lights than none!

She held her hands under the tassles of the shades and smiled gratefully. "Look Peter, you've done all you can. Just won't do, will it? We can't sit all night with our hands up these lights like women's skirts."

"More like a Scotsman's kilt."

"Don't be so gross. How can you?"

"Oh, I don' know. Like this." He slid his free hand through her coat slit

She pushed him away. "Think again, Billy boy. If you think I'm going to expose *anything* here, you've another think coming."

Out the single paned window, chickens clucked and pecked round a black Mercedes parked by the path. Over the roof tops, mist was tinted by the October sun, aura dissolving into the dark marble of threatening clouds. There will be rain, perhaps even snow.

"So, Peter, the FAX was a hoax!" A migraine was gathering.

"Not necessarily. The message might also have been sent here you know, and got lost in transit."

He kneeled behind her and kneaded her back.

"It might be sitting on some bureaucrat's desk at the university, awaiting his pleasure, just like the one you sent Ny with our flight time and number."

"That was all bull! Didn't believe any of it."

"What makes you say that?"

"The confirmation had Ny's name on it. That's why!"

"Jees!" He stopped the massage.

"Means we weren't expected or at least, took 'em by surprise. Did you see what Ny was wearing? Must have been frozen! And this place been got ready in an awful hurry."

A sharp pain shot her left eye and she rubbed it.

"So what's it mean?"

She shrugged. "You tell me!"

"Maybe there's a simple explanation."

"Well you can do what you like, I'm getting a migraine. I'm *not* staying *here*!"

The Foreign Advisor had informed them a banquet of Peking Duck was planned in their honour that evening.

"How are we going to change, Peter? It's so cold, and God knows what lives in there!" She nodded at the bathroom.

He laughed. "Do like we used to in England. Put one thing on underneath and then remove the top one."

"But I must have a wash. I feel...unclean. That place. Can still smell it, feel it."

"Let's see if there's hot water yet," he said, walking into the bathroom and letting the red tap run cold.

"The hot water isn't, no matter what they say. Bring the thermos and I'll try plug the basin."

She handed him the bashed aluminum bottle and he poured the rest of its contents into the sink, plugged with a wad of rough toilet paper around a Canadian dollar coin." Don't pull the plug when you're finished, Ane. Maybe I can use what's left."

She started washing, shaking her head. "God, what have we come to!"

She wriggled into the Indian dress and lifted her breasts into place.

She could hear him splashing the water, humming. His shirt was wet when he emerged. He pulled on a clean one, then an ascot, which he wore so old shirts would fit.

She braided her long hair, flicked one braid down each side and draped beads between.

"It really was worth lugging that dress," he said, buttoning his shirt. "You look very nice."

He stood behind her in front of the mirror and ran his hands down her breasts. "Um, I love the feel of leather. Soft, silky, sexy. Turns me on. Excites me! "

"I'm glad something does!" she retorted, spinning away. "Take me to somewhere warm, Oh Lord and Master, an' I'll be yours forever."

"Think you should wear scarlet lipstick." A cheap shot – knew she hated it.

"And look like a whore?"

"No. It would complement your clear complexion and the beads."

She turned back to the patchy mirror and smeared wide red strokes over her pastel pink. Didn't like red. Made her look cheap! She turned and batting her eyes, flashed him a brilliant smile.

"Boy, are they in for a surprise!"

Outside was dark. The car had gone and the chickens roosted. A street lamp coned miserably onto the cracked concrete sidewalk. He watched for the university car.

Sharp at seven, Ny returned. Out of the clammy cold, into the cutting wind full of coal smoke and to the car – the warmest place since arriving, except perhaps the upstairs hall at the airport.

Foreboding rain filled the sky. It'll snow, Daley thought as he pulled his coat tail in. Mothballs, stronger now, coming and going as Ny moved: his clothes.

Later they discovered best-suits are stored in camphor.

"Ny. I'm sorry, but we'll have to move. It's no good. The rooms, they...well...they're are far too damp and cold for Ane's back."

"There must be a hotel. We'll pay. *Anything* to be warm!"

Ny fidgeted in his seat and looked out the window. Daley wondered if it was a question of saving face; they were committed to paying their expenses in China and a hotel might break the budget. He decided to tough it out as Ane gave him a stern dig.

"I mean it, Ny, we either move or we leave."

"I see what cana do."

Cyclists flickered in and out of the headlights like moths. Daley was puzzled by something different. No traffic sounds: a ghost army on phantom wheels.

The restaurant was an old Western style house, a shadow of its former opulence. It had stained table-cloths and daubs of paint on old wallpaper.

The foyer narrowed to a dark corridor full of garlic. Large rooms with high, naked bulbs and little tables served by girls in hand-soiled aprons, linked through narrow doors. Voices and laughter murmured in the distance.

The beads swished on Ane's suede dress, causing heads to turn and conversation to stop as she swept by. Minnehaha in Manhattan, Daley mused, pleased with the metaphor.

The corridor opened into a bright room full of sing-songing people, cross-legged on cushions around a low table. It was so full of smoke, the naked bulbs shafted like searchlights. Daley's eyes immediately filled and his throat jammed, like mounting the steps to the upper level of the double-decker buses he had ridden to school.

The assembly struggled up and enthused unintelligible greetings. Ane was motioned to a cushion and the table scissored down. Repartee revived.

A man stood and hush descended. The President of the university made to welcome them. He signalled Daley to sit by him, then, eyes closed by a huge smile, he proposed a toast to Canadian-Chinese cooperation and friendship.

He beamed from a clean-shaven, full-moon face and a mouthful of gold-filled teeth. His flat, well-groomed black hair was shiny and smooth. His tailored suit, white shirt and conservative blue tie were more Japanese than Chinese.

He entertained with panache, his words hung on by acolytes. Holding his glass aloft, he delivered the toast in Chinese, to wise nods and serving comments. Clearly he had power, was used to manipulating it, and expected recognition. Daley heard Choi in his ear: "Watch this, man, he's political, an ambitious party appointee."

Daley scanned the table now that everybody was busy. He had forgotten what a smokey room was like. To a man they had American 100's, blue cloud drifting to undulate round the disembodied bulbs.

Never seen such a muddle of clothes. Some suits – academics probably – messaged tee-shirts under windjammers, jeans and running shoes, conspicuous soles displaying dark holes in white rubber. Some half-and-half suit jackets and shallow-collared shirts, gaudy ties, tight jeans and no socks – students probably, maybe post-docs – one foot in China, the other outside.

No females - except Ane.

He smiled at her across the table and bobbed his wine glass. She grinned back.

The man on the other side of the President leaned behind to shake Daley's hand.

"I'm Fleishman. From Switzerland. Spending a year on Post Doctoral exchange. Nice to meet you. Tonight we'll have a good meal - for a change!" He rubbed his hands in anticipation.

The President, still on his feet, turned to the darkened doorway and, sweeping up his wine glass, welcomed his wife.

Though she bowed as she entered, Daley realised she was tall. She showed flawless skin on high cheekbones that emphasised the flare of her eye corners. Threads of age intruded, but her hair, which touched her shoulders, was jet black and thick. A Loren in her prime, Daley mused, now rounding to the over-ripe he found so alluring these days.

Her dress was blue, demeanor gentle, and her wavering smile firmed when she saw Ane. She greeted her with a voice husky. At first Daley thought she was Chinese – tall but Chinese. Then he realised she couldn't be. Her eyes were Western. Dash of native, that's what fooled him. Often they have a Chinese cast. Probably North American Indian.

She fingered her hair behind her ears and settled beside Ane. Realizing he was staring, Daley looked away quickly. The giveaway was her English. No disappeared "l's" or tongueless "th's." They murmured happily like gossiping villagers. Occasionally her eyes would fix him with puzzling candour.

A purple cloth was cracked over the low round table and a large aluminum carousel lowered onto its centre. Silent waitresses in smudged aprons continuously added and took away steaming dishes. Portions were small, limited by the tiny plates and mobility of the passing fare. Succulent odours mixed into the smoke. Some cigarettes had been placed on chopstick holders; others, he was amazed to see, hung from mouth edges like stiff spaghetti, food stuffed past them.

The utensils – chopsticks and a china spoon - impaired him as he tried to fill his dish. After frustrating and futile attempts to capture a mouthful, he used the spoon, much to the party's amusement.

"Try some of this." The President captured slippery pieces of tendon immersed in brown sauce and placed them on his plate. Daley noticed the wife repeat the offer to Ane as the platter went by. He swore the President enjoyed his impotent poking at the elusive morsels. He seemed to watch, eating little himself but keeping Daley's dish full. This ritual "feeding" of guest by host, he was to find common at Chinese banquets.

Chinese music played in the distance as soy and cigarettes circulated. Though the party was loud, even boisterous, Daley sensed something missing – like an orchestra with no brass. No clinking cutlery, no metal on china. Chopsticks made little noise to mark the meal's progress.

He was concentrating on cornering a slippy mushroom in thick gravy, when the host turned to him and asked loudly: "Why is Canada so unfriendly?"

The question took him by surprise and he quickly mouthed a mushroom. He chomped it purposely, playing for time. Unlimited wine had rendered faces red and excited.

His host pressed. "We send our best scholars to Canada and your government insults us!"

The table was quiet.

Daley's stomach sank as he slowly laid down the chopsticks. "As far as I know, Chinese visiting scholars are treated the same as other nationals. They work as equals with Canadians, live in the same apartments, eat at the same restaurants, shop at the same stores."

The grand Chinese was not listening and continued: "Why do you insult us? We send the cream of our students – our future – and you trick them. When they wish to come home, you seduce them to stay." He cracked his napkin in dismissal and turned to the Swiss.

Daley was dumbfounded. He felt foolish, poking at the mixture on his tiny dish, his appetite having vanished.

What's with this guy insulting me in public? The shithead! We make his countrymen welcome, and they destroy our equipment, cook food in our furnaces, hammer tapered inserts into molds backwards, ruining them totally. Besides, wasn't this dinner in my honour and now he's fawning on the Swiss!

He looked at his watch: 8.45. Two more bloody hours. He was shaking, nervously drumming his fingers. Ane smiled across the table and wagged her index finger from side to side; she hated that habit. You've no idea, he fumed at her.

The President blew a long cloud of cigarette smoke and enquired of the embarrassed Swiss, "Is it difficult for foreign scientists to study in *your* country?"

"It's expensive."

"*We* pay for them to go to Canada; *we* pay for them to live there and conduct research *for* the Canadians. And how do *the Canadians* pay us? Bribe them to stay!" He emphasised each 'we' with a ring of cigarette smoke.

Daley stared incredulously at his plate. As he struggled for control, a wild thought intruded: maybe it was an act, a play for the audience. Could anyone be so completely tactless? He wondered if Choi, realising this might happen, had had a belated attack of guilt and sent the FAX to stop them. Well, I'll drink the arsehole's wine, eat his food, and steal his best students and the hell with him! I hope they all stay in Canada.

A sudden realisation leapt at him – *the move*!

He grabbed Ny's arm, squeezing so hard he flinched: "You've got to talk to him about moving, Ny. The Guesthouse is out!."

Ny glanced at the President, clearly apprehensive. "But we opened it specially fora you!"

"Close it again. We're not staying there!"

Ny shrugged his shoulders and continued eating.

Daley had decided it was a night from hell when the next wine surprised him. The Chinese wine had been a sherry but "The Great Wall", a cooperative venture between China and West Germany, was an acceptable Rhinewine, unexpectedly dry. He swished it appreciatively, noting its slow, even roll up the glass sides.

Platters clattered. The aluminum carousel was cleared and replenished with clam-worms, 1000-year-old eggs, and deep-fried live scorpions.

The host served with the encouragement of the assembly but Daley fed himself, moodily declining all offers except the white wine, automatically refilled when emptied in one gulp.

The penultimate dish was hot, cored-apple halves in spun sugar, which were chopsticked, doused in cold water, and mouthed, crackling!

As luke-warm towels sponged away the sticky syrup, spring-onion shoots, small crepes, and fermented wheat sauce were brought to the table.

Ny rose and bent to the ear of the President.

The Peking duck, including boneless feet, was served sliced on plates. Pieces were dipped in the sauce, placed on a crepe, rolled up with green onions, and eaten, cone bottom folded to catch drips.

The head, bisected to display the *choix de fete* (the brain), entered with a flourish. The host chopsticked the morsel, deftly wrapping it in crackling skin pulled back from the beak. He offered it to the Swiss amid much Chinese laughter and encouragement – the ultimate insult of the evening!

The ruckus quietened as the President stood quickly, signalled to his wife, and left without farewells. Moments later he returned in coat and hat and curtly informed Daley they were to move to the Friendship Hotel. Ane's eyes lit across the table.

Back through the dark streets, Daley sat silent. Finally he boiled over. "The toffee-nosed git! Where's he get off attacking me like that? Bloody embarrassing. And that Swiss sod just...just bloody sat there."

Ane laid her hand on his arm. "Thought something was going on but couldn't really hear. I'm sure it wasn't his fault, the Swiss. Probably as surprised as you. After all, the dinner was supposed to be in *your* honour!"

"Bloody right! We take their 'students' who don't know their arse from a hole in the ground."

"Shush! It's not *his* fault either," she nodded at Ny.

He always made mountains out of molehills. A nice shower and a loving bed will help him forget.

The car entered an impressive brick gate, drove down a drive of shadowy trees, and stopped at the double-steps of a porticoed building. Reinforcement showed through the step edges and chipped brick sulked through the stucco sides – the Administration Office of the Russian-built Friendship Hotel. Slow automatic doors opened into a foyer of ill-fitting carpet spreading to the desk where a clerk stamped flimsy forms, then dispensed keys.

Cologne struggled with must.

Large brass clocks with flipping numbers told the world's time on a heavily marbled wall. Berlin and Bangkok were stopped, London was fast, Beijing was right...10.00.

"Room forty-seven. Fourth floor." Ny waved a key in his face.

The chrome-plated elevators had individual buttons – typically Russian, Daley thought irritably – automatic devices that are never quite automatic. Two were out of order. There was a door to stairs opposite, ill fitting with no light in its window. Never get up four flights this time of night.

Ane pulled the wool coat around her and smiled wearily.

"Remind you of Moscow, Ane?"

She linked her arm through, stepping out of her left high heel with a sigh of relief. "I don't care. Don't care if it's a real dump. It'll be welcome if it's warm!"

The burnished doors opened and they jerked to the fourth floor, arriving with a step up. The musty air carried a barnyard aroma and a TV blared martial music on the desk. An attendant perused the forms and checked the key. Behind him was the fridge for the floor.

Satisfied, he led them down the dark corridor and opened the door to a large warm room with a generous bed and a thermos in the window.

Warm. It was warm!

Ane dropped her coat round her ankles and pirouetted, hugging herself, tassels swishing .

"Let's be buggers and call each other sods." She was glowing. He palmed her bum. "Promises, promises," she laughed, dancing away.

"Better move this!" He picked up the thermos and put it on the bedside table.

Thermoses were the only source of potable water in China.

He looked around. The bed, covered with a red counterpane, dominated the space, stretching across the floor. There was a table with two chairs in the window, and a tall chest-of-drawers with a covered TV by the other wall.

Heat was a radiator, covered by the window-ledge on which the thermos had been standing.

The ledge was the warmest surface in the room but the window was cold. He leaned to the bedside table and turned on the radio.

The news was announced to the theme of "Starwars."

"Well, even if the guy is an arsehole, he'd the sense to move us! If he hadn't, we'd have been the hell out of China and he'd have lost all kinds of face!"

She nodded, happy, warm, busy hanging clothes and stuffing drawers, gently humming.

The recent chill made a bathroom visit urgent. He fumbled for the switch and a silver-fish sprinted for the drain. What a muddle! The Russians, for fun, he found out later from Greg, had mixed the colours of the American Standard fixtures so that a pink, free-standing bath squatted beside a yellow throne with a blue tank and a white broken lid. A heavy, jade sink stretched over the wet floor. Never venture barefoot in the bathrooms of China, Greg had warned. The floors were always wet.

He was relieved to see a toilet roll, though he had to remount it correctly. A sign of age, but nobody in his family seemed capable of replenishing a roll, never mind, having it unwind the right way!

Unlike in the Soviet Union, where anything made of rubber was stolen, there were sink and bath plugs. In Moscow, parked cars often had no wipers.

"It needs flowers," she said as he emerged, placing an empty vase in the window. "If we see any, remind me."

She loved wild flowers, knew all their names, country and botanical. Even in winter she'd find spindly ghosts of last summer to brighten their meal.

The duvet-covered bed was luxury. She stretched into its depths and he slid in beside her.

"Hell!"

"What?"

"Me bloody feet went right through. Sticking out like beached fish. Hate when that happens!"

She giggled, slipped out and tucked the duvet over his feet.

Her hand crept to his stomach. "Please, please, mister, can Johnny come out to play?" she giggled in a tiny voice.

She corrected his aim and, after roughness, he entered her soft. She kissed him gently as he slowly filled her.

Basking in remnant euphoria, she couldn't settle, couldn't get comfortable. Soft snores broke the dark silence. How could he always sleep straight away? Men are like rabbits; the buck passes out. Slam! Then sleep. Isn't fair. Sometimes it would be nice to cuddle a while.

She punched her pillow and turned on her other side. She rolled the evening by in her mind mostly with the President's wife.

"She asked the strangest question."

"Who?"

"The wife."

"Arsehole. Not her. Him. What question?"

"'Does your husband like teenagers?'"

"You mean young girls? None of her business!"

"Not that way."

"Then what?"

"I told her, fine, as long as they're not his own, Thought perhaps you'd know."

Her words hung in the air unanswered. I'll ask in the morning, she promised, spooning into him.

WEDNESDAY 25 OCTOBER

Nan's wind-up alarm clock shrilled. Daley was warm, unwilling to straighten his legs into the cold covers. His nose was cold. Just like February in England.

The bell stopped. He sat up and pulled on his socks, cursing the toe-hole. Since Nan died, no socks were darned, so he'd taken to stapling the holes shut. He smiled to himself – works well as long as the staple ends closed over.

He poured steaming water over the two piles of instant coffee and creamer, then took the cups to the bed. He was sitting on the side as she woke. His favourite time this: the relaxed few minutes of the day's first coffee.

"Funny thing about the pills Gypsum gave me for arithma. Wake every morning, hard as a chapel hat-peg, like a teenager."

She laughed, stretching languidly. "Dream on." She liked their play.

Later they watched the day awaken through rain drumming the grimy window. Clumps of cyclists swished water over the barren flowerbeds, an occasional taxi spraying them in turn.

"Don't you think it strange?"

"What?"

"That question last night, you know, about me and teenagers?"

"You heard. Just came up. Talking about families and it just came up."

"Not much of a day to see the Forbidden City, is it? If this doesn't let up, we'll get soaked."

She put down her cup and rocked back and forth, arms round her knees. "Thought I heard Ny tell you that last night. Looking forward to seeing Tiananmen Square, Peter. The Forbidden City runs right into it."

"Probably won't let us in. Still being fixed up."

"Hope they will. Like touching history, walking those flags. D'you think I can bring the camera?"

"Take, *not* bring. Picking up Claire's "bring-taker" habits, you are. In this lot you'll get lousy pictures."

"But it might clear up?"

"Don't see why not: just keep it dry."

The rain had tapered to showers when Ny arrived and, by the time they alighted at the Forbidden City, a brisk wind was drying the wet pavement.

The Forbidden City rolled down to Tiananmen Square, palaces stretching a mile in front and half a mile either side. Halls stretched double-tiered, yellow and green tiled grandeur, with faded blue, red, and white motifs under their generous eaves. Roof peaks emerged from golden open-mouthed dragons and lines of beasts of reality and legend processed at each corner. The sound of traffic penetrated – but only far and light – like Sunday afternoon in a city park.

The large halls followed each other from the North Gate with its Emperor's garden, to the South Gate of Mao and Tiananmen Square. Fanning out from their squat shapes were other, smaller replicas for secondary wives and courtiers, stretching as far as the eye could see.

All surfaces were stone and no plants, save weeds, flourished in the neglected courtyards. Weeds could even be seen struggling through broken–tiled roofs.

Not a blade of tailored grass anywhere.

They reached the central impressive scatter of buildings down the 'Road of the Gods', with its middle path reserved for Deity and right for the Emperor – faded whispers of a vanished past. The flagstones of the way-within-a-way still shone with rain and smelled of wet sea-shores.

One hall held an exhibition of clocks from France, England, Germany, and Switzerland – some few of the China Clock Company – elegant timekeepers of an elegant time, gone for the thousands gawking through the windows.

The hall for the favourite Empress was as big as the apartment blocks.

The Emperor's Hall was the biggest of all.

Daley and Ane peered through the distorting glass at the cold stone floors and faded silk coverings. Outside, the crowds jostled and pushed, cupping hands on windows for a glance of yesterday.

As they stepped down the bricks, Ane asked with a lop-sided smile: "Did I see you making a list this morning, Peter?"

He grinned. "Caught me! Unfortunately lists are fallible. I included transparencies but still forgot 'em!"

"Lucky you brought me, aren't you?"

"What d'you mean?"

"I found the box on the table and packed it."

He squeezed her hand. "Don't know what I do without you," he laughed and meant it.

"You've got us all making lists. I've seen Claire's when she's 'broomhildering' the house. It goes from room to room with heavy ink ticks."

"Trouble is they frighten me. I make 'em so's not to forget, then daren't look there's so much left to do. Real tyrants, lists!"

"But it's so nice to *scratch them out*, isn't it? Feel you've achieved something. The job's *done!*"

The New China Gate was a tower originally built for the Emperor's favourite, the Fragrant Concubine. She would climb each evening to look at the forbidden life outside her Tower of Yearning. Beyond was Tiananmen.

Soldiers were everywhere; the square was barred by a red velvet rope lengthened by sacking twine stretched between two stone bollards, patrolled by a boy scout soldier with a submachine gun. The bizarre restraints jolted Daley. They tried another route, through a garden, but again a soldier stopped them.

So they stood watching a drill squad with metre-long batons. Really like boy-scouts, Daley reflected, with their creased green uniforms, executing karate chops in unmilitary fashion.

"Try a picture, Ane." He stood in front of her. She popped the camera and triggered the shutter, putting the photograph in her pocket.

A baton touched her arm. The guard was holding out a hand, motioning at the camera with his gun. Baton between knees, he turned the unit over in his hands. A small crowd gathered. He shook his head and handed back the camera, motioning she open it.

"Do as he wants. Give him the film."

With a strained smile, Ny was rocking from one foot to another.

She pressed the release. The bottom tray fell open and she

pulled the blue tab, passing the soldier the cassette. He pocketed it and the crowd dispersed.

Ny's apartment was at the end of a dark corridor. It had a happy though cramped atmosphere. His small, rotund wife came forward as they entered. She bowed, hair short, sprinkled with grey. She smelled of lavender, and a cooking-stained smock covered her blue dress. Though she spoke no English, she blurted a rehearsed welcome, gesturing they sit on a chesterfield-cum-bed.

Daley was glad to. His sock had bitten a stinging ring round his toe. His stomach rumbled and Ane glanced reprovingly. He had asked for a Mars bar but she said it would spoil his dinner, so it was her fault he was rumbling.

Plaid blankets were folded on the back of the sofa and oranges tumbled from a dish on the oak coffee table in front of it. Stereo, VCR, and covered TV crowded the window wall opposite. There was a microwave with its impotent plug dangling.

A Swiss clock on the white-washed wall behind them, cuckooed once. He glanced at his watch – 7.45. Slow, just like bloody everything in this country.

Outside the single window, beyond piled bikes and unkempt grass, thunder was rolling like an invading army. Ny served instant coffee – a special treat for visitors.

Place is as wet as bloody Vancouver!

"My son soona home from school."

"And your daughter, will she come tonight?" Daley lifted his mug. The first sip burned his lip.

"I think so," Ny replied uncertainly.

Oh-oh, teenage daughter-dad problems, even in China!

They were shown around the apartment with great pride. The narrow kitchen was full of spicy smells and stood by the son's bed, behind the bikes and piled cardboard boxes that filled most of his room.

The tiny bathroom had no bath.

The dinner table was set in the corridor – pressed into service for this special night.

"My wife froma northern China. She maka special dishes for you."

"Shouldn't have gone to such trouble," Daley protested, but Ny assured him she enjoyed it, a chance to prepare her favourite food. She smiled, nodding as he translated and, unclasping her hands from behind her back, motioned they return to the settee.

Daley picked up the coffee and took a cautious sip. He was puzzled; no daughter's room, not even a bed.

It was now dark outside and the single table lamp cast a cosy glow. The cuckoo clock announced the hour. Mrs. Ny glanced and left to attend to dinner.

"I boughta that in Canada. It goes alla the time. Justa pull its chain."

Impressed by reliable energy. "That's an impressive stereo, Ny."

Ny grinned, clicked a switch and Bach sidled into the room.

"Froma Hong Kong. Alla Chinese scholars from West return through Honga Kong. Buya TV's, stereos, cameras with money saved."

"You managed to save what I gave you!" exclaimed Daley putting down his coffee.

"Oh, yes! Many Chinese people share one home in Canada – very cheap."

"Do you ever play it, I mean really play it loud?"

"Never! Never! Neighbours report – decadent." He waved a hand at the wall behind.

"I see. Is that why all the TV's are covered?"

"Ah-ha. That's superstition. Big eye watches, so cover up."

Strange mixture of myth and the modern.

"You never use the microwave?" Ane asked.

"Nota even plugged! Powera too scarce."

"Scarce?"

"Yes. Every district of Beijing hasa no power one day a week. Too little capacity."

"Why buy one then?"

"Prestige." Ny explained simply.

"I didn't think things like that mattered in China. I mean aren't people all supposed to be equal and everything?"

Ny laughed. "This isa der house for Associate Professor. Students share, six to room in bunks. If they marry, they get a room, so many marry. Assistant Professor she geta one room plus kitchen. Associate – me – one room plus kitchen, bathroom and smalla bedroom; Professor best! – Sitting room, dining room, kitchen, batharoom and smalla bedroom. Very big! Very capitalist!"

"Incentive by shelter." Daley was glad he'd not asked about the daughter – she probably shared a room with six. "So everybody has to use one of these as a bed?"

"Everybody – even Deans. But nota President. He has Party villa."

"He would," breathed Daley.

A door banged and the quiet ticking of bike wheels announced the son. His mother proudly entered with him.

"This isa my son. Kou," said Ny. Daley guessed he was about fourteen. He wore western-style jeans and anorak which he pulled off straight over his head. His face was bright and fresh with exertion and, eager to practise his English, he told of his day with the missing "l's"of Chinese *embouche* and interchangeable genders – a confusion Daley had got used to in Canada.

The youth picked up two oranges, skinned and bulged them into his cheeks. After the sixth elicited a scold from his mother, he sat quietly before the pile of skins. Daley struggled up; the liquid of the day was exacting its toll.

Standing at the tilted toilet, sink pressing his back, he murmured: "Food. I could eata bloody horse. May have to and not know it. Where is the girl? Fashionably late, I suppose."

He looked around. Primitive efforts had been made to "Westernise" the toilet "space." The paper was soft, the seat covered, and the de-silvered areas of the mirror masked by dragons breathing orange fire. A small rainbow throw-rug covered the concrete floor. The mouthful of tooth decay yawning up the basin drain straightened him and, turning away, he washed his hands. He quickly opened the door, took a deep breath of air and re-entered the sitting room, smiling. The anxious hosts were perceptibly relieved.

Ny and his wife seemed to become agitated as the stilted conversation progressed. Pauses lengthened and visits to check dinner became more frequent.

"Ane, bet this dinner's better than last night's."

"Shsh!" She leaned forward to put her cup down and confided: "You're flying low."

He looked down, then around. Bloody sink. He pulled the zip to the first difficult bend. "Could get arrested you know, smuggling a hidden weapon into China." Ane spluttered, elbowing him.

A muffled clump, like the distant closing of an expensive car door, sent Ny and his wife to the hall. As the trio emerged, Daley could see the visitor was a girl. She threw back her hood revealing a colourful headscarf tied World War Two style. As Ny helped with her cloak, he announced proudly, "This is Yen, my daughter."

"T'is a pleasure to meet you," she said, bobbing lightly.

She was tall, slim, about nineteen. Her eyes held him; fawn's eyes, large, deep, more *kwailo* than almond. Her palms were soft but her grip firm. A tan, clear face smiled at him. High cheekbones arched full cheeks to a determined set. A thin gold chain hung around her elegant neck. Chinese...yet not so.

He could not hold her gaze and looked down to the squeeze of firm breasts in her loose shirt and the accentuation of wide hips by the drape of a flared denim skirt. Her calves were muscled, legs bare to ankle.

He looked up again as her lashes flickered. With an embarrassed grin, he let go her hand and subsided into his seat.

This girl was different from her wiry father and roly-poly mother.

Her supple fingers fanned like a Thai dancer's over Ane's dress.

More handsome than beautiful, Daley decided, with a presence the French call "magnifique". "Statuesque" is better, he thought, imagining the cascade of hair hidden under the red dragon, body snaking to a single front knot so tight not a strand showed. Maybe a religious thing – teens are weird these days. Funny, a beautiful woman is beautiful, is beautiful, is beautiful...

He tried to find fault. Face too long? Too rectangular? Definitely not. He was staring and, as if knowing, she gave him a sideways, head-tilted, look. He looked away.

Had he seen her somewhere recently? Not possible. Probably someone on TV. Full of beautiful women, TV. This girl was perhaps the most beautiful he'd ever been close to. She was smiling at him, warm like a winter chinook.

Ny brought a chair and she settled into it, palming her shirt evenly under and over her knees, fingering errant hairs under her scarf edges.

Her mother worried around, picking up peel.

"I love your scarf!" said Ane impulsively.

The girl laughed softly. "Me mother bought it for me. T'is specially woven to tie this way," she explained, one finger on the somnolent dragon head, others circling evocatively.

"She has many hleads, thlat dlagon," her brother explained.

" Mlany," she mimicked, "but only one can be seen when the knot is tied." She made a fist on her forehead, one predatory finger pulsing forward in mime.

Entranced, the brother followed her hand-play. Clearly he idolised her. Different from my siblings, Daley ruminated, as the girl puffed warmth into her fingers.

Ane lifted a blanket from the couch back and held it out to her. "Here. You must be cold."

"No, no, not at all. One gets used to it," the girl shrugged, making faint nipple tracks in her shirt.

"Why don't people wear warmer clothing? They must be cold but they run around in nothing."

"Ah, the cold is yet to come!" The girl played with the small cross hanging on her neck. "Winter clothes will soon come out of storage and these'll go away. There's only room for one set at a time."

As she moved, Daley caught a waft of starch and Pears soap. How did she come by traditional Western toiletries? Probably Hong Kong – like everything else in the room.

"Explains the camphor."

"Space is at a premium in Beijing. So boxes are collected and filled with best clothes folded in mothballs."

Her English had an Irish shadow and was terribly dated. He hadn't heard "best clothes" since leaving Britain in the sixties!

"You must have seen 'em, the cardboard boxes, piled terribly high on bikes, so high you'd think they bowl over!"

The boy took an orange and cupped it in his hands. "Pleople collect, slell. Blig blusiness!"

"Even communism can't exorcise centuries of private enterprise," observed the girl.

Self-conscious about her smile, maybe braces. Bright, white, even. He looked back and she gave him a full smile, eyes shining as though acquiescing.

Her front teeth were a perfect single, almost imperceptable, more like a missing but almost missed little finger.

The brother was peeling the hidden orange but his mother saw and knocked it back into the bowl as she emerged from the kitchen. She motioned them to dinner.

The girl rose to lead the party. She walked with back straight, head high. Definitely balletic. Daley stood, zipped in one movement, picked up her chair, and followed.

He watched the slide of her bum and hummed to himself: "and the cheeks of her arse went, chuff, chuff, chuff."

Rugby-song writers got that right. "Bloody right," as Ray Jenkins would say.

He slid the chair under her, hastily turning to do the same for Ane who wore a frosty smile.

Mrs. Ny had cooked so many dishes, forgotten ones were found days after.

The table centre-piece was a tower charcoal-burner, hissing blue flame and boiling sliced mutton, Chinese cabbage, and beans. The steam was full of flavour, the kerosene whirling Daley back to the pull-down, paraffin-lamp above the scrubbed kitchen table of Tipperary childhood.

The main dish was chopsticked from the tower and rolled with a steamed, Northern China pudding of rice, meat and plums, upended on a platter like an English suet dumpling.

Daley joshed Ny about his days in Canada.

"We think Canada a cold country. It wasa wrong!"

"Oh, dah! You speak English like an Italiano."

"Parts of Canada are always cold, Ny. There's a Four Seasons Hotel in Labrador City known as the 'Two Seasons.' Cold and Colder!" The table chuckled. Mrs. Ny smiled, pleased they were enjoying her food. "What people don't realise is the Niagara peninsula is farther south than Milan. Peaches, grapes, and tobacco grow there!"

Ny lay down his chopsticks, sat back and folded his arms. "I knowa no English when I arrive. So I sit ina restaurant and say 'same as him.' I soona learn Canadian dishes!"

The girl was quiet. The boy wolfed down his food, went for more, demolished it, and went again. His mother waylaid him on his third round, her chop-sticks pausing over his plate like a police baton.

The boy broke the silence. "You lave poritical tlubles in your country?"

"We have Quebec but it's not serious, at least, not often." He smiled as he told a story. Unknown packages were politically sensitive. A newly-graduated photographer, in Quebec City for a job interview, was rushing and had to stop to tie a shoelace. He ran on, forgetting his portfolio, a year's work. He returned to find the street cordoned off and a large crowd gathered. Suddenly there was an explosion. A "suspicious bag" had been blown up – for safety's sake! A year's work Poof!" Daley threw up his hands propelling imaginary fragments as the table chuckled and Ny murmured translation for his wife.

The girl was not amused.

"You don't know what trouble is at all!" A quick glance from her father and she looked down, but her intensity surprised Daley.

There was a loud knock on the door.

The girl's face fell and she sat up, stock still. Her chopstick fell to the floor and she shot a glance down the corridor.

Ny shuffled his chair back and went to answer.

Picking up her utensil, the girl wiped it repeatedly with her napkin.

Daley noticed her hand was shaking.
Ny returned, said a few words in his son's ear, who then nodded at the company and went to the bedroom, emerging wheeling a bike to the visitor.

The girl relaxed like a released bow. She fixed Daley with her bright eyes. "Did you bring any sweets to China?"

He shifted uncomfortably. Why did she have such an effect on him? Hell, he'd only just met her! . "'Sweets'? Oh, you mean candy?"

She nodded.

"Matter of fact, we did. Halloween Mars Bars, cheese and crackers, raisins - as many as we could carry – after Russia. We won't need 'em though."

"And you thought China'd be same?"

"Well, in some ways it is. You have the same business of money forms on the aeroplane."

"We lave two tlypes of money. One flor you, one flor us."

"Oh, Kou. All you tink about is money! It's so insignificant in *real* life."

An idealist, sighed Ane. What it is to be young!

"It looks easy to counterfeit," observed Daley.

"All money clan be clopied by Japanese machlines like luniversity's new one."

"Not Canadian money. The notes have a thin-film ceramic spot. Look, let me show you." He struggled out his wallet from his pocket and held a red note near the flaring tower, moving it back and forth. "See. From one direction it's orange; from the other, yellow. Impossible to copy."

"Leta me see. Clever! Very clever. How?"

"The oxide is thin so light of wavelength half the layer thickness reflects and can be seen. As you change the angle, the layer thickness changes, so the colour changes."

Wind driven rain gossiped on the window, a slow drip betraying a leak as the party returned to the sitting room for coffee.

The orange peel had gone. The girl scissored to the floor in a feline motion.

"I've never flown before and we're goin' to Bojai together." She flicked an invisible crumb from her knee. She'd really come to life since the innocuous visitor.

Ane laughed."Taking off gives me such a feeling of power."

The girl shook her head."Don't like power. Power hurts."

"Lets nota start."

"Oh, da. This country'll be the death of us! You defend 'em! Won't discuss them. You think it'll all go away if you don't look."

Daley sat back surprised for Ny had really pressed a button.

"We're ruled by old men and their old women watch. Miscegenation is rampant. T'is a country for the old. *Never* be free!"

It was the most serious thing said all evening, an unexpected deep in the small talk.

"Do I *have* to stay with Aunt Tanner, da? T'is so *provincial.* in the country. I like the city. Here t'will happen again and I want to be *here*. not in the wilderness!" Her stiff finger hit the table for emphasis.

Moods like Beth's. Teens! Same everywhere.

"You lika mountains."

"T'is *boring,* da! My friends are *here.*"

"You'll maka new ones."

"But there's nothin' to do!"

"You shlouldn't make him to glo if he doesn't wlant to!"

Ny glared at his son.

Tiananmen Flight 67

Brother and sister defend each other. Very different from my progeny. Maybe Tiananmen brought the young together. Daley was ashamed of duelling with his daughters, always confused by the precipitate deterioration into *ad hoc* dictates.

Ny wagged his forefinger firmly. "You'lla go. Know you hava to!"

The girl inspected her fingernails fanned in her lap. "Yes, da. Suppose you're right but still I'd rather not."

It wasn't till long after that Daley realised the entire spat had transpired in English! Most family talk had been Chinese.

A cuckoo broke the awkward silence and the girl turned, hands on knees, to look at the VCR. Daley followed her glance – 10.01. God, doesn't time fly!

As she floated into the dark corridor with her mother and Ane, she turned, and the bulb cast her profile. Daley's breath caught.

Suddenly the girl, hands to the back of her bowed head, unpinned her scarf and passed it to Ane. The wife re-entered the room, hastily rummaged in a drawer and, silk flying – deep blue with gold flowers - returned to the corridor, wagging her finger and tutting at her daughter. The girl spun the corners, held it against her neck and deftly tied it.

Daley was puzzled. Mrs. Ny had been stricken - but over a scarf? Made no sense.

He sat on the side of the bed listening to Mozart on the radio. The rain was coming and going against the window as he rubbed Lanocane into the angry ring round his big toe.

Ane was in the big bed. "Family's a real muddle of English, isn't it, Peter? Ny speaks Italiano, daughter Irish, son Chinese, and wife, not at all!"

"Like an international conference. Obviously she's been among Irish, maybe worked in the embassy or something."

The "Meditation from Thais" slipped into the room and he hummed along, smiling sadly. "Me dad loved this, you know. If it came on the radio, no matter what was going on, we all had to be quiet: family, visitors, dogs, everybody. A peep and he'd round on you."

Ane sat up. "You know, she was expecting us."

"Who?"

"Ny's wife."

"What you talking about? Course she was."

"No, I mean, that dinner. Must have taken her a week to prepare. *She* was *expecting* us." She nodded with satisfaction and lay down again.

"Well, Ny certainly wasn't, was he "

"Please turn the radio off. I'm tired and it's one thirty. "

There was quiet.

"You liked her, didn't you?"

"Who?"

"You know who!"

"Oh. The daughter. Well, you must admit she's unusual. High, wide and handsome. Taller than her parents, isn't she?"

"Don't find that strange. Many kids are taller than their parents. Look at Ian Jenkins. Towers over his mum and dad."

"True. Didn't seem Chinese, though. Face wasn't Chinese, large eyes, pouty mouth. Wasn't flat either."

"She's young. Immature. Unrealistic about money! Pity about her teeth."

She was vexed with herself. Had promised herself not to mention it but there it was, she had. Like an immature schoolgirl. She was too tired to care.

"Wish I'd been that crucifix," he murmured, recalling the nipple traces as he lifted the comforter and slid under.

"Didn't you find it strange she wears a crucifix?"

He stretched his left arm under as she lifted her head. "Maybe it's fashionable to wear western icons."

She snuggled down. "Her English too. So old-fashioned."

"I thought that too!" he said, uneasy at enjoying talking about the girl so much. "Haven't heard sweets' for a long time! Did you see her reaction to the knock on the door?...Scared!"

"Wouldn't you be? I bet she was at Tiananmen and that's why she's going to her aunt."

"Maybe. Seemed political, idealist anyway. Could be why she wears that scarf you know, working-woman style."

"Nah. Teenager thing. Remember when Beth'd only wear your undervests? Had to sew on your name so you would not lose 'em. Besides she gave it to me, so she can't be all that frightened."

"It was dark and she probably knew her mother had another."

She rethumped her pillow into shape. "I don't care what you say. It was a generous thing to do!" She was irritated at her own ambivalence, decided his arm was hurting her neck and was tired of talking about the girl who was too young anyway.

Thursday 26 October

On Tiananmen there was silence. Only in the safety of home did a professor speak, voice shaking like a father of lost children, of the empty chairs in his class. Later Ny explained that in China teachers and students were a permanent family – inseparable. There had been a time when a student-criminal teacher was beheaded for misguiding his charge!

Professor Wang and his wife, who had visited Minster for three months, had invited them for morning coffee before the venue of the day –the Great Wall. The girl came too and was sitting, mug and saucer on her knee steadied by one hand, feeding on a brittle biscuit with the other. She was still drab but magnificent, tight scarf circling her head.

Daley's biscuit was half eaten, the balance in crumbs in his lap. He hated snacks with no table, especially when the saucer slid to the edge of his clenched knees. He watched how she made no crumbs. She seemed to suck the biscuit. He'd seen Mick Lister do the same once with a cigarette-end years ago: fold it into his mouth, close his lips, then fold it out again with a smirk, still lit.

She too spoke of the recent terror, husky voice wavering, eyes liquid, intensity riveting. She spoke of the unsung people of

Beijing who protected the "kids." In lines with linked arms, they surrounded the Tiananmen tents, standing between the students and the provincial army.

For the first time Daley heard the story of the army. Recruited from villages, well fed and guaranteed prestige on return, they were not interested in joining the students. They believed in the regime that fed them. So it was they gunned down the people; yet the people stood, barring their way, held by neighbours. Defiant, the living and the dead standing together.

The girl's voice went soft, so soft it was difficult to hear. Occasionally she lapsed into silence. The company held its collective breath, all the time watching the scarfed head with the faraway eyes.

"We were in the 'Gate of Heavenly Peace'; that's what Tien An Men means, can you believe?" she said with quiet bitterness. The people had said, 'If one drop of blood is shed, the government will fall!' Zhao Ziyang was with us. We were tired, happy, excited."

It was clearly an often told story. Heads nodded silently. Daley looked at Ane. Her eyes were moist.

"On that day, I left the square to attend class. My friend was still sleepin' in the tent but the crowd was waking."

Her hands and fingers mimed her words.

"I passed tanks with big '27's' on their sides and flowers in every metal edge but noticed no change. In class through the open windows we heard the rumble, felt the floor tremble. I ran unbelieving, through banners and ropes, jeans, and people, to the tent. Oh, glory be, the tent!" Her voice broke, fingers waving the air uselessly, settling, clenching and unclenching in her lap as tears remembered that day.

"It wasn't there! A purple bundle of ripped canvas, tracked by a tank, a grotesque eiderdown, hand sticking out as though sleeping. Another friend, still in the canvas, was less than two inches thick, crimson, inside and through." She was lost as the image worked her face and tears flowed freely. Wang's plump little wife cradled her sobs, whispered of her lost friends and those hanged daily in plain sight so all would learn.

She rocked the girl and, leaning forward protectively, spoke of her own terror; of joining the chain of linked arms till her neighbour was knocked from her feet by a bullet; of going down with her so saving her own life; of lying face down, small in the road, a barrage of screams shivering above the squeaks of crushing tanks – not daring to move, praying the rumbling and shaking, screaming ground would fade.

Back at the Friendship Hotel, he sat on the bed, watching through the open door and thinking. It's not real – a play, a reading. Only happens in the world of Lazyboys, TV, and snacks. He shook his head. It happened long before we got here and is over, settled. They would be untouched, except for the stories. Those he could handle. He drew a deep breath and glanced at his watch. 11.30. Their ride was due.

The taxi appeared as the hotel double doors jerked open.
The rain had stopped and the sun was emerging.
Ane grasped the black and white coat around her and bent into the back seat. The girl, sitting in a cocoon of coat, pulled small between them. With a jerk, they were off to see the seventh wonder of the ancient world.
He breathed a sigh – thank God the big sock hole was gone.
Ane rolled down her window.
"You must be joking! It's freezing."
"Fresh. I want fresh air."
At first the traffic was light but it became dense as they left the city down Changping Road.
"Today therea be army control. Thisa road leave Beijing so 'Red-Road.' We hava no problem," Ny assured them, nodding at the flag on the antenna.
At least there's some kind of order, Daley noted as they approached. Bicycles and pedestrians were moving to the right, leaving the main road to motor and horse-drawn traffic. Flow was smooth – search must be cursory. He could see the canvas

covers of army trucks ahead – two, one beyond the other, sideways across to zig-zag the traffic.

As they approached, a mule-cart loaded with coal ahead, was signaled to the left. A control officer saluted them and waved them to the right.

Cyclists and walkers were inspected by two soldiers either side of the right sidewalk.

"Look fora guns with metal detectors, people with people-prods." A soldier was circling an instrument like a vacuum cleaner above the straw of a cart as his neighbour prodded the stooks with a bayonet.

"Provincials. Regiment froma provinces. Not likea Beijing people."

Daley remembered the army of Tiananmen had been provincial and illiterate.

They stopped parallel to the mule cart. Shouts of nervous Chinese through Ane's open window.

The girl, eyes shut and head deep in her coat, was fingering her cross.

Soldiers probed the coal, grunting with each lunge. Young, grim, the Hitler Youth of grainy newsreels.

He concentrated on the cyclists and walkers. They lined, thick like a cornfield, so close one couldn't see through. On saddle, one foot down or standing one knee bent, a jumble of chains, jeans, tubing and tires on staid 'sit-up-and-beg' bikes of old village 'bobbies.' They were swaddled in scarves, sweaters, gloves with and without fingers, coats, long and short, windbreakers and summer rain jackets that couldn't break a breeze, balaclavas, ski-hats and cardboard boxes with ear-holes for straps. The smirking soldiers frisked them, blowing on fingers between. Fast quipping males were quick-checked and the silent females, slow-felt. A husband and his wife, with her blouse open to let her baby suckle, stood waiting. The baby, swaddled in a green and black plaid blanket, blended into her, tiny cheeks working, milk dribbling.

Husband inspected, she passed him the child, momentarily,

baring her breast. The soldier's mouth fell, she hastily buttoned up and stood for his search.

The husband, unnoticed, quickly extracted and pocketted a black object from the baby's blanket and, swaying the gurgling infant in the crook of his arm, tickled it under the chin and baby-talked to it. Daley grinned. Nicely done – the world's oldest ploy.

One mule, legs splayed, extruded steaming buns, piling the road and an army boot. The air filled with stable. The disgusted private, kicked off the pile, lifted the mangy tail and stubbed his cigarette into the offending orifice.

The animal reared as if shot. The cart heaved.

The tethering soldier dropped his gun.

Coal cobs peppered the car then deluged the road.

Ane rolled up her window freshing back the young perfume.

The cart driver, mumbling to himself, black toes protruding socks, ran to the mule and, pulling its right ear, standing tip-toe, murmured into it. The animal stilled.

Daley watched. So drab even mule shit fits.

"All ways froma Beijing searched. Very dangerous. Looka for reactionaries, looka for guns."

The car jerked – their turn.

The two soldiers squatting on the tailgate of the right-hand truck and the two on the road straightened, flicked away cigarettes, shouldered guns and saluted – out of sync. Daley waved like royalty.

"Why'd you do that? " Ane smacked his raised hand.

"Never been saluted before."

As they pulled into the traffic, he noticed the girl's necklace had been squeezed so tight, the cross was bent.

They entered hilly country. Bracken and hardy trees clung to the cliffs as the road wound upwards. The day was crisp, blue showing through the wind-tattered clouds.

The road was a jam of people. Ane asked the car pull over and stepped out, Yen with her. Daley knew – flowers. He watched Ane's determined step and then the girl: the caring, mature woman and the effervescent child.

Ane knew wildflowers by their country names, Ladyslippers, Jack-in-the-Pulpit, Queen Anne's Lace and, his favorite, Baby's Breath. She knew a wood where orchids grew near the haunted bridge at Ribstone. It was a place of wild iris, tiny purple, and hidden nests of birds, a badger set and a fox den. Funny the difference wild flowers make to a room. Not exotic blooms but subtle pastels. She knew their secret for they'd not wilt for days. Whenever he took a bunch, he had to take the roots so the heads would stand. She would scold him – roots must be left!

The car was cooling. He pulled his coat closer, hands deep in the pockets. Flowers this time of year; no chance, he decided irritably.

Eventually they emerged up the road, the girl retying her scarf. Ane had a bouquet of barley, ash berries, and elder bunches – gold, orange, and purple. Daley shook his head, she would go into the desert and return with a handful of colour.

As the girl bent into the car, she flashed him a smile and gave him her grasp. " These are for you."

Well, he had done it! Walked the Great Wall or, rather, climbed it! In windsweeping cold on a salt-cellaring of snow, he had clambered the narrow path between parapets and pinnacles, by step and by steep to the topmost. The battlements lay perpendicular to the lie of the bleak hills. Open watch-towers for smoke signals alternated with roofed ones for garrisons. The latter offered protection from the breath-stealing wind, but narrowed the path to jostling confusion. Every section was signed by its craftsmen.

"What you smiling at, Peter?"

"These." He patted the low rails. "Reminds me of Dave Allen's story about the two drunks on a railway line, ' Never walked stairs so wide! ' gasps one. 'Doesn't worry me,' says the other, 'it's these low handrails!'" She laughed and walked ahead to afford him wind break.

He found breathing, or rather catching a full breath, difficult.

The girl bounced up.

"Why don't you keep up? You should do more exercise – you wouldn't begrudge the breath." She skipped off, laughing over her shoulder.

They passed two soldiers talking to a man with a stick. The girl's face fell like a deflated balloon and she slowed to a walk with him.

Dromedaries lazed in thin sun in sheltered paddocks waiting to pose frozen riders for photographs.

The Chinese had discovered the camera and everyone had one. Ane popped open the polaroid. The crowd stopped and peered over Ny's shoulder as he explained against the wind, the metamorphosis of the picture. The print passed from hand to hand and Ane eventually intercepted it, fully developed. Yen stood on the wall, face turned away, camel visible under her raised leg, as though being mounted.

Daley saw a lady laughing behind a glove, beards were unusual.

Fifty thousand kilometers and he had walked a single one. Ane was reading a plaque, hand on each side as if to keep it still. "How long is it really? In words *I* can understand."

He did some fast calculations. " If it were a bicycle chain, it'd stretch from here to Beijing!"

"Enough stone to wall the world ten times!" read the girl. "Makes our efforts seem insignificant altogether."

They say a man is greater for walking the Wall, but Daley found the cold wind only made relief mandatory – much to the girl's amusement.

" As you get *old*, you must go more often."

He strode off testy – that "old" word again – the cold had let him down.

On the drive back to Beijing they entered a forest. There were fewer people on the cedar shadowed road and they were mostly walking. He enjoyed the fresh smell of the girl. He remembered a skipping girlfriend, as she bent to pick severed poppy heads.

"How can they do that?" asked the girl suddenly, nodding at couples walking hand in hand. "Their parents can't care at all?"

Ane was surprised, "What do you mean?"

"My da won't let me do that."

Another side of Ny, the happy-go-lucky. Maybe he was strict. Maybe she's wild, thought Daley.

"I walked that way, though, with a boy in the Forbidden City. We laughed together. Tis for the 'forbidden,' so we did nothing wrong, did we?"

As Daley watched the tail of the gold dragon on her scarf, an often thought surfaced. Ane is a "listener." Has a proclivity for it. World's divided into talkers and listeners. Everybody wants to talk about themselves. Can even sense them waiting, queueing for the confessional. Most people don't want to hear – except the listeners. Talkers recognized them and total strangers bare their souls!

"He was a sculptor and they hated him. They killed him that day."

Ane put an arm round her, squeezing his shoulder to warn him.

"Funny, I still see him…everywhere. On buses, in crowds, closing elevators, in shop windows – always there, distant, but there…everywhere."

Ane took her hands. "You must take love where you can. Life's too short. Don't feel bad…you *did*…imagine if you hadn't."

The girl recovered like a child. "I hate wearing trousers! Don't you? I'm starvin.' Let's find tuck and gorge!"

That startled Daley. Archaic English. Jes.

Bumping potholes squeaked the springs and deadened outside sounds.

The girl sighed: "I am glad, really I am. 'What is thy substance, whereof are you made that millions of strange shadows on you tend?'"

"No inspection thisa way. Only ifa leave Beijing. Nobody trya enter –all want leave"

Friday, 27 October

Daley was up, sitting at the desk, holding slides against the sunrise, squinting through a magnifying glass. He was assembling his talk. His watch, folded on the table, confirmed it was early – 6.30.

"When will you get some new glasses?" A sleepy voice from the bed. "Think you like being the eccentric professor!"

They were mended with epoxy, bridge braced with straightened clothes-hanger wire and screwless leg hinged by a small, safety pin.

"They function. Besides, you don't mind borrowing them! You've no idea how difficult it is to mend one's own glasses – you can't see what you're doin'."

"I think you enjoy fixing things. More even than getting new ones."

She punched her pillow, then subsided into it. "Think of all the times you've mended mufflers with dog food cans and hose clamps when it would've been quicker to replace 'em."

"It saves money."

"Funny thing is I love you for it. It's you, make-do. Couldn't live with an unimaginative man. New glasses'd make you more handsome though."

Daley looked round the assembling room. The audience seemed to be wearing every piece of clothing they owned, with one concession - fingerless gloves to facilitate writing.

The morning had started in a lounge of deep armchairs and glass coffee tables, sunlight from high windows and the inevitable green tea. He had removed his coat, thinking that, ever on the move, he would keep warm.

Unfortunately, interpreted lectures take twice as long, so, in this room with no heat, he was slowly freezing.

He carried slides in a carousel to save confusion, but the projector was a Russian straight-tray so they had been reloaded.

After introductions, the lecture started – and stopped. The first slide had stuck!

A tide erupted from the front row and he watched their enthusiastic incompetence with rising apprehension. Universal, he thought irritably –everyone's a projectionist!

A hand-loaded "magic-lantern" was set up and the lecture recommenced, brisk delivery reduced to a chilly crawl by translation and expansive explanation.

The end was greeted with exuberant clapping. He rubbed his numb hands and wriggled his toes. The applause was genuine, they stood as it continued. He got a recurring feeling that a fire burned inside these people. Never far from the surface, warming through handshakes, diffusing through smiles.

Ane was waiting outside the antique telephone exchange with its bakelite plugs and deft ladies.

"Went well!" he told her as she came up.

"Something's happened."

He ignored her. "Let's go to the sitting room. I'm freezing. That room was an icebox."

"I've got to talk to you."

"Okay. Let's go there anyway. I have to interview the students in a few minutes and must get warm."

In the room, he stood in a patch of sunshine.

"I had visitors."

"Visitors?"

"I was sitting reading this magazine and there was a knock, so I went to the door and there was this tall, well-dressed Chinese man and a girl with a baby. I told him you weren't here but he wanted to talk to *me*. His cologne was strong – way too much. He introduced himself and his sister. He's a diplomat and his sister's husband is at McGill in Montreal. She wants to join him and he's managed to get her a passport."

"And they want our help, right?"

"She has a letter from our embassy promising a visa but she can't go. Wants us to go with her."

"*Exactly* what Choi told us about! Ny too for that matter! They want our 'protection.' The protection our party can give.

It's dangerous. You didn't say we would, did you?"

"Her husband's never seen the baby! We can go. Where's the harm? She's *got* the visa."

"NO BLOODY WAY!"

"Imagine if you'd never seen Eddie!"

There was a small silence.

"She let me hold the baby."

He took a deep breath and put his arm round her. "Ah, that's it. I love you. How can you be so soft, yet so sensible? You know we must stay out of it. Really could be dangerous. You didn't say we'd do it, did you?"

"No. Said I'd ask you."

"Look, the baby's got its mother, and grandmothers too, no doubt. These people are not like us. They're used to separation. Ny didn't see his family for two years."

"Yes, but not a baby he'd never seen! " She was worrying her wedding ring.

"There's more, isn't there?"

She nodded.

"Okay, lets have it."

"I think it was that man in Hong Kong."

"Which?"

"It was the same cologne."

"Your bloody nose."

"Well, I remember smells and it was the same as the wildman in Hong Kong. The one that nearly knocked me down with the hotel door."

"Doesn't mean it was him. They all wash in perfume."

"No, this was the same – an expensive one."

"But you said he was well-dressed, a diplomat. Other bugger was a tramp."

"Could be the same. I mean, both tall, with long hair."

Ny came in, hands waving. Daley stilled him with an upright hand and told him of the visit.

The forever smile disappeared. "Hava nothing to do with them. May bea trap! I warn'ned you."

There were eight students, some sharp, some also-rans. To a man, they asked when they would hear from Minster. Daley secretly hoped they had heard, at least the good ones, would verify Louisa's FAX. None had.

He was gathering his papers when an unscheduled one came in with stubbly hair, acne, and circular steel glasses. He was wearing sneakers, faded jeans, and ill-fitting overcoat, was nervous and talked slowly. Yen had arranged for them to meet at his apartment and, as they walked, the boy proudly told of his marriage and his luck.

Laughing children, playing in a clutter of waste paper and curling cabbage leaves, made way as they climbed the crumbling steps of a grey apartment block and threaded the bicycles on every flat surface round the door. In the gloom at the top of the stairs, a student knelt on the floor, primus bluely heating a pan of smoking oil. The acrid vapour hit Daley's throat, making his eyes water as they passed a dark, doorless room in which dirty pans and vegetables were being cleaned in an open stone-slab trough, with water draining through a hole to a hole in the floor.

A lockless door revealed Yen and the embarrassed wife, sitting on a quilted bed that dominated the room. They rose in greeting.

She was still scarfed.

"Thought you'd like to see how we live."

The room was tiny and full. The TV on the side table was cosied in plum and surrounded by photographs and knickknacks. A bike leaned on a desk at the foot of the bed, a primus on rickety shelves above its front wheel and thermoses under its chain. Daley thought back to their tiny apartment on Parker Street, Berkeley. They'd been happy, though it was pokey; perhaps there's happiness here too.

The host offered oranges and a cup of Nescafe from a jar that cost $20 of his $60 monthly wage. To his ill-concealed relief, Daley declined.

A pall of urine permeated the room.

"He wants to show you his results," the girl told Daley. The student rose, rummaged under the bed and emerged with a briefcase.

"Can shlow?"

He passed Daley a white, foamed ceramic tile. The bubbles seemed monosize, and the sharpness of the edges suggested it was strong. "It's high quality. Tell me about it?"

"It new in Chlina!"

Ane took *Time* from her pocket and began to leaf it.

"Maybe, but what is original about it?"

The boy looked confused.

The girl took the magazine from Ane.

Daley sighed.

"I mlade it."

"Had this trouble in Russia."

Yen interrupted, wagging the rolled-up magazine at him: "Russians! You always compare us with the Russians! We hate 'em. What do you know about China? The Russian system was mimicked by China." A curl worked loose and looped her eye, "And t'will take time to correct. Some Chinese science is world beatin'. Look at acupuncture. The West is fascinated by it!"

"True, but original research must be just that."

"Dlont lave equipment...no electlic power."

Later that afternoon Daley saw evidence of his complaint at the student's lab.

Weeds fought waste paper between piles of broken bricks and tired yellow buildings. The place looked like an old bombsite.

A drab room containing massive equipment was an octopus of pipes and heavy, braided wires that spread in tentacles across the floor from a squat steel casing. No dials, screens, printers, just manual controls; nothing painted: raw rust with shimmering blue welds. Bright faces smiled at him and showed data from the heavyweight deity. In a machine shop, workers sat reading; some played cards. This was the one day per week the power was off.

The girl took Ane to a *cloisonne* factory. Ane thought they were followed by a black Mercedes before she realised that there were so few cars and so few roads, that everybody was following everybody!

The building was decrepit, its floors traversed by a doorless elevator. The guide explained and the girl translated. *Cloisonne* starts by fusing fine wires into the desired design on a copper or brass base. Then layers of multicoloured enamel are applied. The wires must be hot and each layer of enamel fired before the next. Finally the ware is polished to reveal the original wire tracery divided by remnant enamel.

Ane tied the scarf Yen had given her over her face, bandit-style, against the dust. Yen bent to her. "Bureaucrats decide the patterns. The artists only choose the colours. Party omavauns know art! Huh!"

Ane was appalled by the lack of safety masks, helmets, and shoes.

The open elevator with its white-gloved operator rose to fill the hole in the wall and they rattled to the basement. There, a small, smiling Chinese girl stepped in, carrying a tray of red-hot wires at arms-length. Ane shrunk from the shimmering mass, and as the elevator clunked to a stop, the wires went one way, and she the other!

Craftsmen soldered warm wire into patterns on roughly turned vases. In a back corner, an old man, with a wisp of grey beard and bent back, was using fine brushes and a magnifying glass to meticulously paint a tree inside a glass bubble. Like the man in Kiev, putting gold boots on fleas, Ane thought.

"If you liked it so much, Ane, why didn't you buy it?"
"Weren't for sale."
He took a long drink of the grainy coffee.
"Peter. Isn't McGill in Montreal?"
"Um. Why'd you ask?"
"Just thinking."
She paused...he hated it when she did that.

"That FAX came from Montreal."

"Forgotten that. Don't think there's any connection. Why would the husband try to dissuade us from visiting China? Hell, they need our help!"

She tried to squash the rest of the day into the almost-full page of her diary. She allowed herself one page a day!

"Did you see what Ny's daughter did, Peter, at that student's apartment?"

"Wasn't it a shambles? Every building smells like a urinal. Don't know how they stand it."

"You probably didn't notice. You were so caught up in 'shop.'"

"What you talking about?"

"She grabbed *Time* right out of my hand!"

"She wagged it at me about Russia."

"I don't think that was why, though. She grabbed it before you mentioned Russia! Didn't even want to read it. Just wave it about!"

"Starved for Western news probably. What were you looking at?"

"The Tiananmen pictures."

"Maybe that's it. Maybe they hurt."

"Then why not stop looking? No need to grab it, is there?"

He launched off the bed, walked to the table and decanted water from the thermos into a glass. It was raining again, coming and going against the window, like a garden hose.

"Odd, isn't it. We've been in China four days and I've only given one lecture. Greg said they'd work me arse off, three lectures a day."

"But you only really came to interview those students."

"Ny had nothing to do with that. You'd think he'd have me appearing in every dump possible."

She closed the diary and slid the pencil into its spine.

He looked at the steady rain. The girl was everything she shouldn't be.

He switched on the TV. The screen defocussed to a glowing campfire. He jerked awake as his head rolled. "Let's go to bed.

Full day of China bashing tomorrow."

"Shall I put on my head clothes?"

He smiled. "Too tired to think. Never mind. Don't think I'd be interested in Sophia Loren right now."

"You must be tired!"

"Summer Palace tomorrow, isn't it? I hope there aren't too many bloody stairs."

Saturday, 28 October

They met Ny and his daughter for lunch in the international cafeteria of the Beijing School of Arts and Science. Lunch was cabbage. Like beets in Moscow, Daley reflected, cabbage in Beijing, the only and everywhere vegetable. It lined roadsides, piled bicycles, outside apartments, on balconies, in corridors, on chairs and beside holes in unkempt gardens. In one building they were being reduced to soup by the truckload in slurping vats over roaring burners. The harvest for winter.

Sulphur permeated everything like ungathered fields of the plants.

Still scarfed, white this time, the girl wore round red earrings. Her coat was the bulkiest Daley had ever seen, its pockets bulging like a child's candy-filled cheeks.

"What in the world d'you have in there?"

"Everything!" she bubbled, strewing the table with stones, dried and fresh flower petals, and tickets for functions and places. "These bring me luck. Here's a red one." She held out the sliver of rose quartz. "These bring spring everywhere." She rubbed a few flower petals, then picked up a ticket. "These are useful when da asks where I've been. Show him a ticket and he's happy."

Daley glanced at Ny queuing for their food. Wonder if Beth's ever given me that line.

She shed the coat onto the back of her chair.

"You'll get the skirts dirty."

"Will not so! You're always on about the dirt! Not important, dirt. Neat and tidy's not what matters, it's food, clothes, shelter."

"As long as you're happy."

She fingered an earring. "I was happy...once...in China. At Aunt Tanner's. Loved watching her flowers swinging between my feet. My uncle built me a swing. Nice man, my uncle."

She circled her forefinger on the formica table. "They cut down the tree to make iron and now the flowers struggle with clover butterflies and long grass."

She stood, the chair tipped her coat inside-out on the floor. She righted it and walked off to her father.

Daley watched. Funny about women's bums. What was it Claire said? Boobs are for babies, bums for babes. Definitely.

"Well. That was a surprise, I must say."

"Oh, I don't know, Ane. She gets upset when I mention dirt."

"No, I mean Ny's family has money."

"What makes you think that?"

"Aunt obviously does. A house, garden. Thought people couldn't own property in China."

"Probably if you're in the 'Party' – like Russia and the dachas."

Ny set down a tray of steaming cabbage and the girl passed around chipped plates and aluminum spoons.

Recognizing a familiar pate across the room, Daley walked over and welcomed Greg to the land of cabbages and kings. Greg turned, surprise in his baby blues.

The Swiss scientist from the banquet slid his tray onto the table beside Daley.

"Look, I'm really most awfully sorry about the banquet."

Daley smiled back as if to say it wasn't his fault.

"I hear the new President *is* an A-hole."

"When d'you arrive, Greg?"

"Late last night. Left Hakone Wednesday. Always spend a day in Hong Kong before braving this chaos. Civilization before dilapidation."

"Oh, Pete, almost forgot. This came to Hakone for you." He poked a squib of paper at Daley who murmured thanks and unrolled it.

It was a FAX – *the* FAX. The Ramada FAX, for God's sakes! *Another* copy. Whoever sent it really didn't want us in China! "Who gave it to you?"

"Took it from the notice board."

Greg's forehead wrinkled with concern. "You all right? Look like you've seen a ghost."

"No. I mean yes. I'm all right. Just need some food."

"See you in Hong Kong," his friend shouted after him.

The FAX copy had unglued him. The dissuasion had started all the way back *in Japan*!

He decided not to tell Ane – after all she'd seen it already. He sat down so preoccupied he didn't notice he was in her chair.

"Would you jump in my grave so quick? "She laughed, returning from the bathroom. "Better have something to eat, Peter, before you pass out."

"Today we goa Summer Palace. You willa enjoy."

Hope there's no bloody steps, thought Daley, picking cabbage strands from his teeth.

A road-crew were hand-building a new freeway. A Hitachi digger, bucket tucked in like the head of a sleeping goose rested there beside. Wood was being split, one man above, one below, long saw between.

The girl's freshness floated him to the first girl of that other life –bright, laughing, balancing the sidewalk edge, arms out, nurse's cloak lining swishing the starch of her pinafore. God what they miss, the "now" generation. The magic. The intense highs, desperate lows. Girls just never thought of it, never mind doing it! The exquisite end-game, the accidental touch, words chosen for lonely hours, launched, flight, impact, delicious persuasion. Now a kiss was a given, a prelude to all the way. The magic of goddesses – lost.

They passed a cart loaded with steel reinforcing rod, driver on top, asleep, and a woman with three dead chickens in her bicycle panier. No leather anywhere; mules and donkeys traced with rope were bitless. They set their own pace and, though their handlers had whips, they were never touched but rather startled. The Chinese seemed fond of their animals.

The car coasted in neutral down hills and often on the open flat with no noticeable speed change for the longest time. They drifted to traffic lights and, after passing trucks, conserved momentum by dropping into neutral.

The engine was turned off in traffic jams.

Gas seemed to last forever. Daley noticed they would need some tomorrow, but tomorrow they made a 200km trip on "empty"!

He never saw a gas station.

Ny told him gas was contaminated so organizations had their own, taxis too. There were few cars and almost none was made in China.

Deep in a forest, the Summer Palace of the Empress Dowager, Tzu Hsi, spread around an unexpected lake and up its necklace of hills. Pavilions connected by paths of mosaic cats were covered with leaves being swept by an army of women. One was swatting leaves from a tree, filling the air with brown. Bleached lotus plants stood in empty streams and elegant bridges, carrying the roofed walkways of imperial days, crossed empty pools of cracked-mud.

Along the lakeside stretched the longest covered promenade in the world. Two thousand feet of ceilings painted with scenes in chromatic red, blue, and orange of that China in the south.

Around a corner, a long stairway led up cedar slopes to pavilions stacked like playblocks to the sky. Ane started up with Ny, the girl jumping ahead. Daley sighed and sat on a convenient bench; the climb was out of the question.

The girl came dancing back.

"Don't you want to see? The view's spectacular."

"Can't," he said, resigned to her scorn.

Her nose flared. "Oh, well. I've seen it many times so I'll sit wid you. Mind?"

He shook his head and pulled in his coat but she found a stone and toe teased it. Her cheeks were flushed from the October breeze.

"Have you always had a beard? Makes you look so old."

"Since the early seventies."

"I didn't think you were that old!"

"The nineteen seventies." That "old" word again.

Two birds whirred past, one alighting, chipping from branch to branch, the other fussing beneath.

Say something. Anything. "Can I ask you something?"

She nodded.

"You speak Irish – I mean English with an Irish accent."

"Do I? Must be me Irish friend. We spent a lot of time together."

A deadly lull.

He studied her earrings, crimson on white.

"Man's oldest ceramics, your earrings. Ancient civilizations thought enamels were magic."

"Magic! That's a swiz! Didn't even have to work for it."

He glanced in surprise. "Swiz!" Not heard that for years. Wherever did she get these words?

She came and sat beside him. "Tell me about Canada."

He sat silently gathering his thoughts, then started. "It's fall there now. Ploughmen, trailing a confetti of quarrelsome gulls, turn the shiny folds of earth for next year's promise." His words petered out self-consciously.

"Don't stop."

"Really?"

She nodded quickly.

"Sumac flames, wind chimes lament, contented cats curl, whiskers flicking dreams."

"Fond of animals, aren't you? Never had a pet. I was lonely. Tzu Hsi was lonely too."

"Who?"

"Tzu Hsi, the Empress Dowager who lived here. It's a hundred of your years old now. So beautiful in summer, flowers colourin' everything. A shame you're seein' it so drab. Tzu Hsi, means 'Motherly and Auspicious.' The people liked her but she was terrible homesick for southern China."

She jumped up and pointed toe swirls round the pink quartz from her pocket. "I get lonely sometimes. Do you like me?" She asked so quietly he wasn't sure he'd heard. "No, you don't. You don't like *anythin'* in China!"

He stared, robbed of words.

A sweeper, smelling of turned compost, swished by.

"Who wouldn't like you?" he rushed. "You wear your soul outside. Those steps take my breath, but so do you...so do you." He was amazed. Where had that come from? No idea but he was pleased. He knew she was staring, he knew she'd look away if he looked up.

Ny and Ane reappeared and she skipped off to meet them.

They sat in a cafe of sticky tables and never-cleaned floors.

"Nota eat here...nota good."

The girl sat silent, embarrassed they'd come in, embarrassed the taxi was late, embarrassed with herself.

Daley took a deep breath. The magic had gone. Tenuous thing magic.

He picked up a clay soup spoon and tried to stand it on its dished blade. It kept falling but he kept trying.

"Sure you're *old*! So old."

He glanced up. Her eyes were away.

Definitely gone!

III
BEIJING TO BOJAI

SUNDAY OCTOBER 29

Always breezy, this place, Daley mused: the Gobi, the wind, then dust – everywhere.

"Do you think I'll need me coat on the aircraft, Peter?"

He shook his head. God, his knees ached.

As she laid the coat in the suitcase, a Polaroid photograph fell on the floor.

"It's the one you took in Tiananmen Square. Forgotten it, hadn't you? Pass me the magnifying glass, please. Let's see why they confiscated the film."

"Look at this." She poked her finger at the middle-background. "Behind the squad through the arch in the wall."

A crisp image inside the arch: a black car, door held by a tall young Chinese, an old man emerging with a stick.

The driver was a woman in uniform, epaulet starred, hair pulled in a bun.

"So? What's to see?"

"That man holding the door. It's that diplomat, the one with the sister and baby."

"You sure?"

She nodded firmly.

"Don't think they're the reason we lost the film. That would be too happenstance. The soldier came up behind us. Besides, the car is emptying – maybe thirty seconds! I think it was that we weren't supposed to photograph the army."

"I don't care. It's him – that man – I'm sure."

The Departures level of Beijing Airport was chaos.

The girl was as excited as a child on Christmas eve. The kerosene smell seemed to intoxicate her. A jet wound up and she dropped her luggage and involuntarily clapped her hands. Her scarf was changed for the occasion – bright orange with vivid blue flowers tied like a paper boat.

They passed the sumptuous CAC First Class lounge – bored hostess reading a paperback– and joined the herd overflowing the boarding area. Daley's beard brought stares and whispers as they sat on a windowsill outside the gate.

Twenty minutes before flight-time, the army arrived: four soldiers and two officers. They took up station by the doors Daley assumed opened to the flight tunnel, setting up a video camera and recorder. Their arrival quieted the babble, but it returned as soon as they were set.

Ten minutes before the scheduled flight time, the doors opened and the crowd surged forward. The military scrutinized all documents and, as Daley was getting irritable at the bureaucracy, a minor eruption occurred. A soldier pushed by, documents in one hand, a boy in the other.

"Ah they caughta one reactionary."

A schoolboy, Daley thought. Then he noticed Yen – pale, excitement canceled. Her eyes glanced around like an uncertain bird. Fear. She's frightened.

She touched his arm.

He was surprised and patted her hand for reassurance.

The soldiers were now checking enthusiastically.

Daley passed the passports to the officer in a rough dun uniform with red silk stars. He flicked through the Chinese documents, then thumbed Daley's, the visa falling open.

The effect was electric! He stiffened, saluted and waved them through.

God bless Choi, Ben...every bugger, Daley murmured to himself as they hustled into the aircraft.

The door shut but the smell of kerosene persisted. The aeroplane was a Russian Illyutian 147 with three jets at the back and seats that folded forwards, flat to the cushion. The fold-down table was immovable beyond the upper stomach for all but the most svelte. Daley banged his head as he stood to find the buckle end of his seat-belt.

In the air, the girl's ebullience returned. Full eyes dancing, she skipped the aisle, ankle clicking ankle sideways, to look out the escape door window.

Green tea made the rounds.

Ny pulled his sleeve.

"We fly over Zhejiang province. When twenty I wasa sent there to Hangzhou from Beijing to work factory. My wife sent to country, to farm. She mada food for workers. Did nota see her fora three years." He counted on his fingers. "1969 to 1972."

"Jes, the Cultural Revolution?"

He nodded, eyes serious.

"Your daughter?"

"I lifted metal parts from one line, put them on another. Complete waste of time. Nobody worked. State pay whether you work or not, so nobody work. People sad. They work hard in towns then state senda them away. No family, no friends. Good for professors, they say, learn how people live. Bad waste ofa time, very bad." He inspected his fingers, shaking his head.

He had ignored the question about Yen. Maybe he had not heard, or else he just didn't want to talk about it. Perhaps she just went with her brother. Daley decided not to press him as it clearly upset him.

"We meta by guide from plant. I never been. Factory wasa near Beijing but Mao move from Russians! Move all factories to country."

Daley looked past Ane at the angled wing. Rivets stood out like bolt heads. God, he wondered, why was the West so frightened of the Russians? He recalled the banks of car batteries under the benches of every laboratory he visited in Moscow and their fascination with his pocket calculator.

He looked up and was stunned. The seat-back was draped

with black waves of long hair. His breath caught, his jaw slacked. At first he did not recognise her but then did when she smiled at his confusion.

He had to look away. Knew she knew. How could she not?

"Why'd you wear that scarf anyway?" he managed at the window. "Your hair's nice. Shame to cover it."

"Pollution – tis no good for the hair at all."

He pondered her answer. Made no sense. According to Greg, Xian was much more polluted than Beijing! Maybe she didn't know. He pulled open the flimsy lunch box containing a noodle salad in plastic, a dry meat sandwich, an envelope of soy sauce, and a roll of candy. He played with the sandwich. Her hair had taken him by surprise. It had always been his favorite feminine charm. Ane once had long hair for him.

He popped a candy in his mouth. Menthol froze his throat and nose: cough drops! He rewrapped the tube and slipped it into his pocket. "Throat candy," he told Ane, pocketing hers also. "Not very nice."

He tracked to the perennial problem – titanium. Why a titanium plant? Ny's answer had been evasive, something about an interest in zirconium oxide. He was unconvinced.

The girl looked out Ane's window, hair draping Daley's front. "Will you look at the clouds, so beautiful, angel side up. 'It's a pity beyond telling./Is hid in the heart of love./The folk who are buying and selling./The clouds on their journey above.'" She took a breath. "Not the grey and brown that sads over Beijing, are they?"

The guide book told Daley that Xian was an industrial city, 916 kms south west of Beijing, famous for the army of terra cotta giants that marched under its fields in heavily polluted air.

The intercom came on. "The centre of gravity of this aircraft is in the rear, so passengers in the front cabin are requested, for their own comfort and safety, to remain seated whilst the rear cabin deplanes. Failure to follow these instructions may seriously threaten the stability of the aircraft on the ground."

He and Ane looked at each other as the girl giggled.

"They've got to be joking," Ane breathed.

He was shaking his head. The back-heavy aircraft would tip on its tail, for God's sake – pile 'em onto the rear toilets like so many ragdolls in a barrel!

Touchdown was hard and the sun was blood red.

Xian.

Sulphur penetrated noses to running.

The girl skipped ahead then stopped, breathed in the wind and side-stepped beside him. "My first holiday! Chinese don't take holidays."

"The nicest day's the first."

"I love it when you're wistful," she said over her shoulder.

They were met by a death's-head scientist with an egg-swallowing Adam's apple and permanent smile. He was a bundle of nerves. He shot his cuff to give a limp hand-shake then returned his hands to shoot pocket-billiards – faster as his conversation with Ny increased in volume.

The morose driver gave a quick nod and no smile.

There was a boxed meal and a four hour drive to Bojai, 160 kilometers west. The host lit a cigarette and said something to Ny in Chinese.

"He sorry. Speaka no English. I translate."

With a cadaverous smile, the man opened the van doors and motioned them in. The bags were nearly loaded when a woman walked up, bowed and said in English not used for some time: "Glood evening. I glide."

"Really! On air or what!" murmured Daley irritably as Ane flashed him a stony glance.

She was too thin, but nicely curved under a black polo-neck sweater, faded jeans stretched tight over a feminine bum and a short black leather coat. She wore lavender. All Chinese women seemed to, but close up smelled as though they had bathed in it! The men smelled like they had shit themselves in a tobacco shop. Her hair was pulled back in a bun and the thin smile radiated fine lines from her eyes. Fortyish, Daley decided.

"He surprised," Ny confided. "Thinka he guide but she say she speak English."

The man smiled coldly and returned to bag loading. His face was tight. His grey jacket hung like someone else's, and his shoes shone. (Daley had seen few polished shoes in China.) He started each sentence with a clearing of the throat.

The woman was coolly correct, with bland eyes that danced only for the driver. "How was flight?" she asked Yen, but the girl looked away so Daley replied: "Cramped. Efficient, except for the luggage." He nodded at the pile of luggage in the road, people pulling it like crows at a carcass. She tutted and shrugged shoulders as they bumped off down the street, pollution of Xian inside and out.

The bench was hard and below the level of the spare wheel platform. Any heat will be intercepted Daley noted. Ny and his daughter sat behind.

He motioned Ane to spread Beth's coat over their knees and she sniffed: "Lavender. She's wearing lavender. I'm allergic, remember?"

He squeezed her hand. "It'll pass. Once we get going."

Conversation was too difficult so he cleaned the fogged window and glanced at his watch. 3.00. Bojai by 7.00.

Strange mixture of people. If the guide let her hair down she'd be attractive. She leaned forward, lit a cigarette and blew an invisible cloud at the driver.

Wonder why the hell they sent the man: couldn't guide them up a straight street.

What a pair! A scientist with a death's-head and a severe-haired lady –DHS and SHL – he had a penchant for acronyms.

The persistent gas smell suggested the fuel line was leaking.

Out of town, winter fields rolled to the angry sun now losing its battle with black rain clouds. Walkers and cyclists with crippling loads flitted like bats in the late evening.

The girl was humming happily.

Two-and-a-half hours to go. Darkness filled the windows.

The headlights flicked on and off. Swinging corncobs sheaved like wheat, hung in festoons from trees. Severed stalks were bunch-tied and lined the roadside.

They passed people burning paper houses and paper carts. "Money" of the dead; a roadside funeral, he was told.

Never a sign. Twice, high in the windless trees, shingles with kilometers to nowhere.

Ane sought his hand, lost in very different thoughts. Twenty four years of marriage. Not all smooth: they had had fights, tiffs really, usually money, kids. This girl was so *young*, innocent, unwrapped. Men are so stupid! She shuffled uncomfortably on the seat. Like Claire said, their brains were too low!

Villages reduced the road to a rutted quagmire of rocks and potholes. Old Chinese, most often women, perched on islands in the ooze, awaiting transient lights. All was dark – not the dark of Prussian nights – but of windowless cellars, an all-enveloping black parenthesized by doused headlights.

Around a corner and into a bivouac of Flanders fields' mud. A village square was spread with candle-lit tables bearing vegetables and cooked food.

The van slowed.

Shimmering tents and shadowy mule carts threaded the belanterned melee. Every window had shelves lined with sauces and soft drinks. A pile of people bunched around a TV as a barber clipped hair into the mud at his feet.

Never a gas station anywhere!

Busy pool tables, too large for the rooms, appropriated the sidewalk, forcing crowds into the stream of mud-splashing cyclists.

An old man walked his mule, softly talking, heads nodding together.

No cars. Once a wild animal – two points of light flashing low in the road – then black. Sometimes broken by the branch tracery sky, sometimes by the rutted road. Daley began to feel motion-induced nausea abetted by gas vapour. He pulled the coat round with a shiver. The damp was winning and large drops of the threatened rain slowly splashed the windscreen before becoming a downpour.

Suddenly, Chinese chatter.

The girl stifled a cry.

Ahead was a roadblock. A green truck, white 8341 on its side, was caught in the high beams.

Ane reached, touched, squeezed his hand.

A peasant was being questioned beside, his mule. Suddenly a raised gun gleaming, down on the man's bent head. He folded, hands in hair, mule bending as if concerned, umbilical trace tightened.

Brittle laughter through drumming water noises. Someone urinated on the prone figure. The squat, heavy leader shot the mule which collapsed as a dull report reached the van.

There! Not there! A hand clamped Daley's arm.

His stomach spasmed and his mouth, dry with fumes, filled with unswallowable saliva as vomit rose, spurted through his fingers and sprayed the coat and spare wheel .

He shivered. Awful, *God awful*. Hated up-chucking. Cold sweat popped his forehead and gathered to drip from his nose.

"Peter. Oh, my God! Let me see." Ane wiped his forehead then cleaned each finger.

The mule collapsed again and again before his closed eyes, each time with a heave, dry tearing. Ane gently inveigled the soiled coat from his elbows and dropped it to their feet.

The heaves slowed.

The air was fetid. Nostrils burning with regurgitated eucalyptus, heart beating like a trapped bird in his throat, he tongued the roof of his mouth and used his thumb to squeeze vomit from his beard. He stared at the transfixed tableau.

They sat with pale faces frozen.

The army pulled the mule to one side and rolled the peasant on top.

Daley shook like a wet dog. Suddenly they were real, this army, real and *in his face*!

The soldiers formed and headed up the truck beams.

The arm grip returned, tighter this time.

Chinese babble filled the van.

Ane pulled his coat lapels. "What they saying?"

"Quiet!" the woman warned.

"Make her tell us, Peter! Make her. Do *something*!" She buried herself in his chest.

Ane was sobbing. She cursed him, cursed him for not listening to her, cursed Ny for inviting them to hell. Peter never listened to her, never did. Here they were in the crap-hole of the world with nothing, useless *bloody nothing* !

He tensed.

A colander gun muzzle snubbed the driver's window.

A guttural order – headlights out.

The leader fixed them in his flashlight and shouted at the woman.

Ny whispered: "Wants we geta out."

In this bloody rain!

Ane huddled, tight.

The grip on his arm tightened.

He glanced at it then at the girl: eyes – nothing but eyes – wide, terrified-in-the-torch eyes.

Motion became underwater slow, words unstable. The officer ordered curtly: "Passports!"

Ane seized his hand. "Don't! Don't give 'em. Without them...Oh Peter, please don't."

The woman's hand wagged impatiently.

"We'll be dead if I don't!"

"We'll be *dead if you do*, and it'll be *your fault*!"

The woman slapped them into the leader's hand, then stared straight past him. He pushed the neb of his cap, so the water stream missed his nose, and perused them in his wobbling flashlight.

Suddenly he threw them back and shouted. The squad fell in. The torch went out.

Blackness. Silence.

Gone!

"You can look now, Ane."

Everyone chattered.

The girl sat silent. He father shied words at her but she just watched, deep eyes still. In the paltry light from the dash, Daley saw fear.

Ane was pulling at him. "I don't care, Peter, I was terrified. Never, never been so terrified in my *whole* life."

"S'over, love. Over. Over."

He felt guilty. Just passed them over as told to. She was right, he *should* have objected. Thought of something. Anything. There just wasn't an option. Marched off in the pouring rain to God-knows-bloody-what?

Ny leaned forward and told him the soldiers were searching for a stolen van, full of explosives and reactionaries. It had left Beijing the day before.

Now the road was surfaced here and there. In a black field, eerie flashes like dumb shell bursts illuminated a turned-turtle tractor and its goggleless owner, perched in its innards, mending it.

The van engine missed, went on, missed again, then died. They free-wheeled to the edge.

Out of gas!

The clamor stilled.

"Well! Now what? Not seen a bloody gas station anywhere."

The close sprig of the Ny's hair bobbed a lot.

After a hurried discussion, the man, now christened DHS, left into the night.

"Good job rain's stopped, Ane. Where d'you think he's gone?"

"Maybe knows a gas station."

The woman, now SHL, bent forward and, in the instrument lights, poured steaming fluid from a thermos into its top.

"Tlake. It help."

She extracted a handkerchief, wet it from the thermos, and wiped his face. She slid open the door, manhandled the spare wheel through, and swilled it with the balance of the thermos.

"Thank you. I sorry. Don't know why did."

Ane elbowed him. "Don't do that, Peter! Speak pidgin. She understands."

He nodded. Had a tendency to answer pidgin with pidgin, a habit developed with Chinese students. Had to watch it.

The woman's next move was equally surprising. She lit incense, trapped it in the ashtray, and Christmas slowly replaced stale bile and gas. Resourceful, he reflected, very resourceful.

The company went silent. He dozed.

A heavy engine and lights woke him. The man had returned, knuckling the van side-panels as he came. The woman explained soldiers would take them to Bojai.

Daley couldn't believe it! A few lectures, seeing a few friends, had turned into a nightmare, deepening with the night. The "Boys" that shot for no reason would convey them, cheek-by-jowl, to Bojai.

A canvas-covered truck stood across the track, engine hunting in neutral. A wagging flashlight jumped round its rear.

As they climbed from the impotent van, Daley sank to his socks in the mud.

DHS was standing on the backboard beside the squad leader. Cueing like Joe bloody Davis I bet, Daley thought, sick taste in his mouth and feet now soaked. He squelched to the backboard, threw in the brown bag, then slopped onto it. He pulled Ane up after him, her released feet slurping like soup.

The soldiers pushed them onto the hard wooden forms running either side. The sergeant climbed in last, removing his hat to bow his bald head to them.

They bumped off, DHS regaling the sergeant with a polemic, hands dancing in the dark.

There was a familiar smell of shit and tobacco.

The girl was shivering. At first Daley thought she was cold or jogging with the ride, but, as the sergeant matched a cherooot, he saw her tears in the flare. She was whispering to her father.

Coughing at the smoke of cheap cigars, Daley tried to concentrate on their words.

"Hear...soldier..said? 'You...travel...important circles...My address.' T'will not work now *he* knows, *that man!*"

"Letsa wait and see."

"I know it won't. They'll kill me! That man, I *hate* him!"

"Itsa OK. ...Nota thought of. Changes...needed."

He was sure Ny's smile had gone.

Why speak English. Whom did she hate so much? The leader?

The cab window slid open and, in the welcome draught and still headlights, gaggles of school-children hurried by on bicycle and foot. Off to attend class, he was told. Till 9.30 for self-study and return in the cold morning at 9.00.

Thus, excrement and cheroot in his nostrils, vomit on his tongue and coat, wet socks and muddy shoes, Daley bumped into Bojai.

The over warm suite into which they were ushered was full of grotesque, pre-war furniture, the carpets on the stone floor smelling dank. The Daleys didn't care; it was a chance to clean up. Ane threw her soiled coat in the bath and ran the water.

Daley surveyed the muddle. Left of the door was an art-deco dresser of light oak and chrome. Its rear narrow mirror rose to a central panel.

Two deep settees, one red, one green, lined the walls, right and left with a glass table between. The square ends were closed by deep yellow armchairs, arms towering over seats.

A window occupied most of the outside wall; a cabinet radio and a tall fan stood either side like bookends. He had not seen such a radio since the war; with its large centered tuning knob numbered on its periphery with lines on a protractor.

The fan was hi-tech, vane cage covered with a frilly cosy and available speeds with illuminated push buttons.

No phone. Never a phone in any room in China!

"Well, we've not seen that before." Ane nodded at the large potted plant beside the fan. "Give me your coat. I'll try clean it up too."

The bedroom was dominated by a large bed and matching wardrobe. The headboard of the bed and the wardrobe door matched the dresser. At least they are consistent, he mused. Two dining chairs on either side of the bathroom door completed the set.

He collapsed into a yellow armchair, picking moodily at the mud-caked laces of his brown brogues. He coaxed the bows open, shook the shoes off, then slumped back, ignoring the piles of dry mud on the floor. He'd get trouble but didn't care.

Ane stood before the emptied suitcase on the bed. "Sorry, I've no other shoes but got your slippers. Don't match, I'm afraid. Least one's right and one's left. Give me your shoes, I'll try get the mud off 'em."

He nodded. Wouldn't you bloody know it. Dog again. Always had his bloody slippers. Bet there's an identical pair in his box! His eyelids drooped but every time they did, the garish tableau swooped back and blew him awake. Finally he struggled up and walked through the bedroom to the bathroom, trailing wet-sock footprints on the stone floor. "Going to wash and get out of these clothes, Ane."

Better get some food in him or we're in for a miserable night, she thought, then remembered the sandwiches. Where'd I put 'em? She wondered.

The bathroom was as big as Ny's apartment; the toilet had no seat and the shower no curtain. Water sprang from the lead fall-pipe on flushing and pooled on the floor beside a hair-blocked drain. Threadbare towels hung a wire between the shower head and the unboxed pipes on the opposite wall. He washed in cold water, changed his shirt, tied on a paisley ascot, and emerged chuckling.

"What's tickling you?"

"There's no toilet seat. Reminds me of that Santa Hog affair."

"What you talking about?"

"You know, when the students stole the seat from the Men's, painted it gold and presented it to me like a horse-collar – my Christmas 'present.'"

"So! What's so funny?"

"Well, I heard later, the Dean, taken very short, rushed in and sat in the water."

"And told *you*, I suppose," she tutted.

"No, he didn't. But there's no towels in that toilet, only those hot-air things. So there he was, trying to dry his arse, shirt up, behind cocked into the draught."

"You're joking," she laughed.

He bent over her and gave her a squeeze. She had changed into her Scottish blouse and plaid skirt with its big pin. Her hair was brushed and she was renewing her lipstick.

"Come and have a sandwich. It'll cheer you up!"

They sat in a sofa and opened the greaseproof paper. Gasoline rendered the bread inedible. Looking at each other, they spat out the tainted fare.

"Can you believe what we saw? I mean what we saw happen?"

"I really feared for our lives, Peter. Never been so scared as when that gun came through the window!" She went to the plant in the window and absentmindedly pruned its dead leaves.

"Me neither!" He pulled two tubes of Rowntree's fruit pastilles from the bag, threw her one and opened the other.

"It's really not turning out like we thought, is it? The visit, I mean."

"Look on the bright side. We made it, didn't we? That's funny."

He frowned. "What'you mean funny? Whatever else, it wasn't funny."

"No. I mean that car over there," She nodded out the window. "It's full of people, just sitting."

"People usually do that in cars, you know."

"I know that. But it's off the road and they're just sitting like they're waiting for somebody or something."

The street was dark. It looked cold. The exhaust of the silent jeep parked on the sidewalk opposite, fogged the single streetlamp but the vehicle was discernible, large white 8341 on the hood. He saw a flash where the driver was sitting.

"See that?"

He nodded. "Someone lit a cigarette. Don't worry, it's just the army. They're bloody everywhere."

It hadn't been the flash of a match. Too steady. No. Glasses, maybe binoculars. Certainly not a match. He didn't tell her.

The passenger's substantial form stood into the road. DHS's leader-friend was watching them!

Daley shook his head – paranoid. Paranoid owing to the night. Probably was a match for a stinking cheroot. He closed his eyes to replay the scene but his mind refused; the squat leader was still there.

Let buggers watch if they want to, they're more uncomfortable than I am. Merry wind to their bums, as Nan'd say.

"Poor Yen," he mumbled presently, mouth full of pastilles. "She was distraught. Even more than the others."

"You think so?"

"Know so."

"Well, don't worry, she's young, she'll get over it. Soldiers killed her friends!"

"I began to think it'd never end. Poor unfortunate beast. What did it ever do?"

She knelt in front of him putting her arms round his knees.

"Try not think of it. It's over. Just remember I love you."

"You have odd slippers on!" the girl said, pointing at his feet as she came through the door.

"In the rush of packing, Ane picked one of each!" he explained.

She was in a white blouse and full skirt of large purple and blue flowers. Red and white scarf round her neck, full hair bouncing free.

His chest rose. Her eyes were dancing.

Couldn't remain morose in the face of such ebullience.

Young, he thought. That quick vivid world.

"How can you be so...disorganized?"

He sniped back: "S'easy when my daughter Clare piles the shoes and the dog helps himself. Anyway don't you think they look nice? Another pair at home. He stood up, put his feet together and nodded at them. Read that somewhere and liked it.

She laughed.

"That woman was very brave," she observed to Ane who was running her finger along the window ledge. "Said those soldiers were - how you say - bums?"

"Arseholes!"

Ane inspected her fingers. "Certainly showed a lot of spirit. Thought she was very cold fish till she cleaned you up."

"And gave me a cup of water."

"She mollycoddled you altogether," chuckled the girl with a sideways look

A quiet knock and the guide walked in, followed by Ny. The woman was wearing a tight black skirt and low heels. Striking in black. If only she'd let her hair down. Perfume's too strong, though. Ane'll hate it.

She perched on the high arm of an armchair, lit a cigarette and blew a cloud of smoke towards him. "Lecture tomollow. Two morning, one afternoon."

"They make titanium. I not understand they invite me. Are interested in ceramics?"

Ane glared at him.

"I only gluide. You glo shops," she said to Ane.

"Can I go wid you?" the girl blurted excitedly, hands coming together in supplication. "I love to shop."

Ane nodded, then asked, arms around herself: "Cold. Don't you think it's getting cold? Can we close the window, Peter?"

He pushed up the window then banged it shut past the layers of old paint. There was a man in a light-coloured suit leaning on the jeep and talking to the driver.

Ane sat down. "How can they possibly let boys that age have guns?"

The girl shrugged. "Ti's the age they're indestructible. That's why the old men like them. 'And when the war is done and the youth stone dead, I'd toddle safely home and die – in bed.'"

The woman uncrossed her legs and leaned forward, wine in one hand, cigarette in the other. "They glo village. Young have no job. Offer money join army."

Daley was distracted by her shapely leg and wondered cynically if she did it on purpose. Damn knee stockings. Nylon must be expensive in China.

He looked at his wife. Handled herself well, he reflected. Stoic these nurses!

In fact, the gratuitous violence had taken Ane to the brink. She had wondered whether they would get out of China. Had convinced herself she had been right. It *was* too soon to visit. Couldn't even go to the embassy! Tingles of the trauma returned.

The wine dissolved formality.

The woman asked him: "What West think China tlouble?"

"Hard to know what really happened. The media were full of it but from a distance."

"TV evelywhere."

"Thomas Jefferson said every generation needs its own revolution. What do *you* think inside?"

The woman studied her cigarette. The girl glanced at him, then her. Dangerous ground, he wondered.

Ane rose, went to the bathroom and emerged with a glass of water for the plant and emptied the small glass into it. "Poor thing's as dry as sand."

The frowning guide said slowly: "Not wise, tlalk. Not know who wisten. Still search ladicals. For me start June 3rd. Buses not lun that day. Students steal for balicades so not lun. Saw two 8341 tlucks near New China gate. Full officers so surlound, wave. Soldiers flom compound shoot glass. Eyes hurt."

"I was there," the girl ventured

He looked at her.

"But who started it?"

The girl and woman glanced at each other.

"Hu Yaobang started it," replied the girl in a dusky voice. "He had new ideas."

"You'd lika him, Doc. He proposed China geta rid of chopsticks, usea knives and forks!"

The girl glared at him. "The old men started against him. Must have been autumn '86. He resigned early '87."

"What happened after that?"

"He died."

"Hu Party Secletaly. Give people chance. Plemier Deng tlust. Want *real* change. Legime unable feed people so give fleedom sell vegetables but lose contlol. *Legime* start tlouble!".

"Are you saying they *wanted* it to happen?"

She exhaled a cloud of smoke and nodded.

"Doesn't make sense," Ane said. "How'd students get involved then? They don't sell vegetables."

"Doesn't it always start wid the students! Martin Luther was a student. Students started the Vietnam protests."

"And free-speech as well." Daley remembered Mario Savio on the roof of a Berkeley police car. "You really think *they*, the government, started it– *on purpose?*"

She pulled hard on her cigarette. "Stludents used. Used by lidden faces. After Hu letire, police, army start plactise liot control like South Koleans. Buy TV cameras for...for, how say, plincipal intersections, of Beijing. Government *expect*, Government *want, liot!*"

A pregnant silence.

"Deng *despised* the students," the girl protested. " 'Wa wa' he called *us* 'Children'! Children who didn't appreciate the 'freedoms' he gave us! When Hu died arguing with the old men, that's when *the* march on the square and the troubles started."

"Death tliggered liots Deng need. Then, how say – final stlaw –stludents dislupt Gorbachov visit. Not know who in charge! Dleng lost contlol, left Beijing, let army come." The woman opened her hands wingwise, as if releasing the apocalypse.

Ny walked to the window. The rain had started again and was making little liquid noises, smearing the light of the single street lamp opposite.

"It's raining again," he said.

Don't remember him ever mentioning the weather, reflected Daley. Maybe nervous discussing the troubles. He smiled as "troubles," the Irish euphemism, popped out.

The woman wanted to talk. Her cheeks were glowing. "Stludents in square *before* June. There May."

Daley was surprised. "But that's a month before the demonstrations!"

"Zhao and Li Peng visit then. That night Li Peng order martial law; there *was* lidden agenda, even in May !"

"Tell me about Li Peng and Zhao."

"Lidden agenda!" she repeated.

"Zhao was the Party Secretary," explained the girl. "He also was a friend of the students and in favour of reform. The old men feared him so transferred his power to the Premier, Li Peng, their lackey!" She clipped the last words. Drink did not seem to affect her.

"Pleng explain army use blullets because had no glas. *Lies*. *Lies*! Use glas too! Old men *want* use blullets!"

"The University President, did he support the students, Ny?"

"He was injured in de riots. New President noa problem." Bet he bloody is, though, but you don't want to talk about him.

The girl leaned back on her hands and, shaking hair from shoulders, said: "Enough with the fuddy-duddies. It was an adventure. An adventure like no other! I made so many friends...All day the sky was magic blue; at night, cool velvet. The square smelled to its corners of cookin' from all China. It made your mouth water: boiling soup, frying fish, charcoal fires and everywhere jasmine – even western hamburgers. Noise bubbled. Talkin', shoutin', laughin' all day, all night. Western music – the Beatles, Abba, Bob Dylan, Joan Baez – in each tent, around each corner. People ate in circles, arguing – free, fresh, happy. T'was a time of wonder, a newborn time. We set up boards for messages and at night sang 'We Shall Overcome,' though many did not speak English. We lived in tents. I've read about your camping – the enjoyment of discomfort in summer. Our camp was different, t'was wonderful. Wonderful. I made so many friends. All with the same purpose – a *new* China, *the China of the students, of the people of Beijing.*"

She went silent, blinking away tears.

"That's another thing I don't understand. Why'd the people join the students? I mean in the Vietnam demonstrations, the students were pariahs!"

"Pleople like stludents," explained the woman, extracting another cigarette." Pleople angry at inflation. Not afflord food. Party leaders so corrlupt, people supplort stludents."

"You were there in Tiananmen Square?" asked Ane, pulling her legs under her on the couch.

"See tlank on Changan Avenue, going square, thlough tlaffic light, still – how say – blinking. Tloops, hidden Forblidden City, come out when tank leach square."

"Changan. Is that far from the square?"

"It main stleet. Lun into Square at Forbidden City."

The girl interrupted angrily: "It's supposed to be the *People's* Army! Supposed to be close to the peasants. Huh! We just couldn't believe it!" Her body shook as she smacked a tight fist into her hand. "We weren't frightened by the tanks or bullets at all. It is *our* army after all. *They* wouldn't hurt *us*! We *believed that*! Oh, God, we believed that. We linked arms believin' that. *Were shot down* believin' that!" Her fist emphasized each word, until her wrist folded and she knocked her glass over. "As we fell, others linked and were shot away. Shot away, shot away!"

"Awful!" Ane shuddered, placing a hand on the girl's shoulder.

Daley wished he'd not started in.

He watched her hair bounce gently with silent sobs. Shouldn't have pushed so. He looked away at the rain gossiping on the window.

Hands to her mouth, Ane stood and pushed past, heading for the bathroom.

He followed.

Deep heaves into the toilet.

He sponged her forehead. "Okay, love. It's all right."

They kneeled together for a few minutes, then she said. "I'll be all right, Peter. Just give me a minute. I'll clean up."

Through the door he heard the woman say: "Tloops not know where were. Flom Mongolia. Tired, hungly officers obey or shlot."

He returned to the room just as the girl said: "Sure *t'is* supposed to be our army but t'is *not*. It's the army of *the old men*! No matter they were tired. They were killin' their *own*."

"Not deflending army. Just not flault. As say, lidden agenda. Deng know. Get lid of students that way. Ladio say 'Those not turn in, blought to justice, punished sevlerely. *He* know!"

The girl looked down and traced round the wine stain with her finger.

Ane returned.

"Slorry you not well. Fleel better now?"

Ane nodded. "Let's break out the emergency rations, Peter. None of us have eaten."

She went to the bedroom and emerged with two handfuls of candy. The girl came to a kneel, pushed her hair behind her ears. Have you Rowntree's gums?"

Ane looked at her in surprise. "How d'you know about them?"

She hesitated, then explained: "Da sent them from Canada."

Ane laughed: "I have some." She went back to the bedroom and returned with two tubes. "They're my favorite too. Beth brought some in London and left them in her bag." She nodded at Daley. "He likes pastilles but don't last as long do they?"

The woman shuffled forward and, making to pull her skirt

down, took a box of raisins.

The girl popped two gums in her mouth at once. "Ah, t'was such a time! Such a time." She stood, freeing her scarf and, clasping it round her forehead, laughed. "We wore white headbands like this."

The man walked in.

In one motion, she bent to the radio and turned it on, scarf ends still clasped. As Chinese music wobbled into the room, she twirled and stopped in front of Daley. "Dance with me, please," she invited, taking his hand and pulling.

He pulled back, but her eyes stopped him.

Not danced in years.

"Forgive me if I walk on you feet."

She flashed a smile. "Just dance. *Please*. T'is only me, hold me, dance wid me."

They rocked on the spot, he bending away like a shy, aroused teenager. Her fingers found his. "I need you," she breathed so he wondered if he'd heard.

The conversation – a background hum – continued, but Daley was no longer there. His clumsy feet developed wings and he danced off the ground. She needed him.

The man joined the debate, devouring a chocolate bar. The woman translated for Ane. He was in a white sailor suit with button-down patch pockets, epaulets, a centre vent, and wide-bottomed pants. The ill-fitting jacket revealed a black wool turtleneck with white knitted arms, an animated skull-and-cross-bones stuffing its cadaver's face with Cadburys.

"Like candy, don't they?"
"What were doing with Yen?"
"Dancing."
"I could *see* that. In your head, I mean."
"Trying not to trip her."
"Pull the other one."
"No really, not danced for years, you know that."

"You don't fool me, you know. A soft young body and you're putty, you silly old sod. Well, don't get any ideas." She flounced off to the bathroom.

"She said Ny sent her fruit gums from Canada."

"Wherever she got the taste for 'em, it wasn't from Canada!" she said flatly.

"Where then?"

There was a small silence, then she remembered something: "Did you hear what that man said when you were dancing?"

"No. What did he say? Must have been in Chinese. Can't speak English."

"The woman translated. He pointed out the students had an agenda too."

"What'd you mean?"

"Well, their signs, the ones they were waving, were in *English*. They were in English. Saw 'em on TV."

"So what? Their bloody statue was modelled on the Statue of Liberty, obviously playing to the Western press."

"Don't be so touchy. It's obvious, isn't it? They *planned* for the world to know."

She lay on the bed, covers pulled back.

"Turn off the TV, unplug it, and come to bed," she said languidly. Seeing him with the girl had been exciting.

"That's your dad talking: 'Unplug TV Hanneh,'" he mimicked with a grin. "Thinks TV causes fires. Won't you know, but, if it makes you happy."

"You do fancy her, don't you?"

"Who wouldn't? She's a butterfly."

She kicked him. "For you, she's a Monarch full of milkweed. One bite, you die!" She turned away, leaving him looking at her back.

He clicked the light switch.

The nadir of the night hurtled back – the mule collapse, light-washed road, asphyxiating fumes, white faces, rude gun snout – then the girl swam in. He shook his head and stretched for Ane.

She was shaking and fell - turned into him, wet cheeks smearing his.

He rocked her, murmuring daft little things.
"Don't leave me, Peter, will you?"
"Course not. I love *you*."
She insinuated a leg between his.
"You could never rape anybody," she giggled.

IV
BOJAI TO XIAN TO BEIJING

MONDAY OCTOBER 30

Daley was at the window. Buildings were single storey and muddled; the odd tree bristled, and twigs trembled in the breeze. The jeep was gone, its oil stain filming a puddle. Must have moved during the storm. No dry patch on the road.

It was Monday. Been in China seven days, or was it six? He couldn't remember. Seemed like weeks!

He had given the factory three lecture titles from which to choose two, but they had chosen all three, and he was to deliver the first while Ane and the girl went shopping. She was wearing a below-the-knees, tight black skirt with a side slit. The scarf was gone and her hair, rich in a vertical roll, was corralled by a silver comb.

"See if you can find a salt and pepper for Jenks," he shouted after Ane as they walked off arm-in-arm.

The lecture room was an icebox again, the only warmth his cup of leaf-floating tea. The audience trooped in, its collective breath gathering like fog. The full room smelled of damp overcoats.

He looked round. "Should we wait for the scientist who met us?"

"He return Xian to meet Beijing plane. Pleasea start."

A local plenipotentiary made a rambling introduction and Ny murmured translation. A weak beam of sunlight inveigled a crack in the curtains and illuminated a loose, wooden electrical-connector board on the floor in front of Daley. Two cotton-wound copper wires secured by large knurled-brass screws trailed to it from a wall socket. A black power cord stretched from the other side under the listener's feet to the projector. Like a bloody high school physics lab. These people don't give a hoot about safety!

He walked forward, nodded to the projectionist, and the first slide flashed in. It was intelligible and he breathed a sigh of relief. After a few sentences, Ny signaled him to stop.

This is going to take forever, he thought, gently swishing the tea to extract its dying warmth.

Ny finished, and Daley continued.

Suddenly the picture disappeared and the room plunged into darkness when the projector bulb blew! Daley irritably pushed at an indistinct knot in the wooden floor with the end of the pointer.

The heavy drapes were lifted, the projectionist stood up, threw off fingerless gloves and vanished behind his machine. Daley wished he was anywhere but this cocked-up country of eager amateurs.

His mind wandered to the muddy road, the black night, the hot room, the girl, dancing and smiling.

He looked out the window at the mist on the hills beyond the factory roofs. 9.50.

God, twenty minutes!

Ny strode over to take command, ripping the cotton-wound wires, and a momentary flash overpowered the sun as a distant fuse melted.

A replacement lamp was passed hand to hand to the projectionist. He returned to the scrum, then straightened triumphantly and joined the now-standing help looking at the screen. He switched the machine on with a flourish. Nothing!

Daley couldn't believe it. He pointed at the scorched wires. Ny sheepishly reattached them, then signaled the projectionist. He flicked on the switch and smiled again. Nothing.

The new bulb was removed and held to the sun.

Oh, for God's sake!

"Look, Ny! If there'd been power you'd have felt it, you daft bugger! Go look at the bloody fuse!"

A young man in a white lab coat was hastily dispatched.

Daley looked back out the window. At least his ire had warmed him. Chicken wire was immersed in dirty glass. Must be imported. No way these stupid sods could pull that pane.

The sun was strengthening and chimney shadows were stretching across the opposite roof. The hilltop mist had given way to trees. Winter green. Pastel. Not the chrome green of spring. The projector fan. Power was back.

The lecture recommenced and wandered for a seemingly intermable time, until the final, welcome, slide.

The third and final talk concluded around lunchtime with a close round of polite applause and a rush for the door.

Tea again. This time with the Director and his staff.

Must be in his eighties, neck like a turtle's in a too-big, uniform, walnut face smiling benignly.

He smelled of blankets and stale tobacco from his white, close-cropped hair to his tiny black boots.

The man's hands shook a constant drizzle of ash on his knee. He was a Party man, Ny said – no scientist – a peasant who had marched the long march with Mao and, as reward, confused his days away as the Director of this factory, understanding nothing, smiling at everything.

As tea passed round, DHS hurried in and sat down in the vacant seat the other side of the Director.

Must be much quicker to Xian in daylight, thought Daley.

The man flashed a cadaverous smile, lit a cigarette, then smoothly replaced the stub in the Director's stained fingers as he murmured in his ear. The old man stirred and said something to Ny.

"He'sa sorry van broke and will thank army, for looking after you." Daley thought to ask why the army were still watching them but decided against it.

Polite technical conversation made the rounds as they slurped green tea from unmatched cups.

Ane returned from the local gift shop with the story of an exquisite glass apple with delicately painted wild horses inside.
"Like the one we saw in Beijing; Claire'd love it! I love it! Do you think we could get it home without breaking?"
"Didn't buy it, did you! When will you learn? Too much bloody Yorkshire in you, you know; that's the trouble – too much Nan."
He counted some notes into her hand. "For goodness sake, go back and get it! Course we can get it home. If you like it so much, I'll carry it me-bloody-self."

He never did find out the reason behind the visit to a titanium factory. He was the first western visitor since 1957.

With blinkered logic, Mao had moved "strategic" industries from the population centres so that the Russian enemy of the seventies would have to destroy them piecemeal. Unbending and capricious implementation of his edict had resulted in a series of plants making titanium from mineral to manufactured member, necklacing a valley high in the mountains of Bojai, far from anywhere, far from each other and far from a railhead. Like building ships in Switzerland, thought Daley.

Lunch over, the guide, the girl, Ny, and DHS shepherded him up the valley to visit the spread-out factory, one plant after another. Between and far below, black-dressed Chinese knelt beside a river, hammering clothes on pebbles and poling out construction stones.

The first factory electro-melted titanium ore to produce ingots. These were trucked up the valley to the next, to be rolled into sheet and stamped into plate.

In the first corrugated iron building, the party was confronted by a line of three hundred ton and three thousand ton presses from Germany. Wire guards lay against the walls, impotent. The machines were swarmed by sock-footed, bareheaded workers without safety-glasses.

Now, below the road, the flood deepened and narrowed. For the first time Daley noticed the mountains crowding in, the ultra-craggy, tree-feathered cliff mountains of Chinese paintings. He was surprised. The towering mountains had gravity-defying rocks perched on fissures, cupping the white spray of torrents. Trees latticed the skyline and pelted the mountain sides. Here and there a score through the forest betrayed power line towers – never a road, not even a track. There were cows on the roadside and goats in narrow pastures; but never a wild animal, and very few birds.

A finger of brown in the blue betrayed the power station at the valley head. Rattling trucks, heading up overloaded with coal, passed in a cloud of diesel.

They pulled into the third factory, a pipe plant. Under bamboo eaves, like a prostrate church organ, bristling pipes were being wire-brushed of corrosion by hand, one at a time. It was completely still inside where no machine moved, no footsteps padded - visitors in a midweek cathedral.

"Since tlouble, no demand titanium" explained SHL curtly.

Ane was despondent. "It was gone."

"Told you, didn't I! Thought we'd decided when you saw something you'd buy it. Remember the painted eggs in Kiev that couldn't be found in Moscow and the Pyrennean dolls that were too expensive?"

She rubbed colour into her cheeks with the thin towel. "Don't go on about it. I know I'm always doing it. Maybe we'll find one in Beijing. Aren't you going to change, Peter? You know how formal these banquets are."

"Suppose so. I wish you weren't so parsimonious with yourself. If it had been for the kids or a Christmas present, you'd have bought it like a shot!"

The banquet was another chop-stick fishing competition with

a turning carousel. Wine was a sweet, young Chinese sherry but dinner was a culinary extravaganza, as though the provincials had decided to outdo sophisticated Beijing.

Phoenix in the Snow was a complete chicken, naked of feathers with head, glazed eye and comb nested in a snow foam of uncooked egg-white. Its brownly boiled flesh was to be chopsticked off as it circulated. Wary of uncooked egg, Ane declined, but was joshed into trying Dragons Playing in the Snow: small cuts of eel in a dark brown sauce, hiding in a drift of egg-white. Tiger Fights Dragon was succulent until unmasked as cat cooked to a crisp in a wound-around snake!

The Leader was never without a cigarette: smoke curling blue from his brown-stained fingers. He didn't really smoke, but rather kissed the cigarette.

Daley and Ane were walking with coats over arms, down a stone corridor in the administration building, watched from each wall by sepia photographs of past factory dignitaries.

"Trouble with these dinners is they never fill you. A continuous stream of bloody *hors d'oeuvres*. Difficult to get a good mouthful."

"Got your Gestapo shoes on, haven't you?"

"Only ones I have, remember?"

"Make too much noise."

"Really? I rather like it. Gives the feeling of being here. An imprint after you've gone, if you like."

"You've too much imagination! It's an annoying clicking is all."

"Aren't we picky!" He complained, wondering what had got up her nose.

The girl, he decided. That's it. Paid her too much attention. "Listen, there's a river in the valley over there, Ane. Saw it this afternoon. Looked walkable. Ny's gone off to see his sister, so fancy a walk?"

"Time is it?"

"Seven."

"Can we get there?"

"Think so. Saw people washing and gathering stones. They got there somehow."

They walked towards the darkening trees. Behind, the sun was setting like a burning city, while ahead a faint full moon through the fuzzy hills threatened a cold night. After ten minutes, the fresh smell of fast water filled the air and chattering shallows betrayed the river. They broke out onto a pebble–beach where he had seen women washing clothes.

"Feel that." He passed her a stone.

"Like a prayer-stone, Peter. We collected 'em as kids, used as taws when we didn't have any. Weren't as good though. Weren't round."

"I just used to save 'em but me mum would get mad at the holes in me pockets, so I only carried a small one."

He slipped it into his coat pocket. The air was full of the scent of just-caught fish. The river shallows chuckled but no evening birds sang. He shivered. She linked her arm through for warmth and they walked over uneven stones, clumps of grass and dead flora.

He pushed his hands deep into pockets. "What you think of this lot?"

"You mean our hosts? Gives me the willies, the one that looks like death with a permanent smile."

"Bugger likes candy bars. Doesn't fit though. Doesn't speak English. Supposed to be a scientist but didn't turn up at my lectures."

"Maybe busy, someone must look after shop."

"Ny said he went Xian but he turned up for tea. Crony of the Director, you know. That could be it. Maybe he reports to him – the politico of the party, like Russia."

"I like her."

"She's not in the inner circle. Not invited to tea or anything."

"Probably really is a guide. Ny's never been here you know."

She pulled on his arm as she tripped.

"Something doesn't ring true though. She was in the Tiananmen demonstrations but she's not a student and seems lower echelon. How'd she get to Beijing?"

"Maybe guiding someone like us. On vacation perhaps."

"They don't take vacations."

"On business then."

"Maybe! Bothers me though."

She stooped to pick up a stone.

"Don't start collecting Ane. S'getting dark."

"Remember this?" She ran her hand up a tall stalk of grass and showed him the ear cupped in her palm, "A tree." She broke the stalk and held out the ear. "A bush." Then she threw it in the air with a flourish, "leaves!" She laughed as the seeds clouded. "Remember playing it with the kids."

There was a comfortable, crunching silence.

"I still think we're being followed?"

"What d'you mean, Ane – still?"

"That jeep last night."

"Just an army patrol stopping for a smoke."

She counted on her fingers: "What about that man in Hong Kong, those black cars in Beijing, that FAX, the missing passport. Doesn't it strike you as strange?"

"FAX is a puzzle right enough. All I can think is there really was a communications breakdown between Minster and Beijing."

"I don't believe that."

"Wait a minute! Don't remember seeing handwriting on Greg's copy."

"What d'you mean 'Greg's copy'?"

God, hadn't told her had he!

"Are you saying Greg gave you a FAX?"

He nodded.

"Where'd *he* get it from?"

"Hakone."

"Hakone!" she repeated. "They really did try to stop us didn't they? Whoever *they* are."

"Look, I'm sorry I didn't tell you. But don't you see, it proves the Boadicea message was written in Hong Kong."

"I thought you said that already, assumed it was a mistake."

"That's right. But let's say it wasn't a mistake. Never checked the back; if it was written on, it would show through."

"We were rushed."

"Remind me to check 'em. That man in Hong Kong may have been watching for Westerners and followed us back to the hotel to steal our passports. They are valuable."

"What's that got to do with the message?"

"Nothing. But let's say there is a hidden agenda - God, can't believe I said that! - and he was following us. He could have written that message. Could be friendly, you know, could be trying to warn us. After all, it says, 'Beware.'"

"But why so cryptic? Boadicea and Long John. A woman warrior and a bourbon whiskey. Why not come straight out?"

"Don't know. Maybe he's a crossword fanatic and it's an anagram. Maybe he was nervous that we'd ignore Louisa's message and wanted us to be careful."

"Then he wouldn't steal the passport, would he?"

"That's the trouble. Theories don't mesh. One's friendly, one's hostile. All I can think is the passport was there and we missed it. It'd be hard to see you know. Dark blue under the bed."

"So why trash the room? Look, you can explain all you want. This is not just a *simple* lecture tour."

A fresh gust lifted her hair off her shoulders.
The path veered back to the river; its noise made talking difficult. His legs were getting cold.

She squatted to wash a stone and was handing it to him, when she stopped, stood and shouted in his ear. "What's that?" She was pointing across the river.

"Looks like Yen. Her skirt anyway. Who's that in white with her?"

He surreptitiously dropped her stone. "It's him, I think, DHS. Was wearing a white suit, remember?"

"He just pushed her against that tree, Peter!"

"S'not our affair."

"You said she hated him."

"I said she was frightened of him."

"Then we'd better help her!" She set off upstream, splashing on immersed stones.

"Hey, wait. Nothing to do with us! Stop! Shit!" He stumbled on a large stone, planting a shoe in deep water to keep balance.

He caught up. "Wait. Just wait, will you!"

She stopped, breathing faster. He tried to assemble a breath. Sodding sliding stones. The hell with this!

"We should stay the hell out," he gasped, pushing the hair from his face. "He's bloody army and we know what those bastards can do."

"Don't Daley me! We're wasting time. Stay if you like. She needs help and I'm going."

She turned and set off, pointing and saying over her shoulder: "That's a bridge!"

He peered into the gloom. Stark against the steel sky, a skeletal structure spanned the river, invisible piers turning white water.

God, I'm out of shape! Got to get rid of this bloody belly, he cursed, as it bounced like a water melon. How the hell did she let herself come down here with him? Bloody asking for it! Serves her right, he decided savagely.

He cursed Ny, his family, his failing breath, and his own stupidity as they scrambled up the embankment pebbles.

They stood panting at the top. She put an arm on his back as she regained breath.

It was a railway bridge, old track overgrown with grass and weeds. Derelict. Naked rails warped into the gloom across the river. The ties were set far apart under the rails; roaring water flickered white between and below.

The air was cold and fresh, full of pungent crashing water.

She sprang to the first tie, looking at the next.

No way!

No way she could jump it, even with a run. They looked at each other, then cast around in the long grass.

He cursed the heavy overcoat that made motion difficult. An overgrown tie cricked his ankle. They wrestled it loose with the sudden wormy smell of wet soil then wobble-toppled it across the first two ties. It thumped, bounced, almost fell through then stayed, tilted. He knelt, and with irritable grunts – soaked, wet hair in his eyes – ponderously manoeuvered it with Ane pushing feverishly beside. It straightened.

A quick nod and they doubled across.

Squatting on the second tie, they pull-slid it forward, fingers slimy, impotent, emitting little sounds.

The close roar drenched totally as they forced its wagging end, across the gaps. They leapt the last to large-stride down, slaloming through pebble avalanches, wet coats flapping.

The man took off.

Ane ran ahead, splashing pools, sliding stones, arms waving.

He followed, breath pumping like a steam engine, running as if hip deep in seaweed.

Full moonlight caught her as Ane stumbled up.

Soft sounds, sob sounds. She was smoothing frantically at her skirt with a white cloth as if invaded by ants.

Seeing Ane, she pushed the cloth into a pocket, closed her voluminous coat and mutely fell into Ane's outstretched arms with heaving shoulders.

Daley crunched up, pushing rat-tails of hair from his eyes, gulping like a beached fish.

The girl was half whispering, half sobbing: "Thought I'd take a walk. *That man* followed me." She shivered.

"What possessed you to walk this bloody late? It's dangerous."

She glared at him. "Since when is *my* country dangerous? Since when is the night taken? Since when must we run from the old men and their lickspittles? Since when..." but the last 'since when' dissolved in her failing breath.

He reached out to touch her head, but missed.

Holding the lobby door open, Daley murmured to his wife: "Maybe you should stay with her a while, you know. Alone she may, well...See you upstairs."

She nodded and led the girl down the hall.

He glanced at the wall clock. 9.30. They'd been out two and a half hours.

He had changed and was hanging his coat over the radiator when Ane returned.

"She OK?"

"Upset but all right. Is there hot water, Peter?" She gave him a peck on the cheek as she went to the bathroom. The shower hissed and she started to hum.

"So, bit of a satyr is he, DHS," he mused as she turbaned the President towel round her hair and sank into the couch opposite.

"Suppose you think she egged him on, don't you?"

" No. Think he has some kind of hold over her, though. Puzzling. She's frightened, yet seemed resigned. When rape's inevitable, relax, minimize the harm."

She flounced back to the bathroom. "I can't believe you said that! You're all the same, you men. God gave you two heads but only enough blood for one at a time!"

"Where's that FAX?"

"Look for yourself."

"Oh, for God's sake!" He had inexplicable trouble finding things and would have to suffer humiliation as she pulled it from where it was all the time.

"What were you wearing when we met Greg, Peter?"

"The Harris Tweed."

"Well, then!"

On the table, smoothed side by side, they were identical. He turned them over. Embossed through the one on the left was the inside-out message.

"Bingo! I was right! The one from Hong Kong's written on. T'other isn't."

"So how far ahead are you? Know what it means? Know who wrote it and why? No! Know squat 'cept it was added in Hong Kong."

"Well, that's worth knowing. Besides, whoever wrote it is a friend."

Tuesday, October 31

Morning was cold and clammy. Ny came to Daley at breakfast. "Daughter musta return Beijing. Aunt sick. Cannot stay."

Made sense; after all, DHS lives here. It kept making sense till the girl looked pale. She flashed him a wintry smile and began whispering to Ane. Suddenly she stood with a scrape of chair and left. He turned to Ane but she gave him a quick look, shook her head and continued eating. He contained his curiosity until they were back in the room, packing.

"Whatever you do, don't tell Ny about last night."

He was surprised. "He doesn't know?"

"No, he doesn't and she'd rather he didn't!"

"Jes. The aunt must *really* be sick."

She looked at him but said nothing.

Daley hefted the luggage to the lobby and Ny loaded it into a different van. They waited, Ny and Yen in the rear, DHS, the woman and the driver in the front.

No Ane.

What the hell's keeping her. It's bloody cold and we won't get warm till they run the engine. He pulled his overcoat tighter, hands deeper in the pockets. It was still damp. So is bloody everything. He located the smooth stone and squeezed it.

The weak sun was making its way into the bricked courtyard. Trucks, thumps and factory squeaks intruded.

Eventually Ane emerged with the brown bag, slid open the side door and sat beside him.

"What kept you?"

"Tell you later."

She looked shaken.

Thin snow occasionally spun ahead like smoke.

The place of mud where the army had found them was pointed out as was the site of the roadblock. Of peasant and mule there was no sign. Daley closed his eyes to conjure them up, as if lingering in the local air.

As the door of their hotel room in Xian shut, he could no longer contain his curiosity : "Well! What kept you this morning?"

"Just as I was leaving, this woman came up and insisted on talking to me. At first she made no sense but she hung on. Wouldn't let go. Then I began to understand. She was asking me to take care of Yen. ' Me aunt, ' she told me. ' Yen danger. Beware him. She bad person! Plotect. ' Funny thing, Peter, she was tall – taller than Ny. Women of his family must have tall genes."

"Did she look sick?"

"No. She ran up the stairs to stop me!"

"Then I don't understand. We've an aunt who's sick but isn't. Yen should be happy to return to Beijing but isn't. Fact is, I think she's downright terrified!"

He mumbled into the bathroom, straightening the towels on their rack, catching and stopping himself. Everything tidy, piles hidden. Orderly. A desire to leave things neat. Getting on Ane's nerves, his tidying things.

The soap was on the bath edge and, as he picked it up, he saw a spider take a run at the slippery sides. He hung a towel down the side of the tub, coaxed the scurrying insect onto it with a toothbrush then quickly pulled the towel out. The spider ran off, rescued.

Afternoon was the terra-cotta army of Xian.

The rain let up and a breeze shook the naked young trees. The air was still full of coal but now country-leavened with the smell of wet hay.

They left the hotel at one-o-clock.

He noted that everybody smoked and idle shopwomen knitted. He saw seven men manhandling a dump-truck, its hydraulic system either broken or turned off to save gas. A bootmaker on the sidewalk pedaled an upturned bike, polishing shoe-sole edges.

Dirt, dust, mud, people.

They passed washed-away mud walls. Badminton shuttlecocks winged the sidewalk over a bound goat bleating in the brown October grass.

Cold weather had rung down down-filled heavy curtains in shop doorways and next year's corn hung in stooks from roofs and roadside trees. (Vacated stalks were stacked along walls for the February festival of the Year of the Horse, or for crushing into potholes deep in the road.)

Drying seeds were carefully laid along roadsides, the yellow carpet turned continuously and respread by a peasant guarding against pedestrian, car and bike.

They motored 40 kilometers from Xian to the resting place of China's first emperor, Ch'in Shih-huang-ti. Ny leaned proudly forward from the rear seat: "Emperor buried in thata hill. Fifty meters high, all earth, built by men!"

The woman gestured out the window. "See behind, Mount Li. He bellied between mountain and liver. Wind and Water. Keep away evil spilit."

"Nota only things to keep away men. Many robbers killed by a hidden arrows of automatic bows in thata hill. Even thesa days dangerous. Tomb not yeta opened!"

"Still not opened! Surely there must be maps, records, something."

Ny shook his head. "No. Construction people imprisoned in tomb. No-onea come out; no-onea know secrets."

"Jes. When was it built?"

Ny sat back grinning sheepishly, eyes defocussed as he calculated in his head. The woman answered in the bland voice. "210 BC, your lears."

"Incredible, more than 2000 years ago!"

There was a pause, then the girl spoke for the first time: "They're not the only people buried with the emperor."

"What d'you mean?"

"His barren concubines are also with him."

He couldn't resist teasing her.

"What's a concubine?"

"A wife. The Emperors had many."

"Hmm. Must have been nice being an Emperor."

"Typical! Typical man! Men are all the same. All you think about is sex. There are other things, you know."

Ny broke in: "Automatic bows shoota two hundred meters. You see ina exhibition." He nodded at the huddle of approaching buildings.

They entered a wide square, lined on one side by official but empty shops and on the other by jostling vendors.

Thus they came upon the eighth wonder of the world.

"All discovered ina 1974 bya farmers digging water. Founda ceramic men, never stop digging since! Chinaman. He love dig," Ny laughed.

The girl's morose mood lifted.

They pulled up outside a modern building and the woman went inside for tickets.

The company disembarked to stretch, the girl sitting on a low wall surrounding a bed of spindly trees. Stretching her legs out, she lay back, eyes closed to gather the weak sunshine. Her hair lifted on the wind.

DHS walked over, hitched up the back of his trousers and put his foot on the wall beside her, shooting his cuffs and smoothing the left wing of his thinning hair. He said something and she gave him a chin-up look. He adjusted the crease of a pant leg and smoothed his other wing of hair.

"Seen buggerlugs, Ane? Preening like a bloody banty-cock."

"Don't like him; no, I don't trust him. Still don't know why he's with us, 'specially here."

The girl swung her legs up and back in turn and, with a shake of her head, stood up and left him, leg in the air like a dog with no tree. He self-consciously lifted his leg from the wall, brushed its creases one at a time, then ambled to Ny, who was standing reading a poster. Ny's smile froze at his first words. Their conversation became animated when the man gave him a brown envelope which Ny seemed unwilling to accept.

"Bugger did go off to find help, Ane."

"Don't care. Seems to me, he was stranded too. Besides, it's because of him Yen can't stay with her aunt. I'd be mad too if I was Ny."

The woman reappeared, waving tickets.

Under a curved roof stretching farther than one could see, lay a vast expanse of earth. In the foreground people circulated round wooden stairs and along walkways at the top of a plywood wall. The low hum rose to a hollow din. The air smelled of freshly turned soil. Daley read the plaque over the jostling heads. By 221 B.C. there were 500,000 laborers working the site. When the Emperor died, his body was entombed in the wooded hill which they had passed and his army, his cohort for heaven, was encapsulated here. In 206 BC rebels plundered the pits and burned it.

It took his breath away.

Before and at him, marched three echelons of grim-faced giants. Individually the figures were tall, resolution etched in their aspect but *en-mass* they goose-pimpled his back. They *pressed* forward. Undeniable, unstoppable. Three columns of eight foot infantry. He had a tangible impulse to turn and run as terror mixed with awe, and with rooted-to-the-ground admiration. This army of seven hundred was unswervable – a sea of faces – eyes straight ahead, a coiled spring of straining devastation. The columns were punctuated by huge horses pulling burned-away chariots which, though gone, still rumbled on, the ghosts of their wheels etched black in the clay floor.

Rough-fashioned walls filed the three echelons, tops still imprinted with the burnt beams that once held the roof over the silently marching host.

Each face was different, each uniform unique.

So real were these terracotta greys that Daley swore he detected movement: a swinging arm, a marching foot. Maybe a hand! A sash!

The girl was standing perfectly still, wide eyed with wonder.

As this first overwhelming impression calmed, he inspected the individual statues more closely. Like Napoleon's Old Guard, they were heavily mustached but wore no demoralizing busbies. Their heads were bare, hair pulled to a bob at the back. The phalanxes in front of him wore no armour and didn't carry shields."How come no protection, Ny? Seems foolhardy."

"Ah, these ara men, not officers. Officers weara armour." He pointed at the figures behind a disappeared chariot. They wore a simple front apron of overlapping metal leaves from shoulder to midriff, string-tied at the back. "They travel closea to front to discipline cowards by cutting off heads. See! No helmets allowed!"

The woman had been listening. "Almy light. Almy *never* defense. Almy attack. Bowman splead sideway, continuous fire. Soldier lun at enemy – never stop. No plotection needed. Light for spleed."

Daley shivered, then shuffled with the crowd to the edge of the Command pit. Here officers, runners and guards, guiding the huge army, were frozen in workmanlike bundles in a much smaller area.

White coated archeologists buzzed between, brushing dirt from wrinkles and unearthing new remnants. The headless lined the earthen wall edges, queueing for resurrection.

SHL came and stood beside him. "Puzzle with almy,"she said, nodding at the staff below. "No clommander. He never flound. Horse carriage there," she pointed, "but he never flound."

"Maybe rebels took. Best way stop hated Emperor enter heaven."

"No. Nevler there! *Pleople* never put, so army *never* flight. Emperor *never* lenter heaven!"

He glanced at her in surprise but she turned away. Strange thing to say. Much more likely he was stolen by the revolutionary army that had ransacked the pits. What better way to get back at a hated dynasty?

He walked back to Ane, Ny and the girl at the main pit. The woman remained nervously at the rail.

"They look so *real*," Ane was saying as he came up.

The girl leaned far over the rope to touch a grey head in the first row. The post wobbled. Daley caught her quickly, but released her as fast.

She blinked at him: "Once we were so great as to create such an army! The army now crushes the people. Would be better altogether, immobile like this one."

Ny glanced at the man but he need not have worried, DHS was deep in conversation with SHL.

They emerged into the cold at three-thirty. It was overcast. A chill breeze cracked the flags and drove hands deeper into pockets.

Unzipping the hood in his coat collar that still smelled of vomit and gas, Daley pulled it over and pushed errant strands of hair underneath.

The vendors swarmed.

"'Allo, Mr!"

"Cheep! Little money, Mr!"

"Real cheep!"

"Cheep."

"Cheep. Mr. LOOK AT ME ! Mr!" said one, grabbing Daley's chin and, on tip-toes, turning his head to urge attention.

The desperate vendors waved brightly coloured jackets and quilts, plastic birds that could be blown into nightingales, balls with pull-strings that mewed like a cat and threatening kites which, if they couldn't fly, could terrorize.

Grey miniatures of the army inside were waved under their noses like thuribles at a lunatic mass. Some were in dusty red-velvet-lined boxes, some in string bags.

All were covered in yellow ochre dust, as though a country-wide wind had swirled up, stripping soil from the treeless fields, fading and unloading its burden into all crevices and creases. Dust gritted in Daley's mouth and yellow teared his eyes.

Ny and DHS wanted nothing to do with the market. Woman's work, Daley decided, wishing he could get away. SHL became more animated than he had yet seen her and bartered vivaciously with her angry countrymen.

"Help us make the foreigners pay! "the vendors censured, but she persevered and emerged with a dozen string-bag armies at fifty cents each, plus a larger one for four dollars.

Not to be outdone, Ane bartered with hand-signals for bright quilts with extant insects in rainbow fields. The girl laughed and skipped with her from stall to stall.

The vendors scented "real" money and vied to undercut one another. Ane wrote a price on a piece of paper and passed it to them, they in turn crossed it out and wrote a new price. Never a word was spoken just gesticulations and nods. The final price was underlined by either party

The girl went running to Daley. Ane had bought two bed-size quilts for four dollars each, reduced from forty. She was beside herself. "It's the free-market and t'is wonderful. Never have I seen one before at all, only heard of 'em. Like sex in school." She blushed and turned away.

Enchanting. Just enchanting. Daley caught a quick breath as he watched her dance back to his wife. God. Why now? Why not thirty years ago!

WEDNESDAY NOVEMBER 1

At nine-o-clock, they left without seeing their hosts, who had already returned to Baoji.

Daley struggled with the pollution. Never thought I'd be glad to get back to Beijing.

Ny took their documents and returned with the Boarding Passes. Daley hastily repocketed the passports.

There were no designated seats! A bloody free-for-all. The gate opened and the crowd surged forward in a lump onto the dull runway.

Ane linked her arm through and smiled up at him as they

shuffled up the steps to the Ilyutian 147. Half-way up, the intermittent rain became a continuous drizzle.

Daley looked around irritably, drops forming on his nose. Light was visible through the idling engine pod at the tail.

It's not possible! No way could light be seen *through* a gas turbine!

She felt him tense and pulled at his arm. His smile reassured her.

Blades were scraping shrouds in lazy showers of sparks and nothing, absolutely bloody nothing, could be done. If he raised the alarm, they'd be trampled. He ducked in the door. Perhaps the impingement'll stop when the engine is at operating temperature and the blades are tight, he reflected, trying to dismiss the image as it disappeared from view.

The flight to Beijing was like the subway in rush-hour Tokyo, made more immediate by the narrowness of the fuselage.

The girl was quiet.

Daley was puzzled. She was returning to her beloved Beijing. "It would happen there again," she had said.

It was dark when they entered the drive of the Friendship. The girl's hair was again totally covered. Daley looked at his watch. 5.30.

The girl rolled down the window and gestured for him. As he bent, her face came to him. A quick brush kiss, then halting words in a dusky voice: "Goodbye. Don't forget me, Peter."

He straightened as if stung. Her mouth trembled and a bright spot ran her cheek as she turned away.

Goodbye! Gone?

His throat was full. He jumped as Ny grabbed his hand, pumping it like a rag doll . "Seea you tomorrow. Acrobats. You enjoya very much."

He stood. Watching where she had been.

V
INSIDE: BEIJING

He stood staring at the empty gate, willing the car back, willing unwound the sudden of it. Gone like a blown candle.
His vision blurred. She'd kissed him, hadn't she? Her softness still burned his cheek.
A distant horn sounded. He shook like a wet dog then turned to help Ane with the luggage through the lazy doors. Warmth overtook him as he bent, squeezed her hand off the case lead and heaved it with bitter power.
Must have seen it all, he thought glumly as they stood by the elevator, hurting but not saying.
Maybe she didn't know. Too obvious. The transparent infatuation of an old man. Wouldn't hurt her for the world. Their eyes met; he smiled.

"Good job our bellies fit," she giggled as they stood close in the shower. "Looks like I'm pregnant!"
"Can't be. Only got a starter's pistol!" he joshed as he soaped her. Funny, how loss makes you appreciate what you have.
"Doesn't work very *hard* these days. Must work for a raise!" She tapped his appendage and, realizing what she had said, they laughed uncontrollably.
"You've fallen for her, haven't you?"
"What'd she see in an old fart like me?" he said, but he did not believe it. Been more alive last week than for a long time.

"You haven't answered."

"Girls often try it on with old men. Safe, and they know it. Suckers I suppose. Nobody likes to be *old* you know. Anyways, it's over."

She turned so he could wash her back.

The hot water had reddened the scar over the prosthetic rod inserted after her fall from the horse. As he sponged it, he realised he loved her–that hadn't changed. Could a man love two women?

"Don't rub so hard," She pulled him to her by his buttocks. He gave her a final, softer stroke.

"She's gone. I'm not mad, just glad."

"You're upset!"

"No, I'm not! Really!"

"Yes, love."

He reached for the towel. "Look, love, we leave day after tomorrow. Maybe we'll never come back. Let's enjoy Thursday, our last full day in China: no commitments, no Chinese till evening. Let's go shopping. You enjoy bartering."

God, I hate shopping.

She picked up like a child." We could go to that parade beyond the Beijing Hotel, the one Ny told us about."

Thursday, November 2

A rattling in the street outside drew Daley from the bed to the small window. He could make out a van, its driver assembling a set of Old-Bailey scales. A platform elevator rose out of the road beside it. Two bell boys stepped off and stood huffing ghostly breath through their fingers. The driver returned to the van and emerged carrying a large bamboo basket of tail waving fish. They were weighed and after an exchange of words and money, the boys and fish decended. Synchronized steel covers closed over them.

He was sitting on the bed carefully threading a new pantyliner into a tartan ascot. "Better put on a warm jacket, Peter. Looks cold an' that suit you use for lectures is too thin."

"How about the Harris Tweed?"

"Sounds good. I do wish you'd get some new jackets; your old ones won't close now, you know."

Always on at him to get new clothes. Nothing wrong with the old ones; not worn out or anything, just wouldn't close. Nobody noticed unless he buttoned them.

He emptied the suit pockets onto the table: coffee, sugar, diary, cheque-book, passports with tickets inside.

A passport with no ticket – three passports.

He blinked. *Three*! Definitely! Two with tickets, one without!

He fanned them. How could there be three? She'll kill me.

He stared out the window, suit jacket dropping to the floor. Creeping senility? There all the time and I just didn't notice? Deep pocket after all – stuck in the bottom.

I'll tell her if I have to, but why bother? We'll be home soon and it won't matter. A creeping tightness spread from his bum to his stomach. Surely he'd have noticed when he transferred them from the tweed to the suit before lecturing. He tried to remember by approaching from both sides timewise. But nothing came back to him, only a rush of events muddled like multicoloured taffy.

She walked from the bathroom. "How'd I look?" She twirled in a sensible wool skirt with a high necked blouse under a plaid cardigan. "Only unworn outfit I've got."

"Fine. You look fine. Warm."

"Put my knickers on inside-out. But not changing."

He glanced at her.

"Don't you remember? It's bad luck. Think you've forgotten all your Yorkshire."

"Just so's you won't be cold."

"Why don't you take more care of your clothes? Anybody'd think you had a wardrobe full." She made to pick up the guilty jacket, but he swooped it up first, stuffing the incriminating documents into the inside pocket.

"Won't we need those?" she asked as he hung the suit in the closet. He carefully extracted their two, standing in front, then turned with them in his hand, held up for her, before wriggling them into the Harris tweed.

Ten minutes later, well muffled, they set out to walk to the shopping section on Changan Avenue beyond the Beijing Hotel. The heavy grey clouds had lightened but there were gusts of cold wind. At first the road was quiet, but beyond the massive Beijing Hotel the road was busy with buses, cars, and people.

The air was heavy with diesel.

A crowd lined outside a cobbler's shack waiting for shoes to be mended on the spot.

Every shop seemed to sell black leather coats.

They passed a greengrocers. Beside was a large emporium, its name in English: Gift shop. Five storeys high.

Ane went in.

Daley examined the magnificent antique *cloisonne* in a crown glass window. Maybe...

He ducked inside to find every shelf and square inch of floor and glass-cased counter piled with rainbows of jade, *cloisonne*, jet, ivory and porcelain.

Slow-working salesgirls circulated as he examined regiments of eggs, eggcups, chopsticks, and chopstick holders – never a salt or pepper he wanted for Ray Jenkins.

Then he noticed a pair in delicate *cloisonne*.

The quest was over!

In the corner were a display of open boxes. Each contained a large brush, a crimson bar of paint, two jade columns and a large black slate palette. Personal-Seal Sets! Wasn't that what Beth wanted?

Ane joined him. "What'cha got, Peter?"

"*Cloisonne* cruets for the Jenks and a Seal Set for Beth."

"You know Margaret's told Ray to stop, to collect something else, don't you? House's getting too full of 'em."

"Don't tell me that after we've had so much trouble. What's he going to collect now?"

"Don't know."

"Hope it's not big, "

"Well, I did okay. Got the Christmas presents for Word Processing." She tapped a red bracelet under his nose.

"Nice. They'll like 'em."

He watched the girl slowly counting out notes from her electronic till and sliding abacus balls back and forth on their wires to do her sums.

"Eddie'd like one of those."

"What?"

"That ball thing she's adding up on."

"You know, that's not a bad idea, a sort of ancient computer."

She sighed. "It's so difficult to buy for him. Loves computers but s'got everything that's not expensive."

The girl returned with his change and he waved at the abacus. She backed away, puzzled. He leaned over the counter and picked up the well-worn instrument.

She shook her head.

"No. Don't be frightened. Just want to buy it."

The only man on the staff came over, laughed loudly and sing-songed at the girl. She took the abacus and began wrapping it with sheets of paper as Daley counted notes into the man's hand.

As they left, the girl was leaning on the man, giggling uncontrollably.

"What's so funny?"

"Dunno. Suppose its like goin' in a shop and buying the bloody till!"

"Peter, Let's try Tiananmen again."

"My legs are tired."

"Walking's good for you."

"The army will probably stop us again."

"S'worth a try though, isn't it?"

He nodded. It was useless to argue. It was a long way and it was cold.

They set off at a fast pace to keep warm in the chilly street.

Wangfujing Street was busy until they reached the Beijing Hotel ten minutes later. As they turned along Changan Avenue, the crowd thinned. The shops disappeared. Now there were large buildings behind impressive iron railings and militia-guarded gates. Silent worshipers stood* besides trees, head bowed, mumbling in another, quieter world.

Some men were standing round a bicycle, pedal on the curb. A black and white grosbeak on the handlebar was hopping from claw to claw, one leg looped with twine. An occasional sunflower seed was tossed and neatly caught, crunched in the air as it re-alighted.

In the distance busy Tiananmen rumbled.

Now large sandwich boards advertising tours to "six-monuments-in-a-day", impeded the pavement. The tour buses were up the bushed driveways and hucksters waving tickets approached passers-by – especially the few westerners – offering tours "cheep." One man in a long coat was very persistent.

"Not interested. Sorry," Daley kept saying slowly to the hucksters.

They walked over the uneven flagstones brushed of leaves, the smell of diesel rising. More open now, the gusting wind had a sharper edge.

They reached the congested Changan-Nan Chizi intersection.

"Stleet 'tlanks' came down?" He mimicked the woman.

"Think so."

Crossing the road, even with the lights, was frightening as audacious cyclists swarmed forward from cars and buses, forcing pedestrians to thread them, never stopping, never hesitating, pressing to the other side.

"Think they judge your movement, Ane, and flow around you so don't stop moving!"

She'd managed to find presents for their friends and he'd even found a salt and pepper and the seal set. First time he'd ever found anything, she smirked.

Half a kilometer further Changan suddenly widened into Tiananmen Square.

It was a totally tarmacked airport with nothing but people. A tide of black hair as far as the eye could see, hedged by distant tiny buildings two inches high. One stood out, the Great Hall of the People with its red monocolour wall and its Mao.

A class of little girls in red and black anoraks jogged by, watched by a swooping hawk kite barely discernible in the low grey.

Daley inspected the pavement for tank tracks. Thought he detected faint traces filled with matching concrete and "weathered" to merge.

Ane stopped and said: "You can almost feel the rumble, can't you? The fleeing students, panic, their Statue of Liberty watching."

"*Goddess of Freedom*, you mean. That's what Yen called her."

"This is a killing ground Peter. Mustn't walk it like a park." She had tears in her eyes.

It's a land where to pretend that everything is civilized is a way of life. Barbarism is the response to existence. Looks so ordinary he mused, watching the kite swoop and climb.

She squeezed his arm and swung her heavy bag towards a large statue in the distance. "Let's go see what that's about."

"It's so bloody cold."

"So, let's move quicker."

They strode to the "Martyrs of the Revolution," a hundred-and-twenty foot pile of stone giants with coarse angular faces, led by an inspired youth and a girl with single massive bare breast. Probably signifies nurturing, feeding the revolution, he mused. Still, he decided, inspecting her more closely, it's fuller than most I've seen in China. More like Yen's loose beauties.

There were a few thousand people in the square but it seemed empty. The bitter rain was loaded with ice.

"No sign of the army, Peter."

"Some areas seem closed though." He pointed at the distant rope barrier, then his jaw dropped. "Jesus!"

He stopped dead, swinging her round him.

"What's matter? You all right?"

"No, no. I'm okay. S'him. Over there. That man – *DHS*!"

"You're joking! Where?"

"Don't look! Could swear it's him. He turned when he saw me. Think he was watching us."

"Can't be!"

"Well, now he's just bloody standing."

"Can't be him though. Must be somebody else. I mean he's at the lab in Bojai. You sure?"

"Pretty sure. I'd know that bloody death look anywhere. Can't be two buggers like that!"

She pushed her hair from her face. "Don't think he's been following us do you?"

He glanced quickly in the direction of the suspicious figure. "Following us? Why the hell follow *us*? S'probably just a coincidence."

He shrugged his shoulders and said quietly, not taking his eyes off the man in the near distance: "Look. Let's see what he does when we move. Those shops over there." He nodded towards a clutch of buildings on the periphery of the square. "Let's go. See if he follows."

They ambled with simulated nonchalance past the line of poster kiosks and entered a government gift shop. It was empty. They always were. It smelled like an unaired Victorian sitting room. Its ware was expensive, prices fixed and assistants surly.

They huddled behind the plastic-covered *cloisonne* vases in the dusty window and watched the man.

At first he stood looking round, pushing back the hair blowing in his face. He seemed uncertain. Then, as if making up his mind, he walked slowly to the poster kiosk in front of the shop and stopped behind it. They watched him reading the flyers.

"It's him for sure. Bloody snooker championship in progress."

She pulled closer.

"Leastways, we know and he doesn't."

The man was perusing the shop. Ane pulled back as he came round the kiosk.

He smoothed his flattened hair one side at a time, rain dripping from his nose..

"No doubt at all. Question is what to do."

"Look, Ane, I've an idea that might just work."

"Enough of your bright ideas. Let's go back to the hotel."

"Exactly. We'll go back to the hotel."

"Thought you said - "

"I did and we'll go back to the hotel."

She hated it when he did that. "No, you don't! Tell me?"

"Not yet. Wait and see."

That was worse. She scowled.

"Look," he shouted over the fresh wind. "No matter what I do, just follow, okay. Follow. Don't stop, no matter what."

She tossed her head angrily.

They stepped out, hoods and collars up, not looking back.

As they went back to Changan and turned into the busy Nan Chizi crossing, the rain stopped and the wind dropped. He threw back the hood and finger-combed his hair.

The lights were red. "Remember, no matter what." He squeezed her arm and felt her shiver. The lights changed and he jerked her into the rush of pedestrians and bikes.

Half way across, he stopped.

A small woman, hair in a white scarf, passing behind him on an old bike, hit his leg and, with a little cry, fell off. Immediately bikes piled as far as he could see, a domino cacophony of metal impacts, shouts, screams, thuds, and thumps.

He grabbed the outstretched hand of the little woman and jerked her upright. She yelled at him, waving her arms.

Ane was shaking. He pulled at her arm. "See that, Ane! All over bloody place. I just stopped and bingo–like bloody ninepins – all over bloody place! Knew they would. Knew they would. Bingo! All over place," He laughed hysterically. "Sod'll not cross till that bloody lot's sorted out."

She scolded: "You could have been hurt. Should have told me."

He shook his head.

"But you could have been hurt."

"If I'd told you, you'd a' stopped me. So I didn't."

"Well, I wasn't hurt. Not seriously. Timing, you know. That little woman – there she was. Bingo! Over she went. And over the bloody lot went. All over the place. I knew, you know...knew it'd happen if someone stopped in the middle. Bingo – all over the place!"

"For God's sake stop saying that."

"Well, I did and it did!" He was shivering with emotion.

"You're limping. Thought you'd not been hurt."

"Nothing. Don't worry."

They hurried back down Changan towards the Beijing Hotel. His leg did hurt but he ignored it as it slowly went numb.

Five minutes later they were passing the tour buses again.

"Oh, bloody hell, Ane. It's that fella again. Look, he's seen us. Just keep walking."

The man angled to intercept. Daley glared and waved him away but he persisted, finally running in front and holding out a paper.

"What the hell!"

Ane unraveled it as they walked, step for step on the uneven pavement, like a four-legged race.

She held out the paper to Daley.

It was covered with scratched out numbers, one underlined.

"What is it, the fare or what?"

"One of those pieces of paper from Bojai. No. Sorry. Xian."

The man stood in front of them with an uncertain smile.

"Look we can't just stand here. He'll catch up."

"Can't understand it."

"Is it that woman, SHL, you know, the glide?"

"Can't be. She wasn't with me. No. Yen was."

His heart leapt. "Yen."

"Gotta be."

Stunned as if hit, he couldn't focus, couldn't think.

"She's trying to contact us, Ane. *Us*. You know, secretly."

"Oh, for God's sakes! You've been watching too many movies. It's just a ruse to get us on the bus."

"No. Don't think so."

"You wouldn't, would you?"

"Well, I don't care, I'm off up there." He waved at the hidden drive beyond the bushes. "Don't look so down. If we dodge up this drive, he won't find us anyway."

"Unless he's already seen us. Which case we'll be sitting ducks."

He was set and stepped out, heels tapping in rhythm with his humming. "I'll see you again. When the sun breaks through again." Back! She was back!

The cold wind warmed as momentary sunshine danced on the windows of the grey office buildings.

She ran after him. "You don't fool me, you know. Enough of this knight errant shit."

He ignored her.

"Well, on your head be it!"

Alive again, crunching heel muffling leaves. He wanted to plan his first words carefully. She'd admire that.

Around a corner, masked by a close knit hedge, was a crimson bus with black windows.

The huckster had disappeared.

Daley stopped on the first step and quickly passed his comb through his muddled hair. Pulled through a bloody 'edge backwards, he grinned. Bloody coat smells so he took it off and dropped it on the chrome safety-rail.

Inside was light, but the windows were misted. Stale cigarette smoke and new plastic hit the back of his throat, but he shuffled on, sideways, down the aisle, Ane sourly following.

There were a few passengers waiting to visit the six-monuments-in-a-day.

She was sitting in the centre of the back bench seat.

Heart in his throat, he dropped into the convenient aisle seat ahead of her. She was looking past him, tear traces tracking her cheeks, arms stretched to Ane.

Ane's grim look dissolved like summer ice cream. They embraced in silence, the girl making little noises, as Ane reassured her.

He was piqued not to be acknowledged.

Yen was pale, as though she'd had little sleep. Her eyes were wide and liquid, tired shadows under them like shroud folds. She was nervous, dressed in a faded blue overcoat, jeans and off-white sneakers. Her scarf was faded gingham.

She kept wiping the window to glance out. She held Ane's hands so tight her knuckles blanched.

"You've got to help me!"

Ane drew her in by the shoulder.

Slowly his sulk evaporated.

The girl was now smiling, big eyes wide, cast utterly for him. "We'll help, if we can. You know we will, Yen."

Her eyes flashed the window. "It's become very dangerous for me here. Shouldn't have come back at all. Please. Only you can help. Please take me with you!"

He didn't believe he had heard.

"What?"

"Please take me with you."

"What, back to the hotel?"

She shook her head.

"Anywhere out of China! Canada?"

"You gotta be joking. Can't be done! Look, Ane, tell her."

His wife looked at him in silence.

And this had been *his* idea!

"Look, Yen, if there's anything we can do - I mean, realistically - Just say. But we can't take you to Canada!"

The girl's fingers twisted in her lap.

There was an awkward silence.

"You've just no idea. I mean. Visas, passports, Embassy. Christ! You've no idea how bloody dangerous. S'out of the question. Impossible!"

Ane took over. "Yen, look. Tell us. Why not tell us?"

Daley made to speak but she stilled him with an upraised palm.

The girl licked her lips nervously. She murmured: "Somebody's been talkin'. My friends in the English class are disappearin' and when I ask – well!" She glanced quickly out the window, eyes blinking fast. "' They've gone to the country,' they say. I know what *that* means. I'll be next, don't you see? Please help. There is no one else."

She spoke low and fast to Ane, beyond his hearing so he studied their heads with rising consternation. Exactly what Choi had warned against. Take me to bloody Canada. He wondered cynically if this was her plan all along.

The rain fit his mood.

"Peter, we've got to help, but can't tell Ny."

"What! S'impossible *and you know it*. Tell her for cryin' out loud!"

"You don't understand."

"No, *you* don't understand Ane, or don't seem to bloody want to. Christ, I thought if anyone would understand, you would! Remember what Choi said? We can't."

Their eyes held.

"Now listen. They're watching the embassy, so visas are impossible. She probably doesn't have a passport. Never flew until Xian. No, as Ian Franklin'd say, it's too big an ask."

"But you've got to! You really don't understand."

"Why do you need it, Yen, our help? Tell me. Why? What don't I understand? Why you in trouble? You ask us to put our lives on the line without a *why*. Why you so special? We're in the land of a billion and you can't 'disappear'?"

Her eyes glinted. "I can't. I am Liberty. 'Give me your tired, your poor, your huddled masses yearning to breathe free.'"

His jaw dropped. "She's lost it! Babbling. Quoting poetry, for God's sakes."

An involuntary growl rose in his throat. Like every bloody thing in China, swallowed into warped reality. "Look, Ane, let's face it. We leave tomorrow. If she needs money, okay. Otherwise there's nothing to be done."

"Peter, we've got to. Got to help her. At least to Hong Kong – whatever. But we *must*!"

She took his hands but he pulled them back.

"Peter, she'll be killed if we don't. We've got to try."

She was cool, paler but calm, lips thin with determination.

"Don't get bloody calm on me. Hate it when you're calm. You bloody well know, don't you? She's told you hasn't she? She's told *you*, *why*, and you're not going to tell me, are you?"

She dropped her stare.

"Christ! I knew it. Another bloody ring-in-the-shoe job, isn't it? Don't tell the silly old sod 'cos he'll panic. Don't you realise we could get killed or worse and it'd be your fault. I can't believe it. Surely you can tell me. I am your husband."

She gazed at him in steady silence.

"Well, on your head be it!"

She remained silent but was struggling with tears.

His feelings confused him. It was impossibly dangerous, bloody silly to even consider. Maybe she was right. Better he didn't know. Piqued, though, that she'd expected him to refuse out of hand, to vacillate, unload responsibility. He mumbled irritably: "You just don't trust me, do you?"

"It's not that. Really it isn't. Look at me. You've got to trust *me*." She lifted his chin and caught his eyes directly. "Trust me!"

There was silence for a minute.

"Okay. Let's walk the problem, shall we?" He looked directly at Yen: "Do you have a passport?"

She shook her head.

"I don't care, Peter. We've still got to help. You've got to help."

"Oh, for Christ's sakes, how?"

Suddenly a tremendous thrumping shook the floor; the engine had started. The seat backs vibrated irrepressibly, so he stood up.

"Is DHS there?" Ane shouted in his ear. He gave her a startled look. Completely forgotten the man from Bojai!

The question made the girl jolt as if hit. She knew their acronym. She grabbed Ane's arm, eyes wide with terror. "You've seen *him*? You brought him *here*! To me."

"No. We lost him. We think he was following us but weren't

sure. Anyway, there's nothing to worry about. Really. Nothing."

The girl quickly wiped the window.

"Don't worry. We lost him," said Daley. "Look. We'd better get off before the bus goes. We're going to the acrobats tonight, Yen. Come with your parents. Maybe we'll think of something. Oh, and bring a small black and white photo, and don't be smiling."

He was relieved to get time. An idea was forming, refusing to stop developing in spite of him.

"Why?" Ane asked, uncertainly pulling at his sleeve as they ploughed up the bus.

"Why what?"

"Why bring a photo?"

"Oh, I don't know."

Now you can be in the bloody dark for a change. Tit for bloody tat!

As he donned his coat, he glanced at the lonely figure. His breast ached. God, did I lay into her! He felt wretched. She looked so small.

They dismounted, the door closed and they watched the bus slowly roll past. Now she was gone, it all seemed so impossible.

"Thought of something, haven't you?" Ane asked.

"Look, it's two-o-clock. Better get on. Yesterday's history, tomorrow's mystery, we've got today so we'd better use it!"

"Why was she so adamant Ny shouldn't know? I don't understand. Pretty suspicious, don't you think?"

"No, I don't. Think about it! If Beth was skipping town, would she want you to know? Probably not! You'd only worry an' try to dissuade her. Better you don't know."

"Suppose you're right. But we'll need his help if anything's to be done, so how can he not be told?"

"I'll tell you right now what he'll say."

"Exactly. That's another thing that makes it impossible."

"You'll think of something."

There it was again, that innocent confidence. "I dunno, Ane. Maybe's there's something but I need time. Time to think."

"Why d'you need a photograph? Tell me."

"She'll need a passport, won't she?"

"Yes, but you know she doesn't have one. It's not fair. Shouldn't be getting her hopes up like that. She really thinks we have a plan."

"How the hell can we? You know, I can't believe she asked. Just can't believe it."

They speeded up.

She pulled at his arm and blinked up at him. "Look, Peter, you've no idea. Really you've not."

Yen's eyes – sad, beautiful – swam back. He shivered.

Two Daleys walked away from the bus, away from her: the romantic Irishman and the Canadian engineer.

"You've really have thought of something, haven't you?"

"Come on. What was all that crap about liberty anyway? I know she quotes poetry but that was bloody ludicrous!"

"I know you too well. Can't live with a man this long and not know. Tell me!"

"You're always saying that. You tell *me!*"

He'd decided he wasn't going to tell her. He was going to wait. Besides, he had to think it through, make sure of it.

Their fast pace had slipped his sock underfoot. Damn lace must have bust again!

"Well, we do have the extra passport, don't we?" He immediately bit his tongue.

She pulled him round and brushed a drop of rain off the end of her nose. "What d'you mean, extra passport? You know we don't."

"Look, I'm sorry. I was going to tell you. Well, somehow it didn't matter. Not then anyway." She stared at him, waiting. "I found Beth's."

"Holy God! Now *who* doesn't trust *who*? You found it. What d'you mean *found* it? Where? How could you have found it? It was stolen."

"I know. I thought so, we thought so. Anyway, it wasn't. In me suit pocket all the time. I was going to tell you."

"No you weren't!"

"Look, we can't hiccup along like this. He's sure to pick us up."

"No, listen. Your suit! How could it be in your *suit*? You only wear it for lectures. Never even took it out of the case in Hong Kong!"

He shrugged. "Flew in it, remember. Just kept wearing it. Harris jacket had sick on it. You have a point though. Don't ask me why. It's all a bloody muddle."

He was fed up with the whole thing. All he did these days was try and explain enigmas. "There it was, with the other two, when I emptied my pockets this morning!"

"Just *this morning*?" He nodded. "I know you pooh-pooh it but I really think something's going on."

"Beginning to think you may be right but lets face it, we leave tomorrow. We've got it back. There's only tonight." He looked around quickly. "Let's keep moving. Don't know where that bugger's gone but he's sure to guess we'll come back this way."

The street was becoming busy. He pulled his hood tighter against wind fingers full of rain.

A leaf blew in her face and she batted it away. "You're going to help her, aren't you? Knew you would." She leaned happily on his shoulder.

"It's bloody daft, you know. I mean it isn't even Russia. These buggers are totally unpredictable. Look what happened to that poor mule on the road. Least the stupid sods in Russia were consistent!"

"D'you think the Embassy'll help Peter?"

"No way! Remember the brother's sister? They watch the entrance. No, only chance is to hide her in plain sight, sort of like that fella at Ray Jenkins's factory."

"What you on about Ray Jenkins's factory?"

"This old man used to take a wheel-barrow of rubbish home

every night from the factory. At first the guard stopped and searched him, but as it was always metal turnings and wood ends, he gave up and to just nodded him through. Finally after three or so months it got too much for him. 'Look George,' he said, blocking his way. ' Tha must be taking summat. Promise I'll do nowt, what you nicking?' 'Wheel-barrows!'"

She giggled.

"That's what we must do, steal a wheelbarrow."

They walked on in silence.

"She looks western, doesn't she? Thought so since we met her. Amazing what a bit of makeup can do."

"Hide her in plain sight," he murmured to himself.

The pace quickened as ideas flowed. She unhooked her arm and enumerated on each wet finger. "She could use Beth's passport, wear the Indian dress. It'd fit her with a bit of adjustment. Skirt's full so that's all right, but top'd be a bit loose. Could fix that at any rate. It's certainly blousy enough to be western, not slinky like their dresses, is it? She could easily be Canadian."

"A *lot* of adjustment! She's considerably less endowed than you! Fill her out with pantyliners," he laughed.

She rang his arm. "You are awful, you. Fancy thinking of that. The dress won't be on her photo so that'll look authentic. I suppose we'll have to fill her out. Chinese have none, do they? Remember Louisa's ' two fried eggs'? They'd never take her for one of them if she's big!"

He gave a cynical smile. "Fooled by tits. Still, one thing's in our favour. People in Communist countries hate attention. Fact they go to great lengths to avoid it. Remember that Russian woman and the lightbulbs? No way was she goin' to ask for new ones when I broke 'em all, trying to get the bedside lamp to work. No way!"

"Ane, do you have any of that clart here?"

"You mean hair colouring?"

"That stuff like thick green soup you plaster on your head and leave for a hour."

"Henna? Yes. Why'd you ask?"

"Well, the one thing that's totally Chinese is black hair. Jet black hair. Would that stuff colour hers?"

"Maybe. It's 'Chestnut.' Turns my hair red."

"No, it doesn't. Light auburn more like."

"It'll look funny."

"No, it won't. You use it to cover grey. Her black'll probably go brown. If it looks natural, doesn't matter what colour it is. Except black," he added with a shrug.

She skipped a step, happy now. He was thinking."Another thing, her English's good. Could pass for a westerner anywhere."

"Funny that, isn't it? Irish-English. You're right about the dress. She'll need western underclothes too. Pantyhose. What could be more western?"

There was a short pause.

"I don't have any spare ones...well...good ones. They're all like these." She showed him a badly laddered knee. "All I have are your head-clothes, you know...black stockings and things."

"Don't like those, do you?"

She shook her head.

"Look at it this way. You're a gourmet cook. It's no different, just presentation is all – for the eyes. Sort of an exciting frame for a picture. Anyway, lend 'em to her, she'll look good in them."

She punched his arm.

"Well, what could be more western, I mean, Playboy, Penthouse an' all." His mind was stroking the delicious sight.

She settled into his step.

Twenty minutes later, they entered the Friendship gate. It had stopped raining, so he undid the chin string of his hood with difficulty and flicked it back. He was tired.

"You need your puffer? I can hear you from here."

They were soaked. Hadn't mattered before, now he couldn't wait to throw off the malodorous coat and towel himself.

On the fourth floor he accepted the key from the attendant at the desk with a curt nod, opened their door, swung off the wet coat as though infected and dropped the purchases on the bed with a sigh of relief.

He cleared a space on the bed, chose Beth's passport, opened it, and cocked it to the light to see.

"We're too old for this." He walked to the big window.

Through the skeletal trees, the fading sun rippled crimson fingerprints on the clouds. Bleak, he thought. Winter bleak.

"We never admit it, but we are old. Not inside. Only twenty-four inside, but outside gets old, malfunctional, incontinent, and we just can't believe it. This," he waved the passport, "is a game for the young."

"Look, you're as young as you feel. Besides, this requires patience and the young have none! No, I think you can do it. I've watched you meticulously glueing broken porcelain."

"Well, look at this embossed seal of Canada. It enters the bottom right of the photo, the rest is in the page. Have to think of a way." He rubbed his fingers round the imprint, wondering how blind people ever made sense of braille. "Good job it's old style they encapsulate the photo page these days. This one's glued. Paper's thick too. I wonder. Listen, put your coat back on, we're off shopping again."

She laughed: "I don't believe it. You shopping! *You're* suggesting we go shopping! Wait till I tell Claire!"

"Not for groceries! Other things, things we're going to need."

It was four-o-clock as they joined the rush-hour crush past the Beijing Hotel with its silent, statuesque mannequins in tall windows. They headed towards the shops. Overhead, the crimson clouds were scurrying to strangle the sun. The over-full drains yawned decay.

"Those dreadful candles. Remember the black ones. Where'd we see 'em?"

"Third floor shop, I think. Why? If you think I'm taking those monstrosities home, you've got another think coming."

"No. Need one, is all."

They fought their way up the stairs and down again, stubby candle in hand.

"Now I need a potato," he announced as the traffic-light changed.

"A what? Wait!" She ran after him.

"You'll see," he said, adding provocatively, "it's the only veg with no centre seed."

"There's that greengrocers."

"Right. They should have some. Do they eat 'em in China."

"Mrs. Ny had potatoes."

He grabbed one from the fast diminishing pile and paid with eagerly snatched, coloured money. The change was pastel but he didn't care. The potato was large and firm.

They were back by six, winnings piled on the bed beside the rest, sealbox open, contents spread around.

"I'm goin'a need the gold foil from that Caramilk.".

She made a small tear. It peeled easily and finally she won the entire film.

"Now find me a couple of paper clips please, Ane." He thumbed the spine of the passport flat.

She passed him the tiny box.

Gregarious buggers, paper clips, he reflected irritably. Always dangle relatives. He wriggled two free and clipped the pages open.

" Need a scalpel."

"I have a razor."

He looked at his watch. "What time is Ny coming?"

"Eight-thirty,"

Two hours, he thought, as he inspected her shocking pink razor. "Can go like this can't I? It'll be dark. Don't need to change."

"Well, I'm changing. Your coat's soaked and those trousers are wet. You'd better change them at least."

He nodded silently, preoccupied.

He gently sawed the blade under the photograph, taking care not to damage the page. After working three-quarters round, the image popped and the virgin seal was revealed.

The emboss on the photograph was extant, the back side depressed. He eased the foil into each, reproducing the image with a pencil eraser then lit the candle and, when the flame was full, dripped wax into each gold "dish."

She sat on the bed, leaning on her arms, silently watching.

"It's funny. You always need the help of your tongue. Bet you don't even know it's out."

"Wanna help? Go to the fridge behind the floor clerk and get me an ice tray."

She flounced out of the room.

After a few tries he found that by holding the candle close to the page he could avoid solidified seams. Carefully covering the bottom of the shallow receptacles with an even layer of wax, he let them set.

The upper and lower plates of a seal punch.

The top surfaces of the wax were rough but those on the gold faithfully replicated the seal.

He replaced Beth's photograph on the passport page, pressing it hard to reactivate residual glue. Just in case.

He sat back with a satisfied grin as she returned with the tray of icecubes. He placed the images, gold side down, on the ice tray and gave them to her to return to the freezer.

Now the visa! Hope Beth won't mind a second-hand seal set.

A more difficult proposition, he realized, examining the page of Ane's passport.

His plan was to mimic it by using a potato, just as they had as kids making stamps on Mrs. Pickard's front step . He cut the potato in half along its short axis and placed the halves on the wooden ledge above the radiator, face down.

The visa had a faint blue locator line and a pink circle-stamp overlapping its bottom. The stamp was a Roman wreath framing a ring of Chinese with a large centre star and two smaller stars either side, and four smaller stars below. The blue frame contained, in English under the number and "VISA", "GOOD FOR ONE ENTRY", "VALID UNTIL" and "FOR EACH STAY 030 DAYS." The Chinese translation completed the writing and the whole was boldly signed.

The frame and its words could probably be Xeroxed – the lightness of the ink avoiding betrayal of colour – but the stamp would be a problem. He took a quick look at his watch. 7.30. More than an hour dicking with the photo seal.

Ane went to the bathroom and he heard the water running. She started to hum.

The contents of the sealbox were still strewn across the bed, herded aside for her to sit down. He took the palette stone and rubbed the red paint block with the wet sable brush. Further watering produced an acceptable pink. Maybe, but it'll have to wait for Ny and his access to the university copier.

" What you doing with Beth's seal-set. All these years I've laughed at your make-doing," she laughed, towel turbaned round her head. "It's the challenge you know. You're like Peter Jacob, our mechanic. He loves to rebuild things. It's a defeat for him if he has to buy new! It's wonderful to watch!"

It was the best compliment she'd ever paid him and he sneaked her a sideways smile.

She was very careful not to praise too much. That way it meant more.

He unfolded the flimsy tissue page nested in the passport.

All cash, travelers cheques and valuables were listed for checking on departure. She'll need a Money Form!

He examined the paper, rubbing it between his finger and thumb, then holding it to the light. It was the flimsy tissue. Where could he get anything like this, he wondered, stomach sinking.

As if reading his mind, Ane bent into the brown bag and extracted a transparency box." Aren't you glad I think of *everything*?" she declared smugly.

"Transparencies. I don't understand. How can they help?"

"Look inside."

"Hey, aren't you the clever one!" He pulled off the top plastic sheet and extracted the separating tissue, held it up and shook it.

He put his arms round her bum and gave her a squeeze. "You're a blood-alley, you." His groin reacted and he hastily relaxed his grip.

"Did you play taws?" she asked.

"Aye, but mostly washers. You know what we need for this lot?"

"What?"

"A laggie."

"What's that?"

"A year-old conker

"Never played conkers. It's a boy's thing."

"Well, what we need is a vinegar-soaked, oven-baked laggie, hard as steel. Beat anything!"

There was a little silence.

"Forgotten what I was on about. Oh, yes, must be crease-free so it can be folded once. These are perfect."

He went to the window and looked at the falling night. Not many lights for a city. It's all going to depend on Ny and his copier and we're not even supposed to tell him. His exasperated fist met his palm with a pop and, surprised by the unexpected sound and hurt, he stared at his hands for a moment then turned back to the room.

It was 8.20.

The foggy night was heavy with sulphur. A million three-ring coal stoves belching as Beijing tried to get warm. It reminded him of a Leeds smog in the fifties: conductors walking ahead of creeping double-decker buses waving a hankerchief to guide the blinded driver.

The ride through the evening streets of Beijing was like underwater slow-motioning through endless shoals of people, appearing and disappearing.

They stopped at a large, ill-lit building stretching tall and black. The street was cobbled and slippery. Ane held on to his arm. His teeth chattered.

Making his way with the throng, Daley was pushed and caught his coat hood on a fire extinguisher hanging at shoulder level. He lifted the waterproof. The cylinder rocked but did not fall. As the crowd thinned, he saw Ny in a nest of seats he was defending.

Daley wondered if the bloody lot would ever sit down. Ane pulled his sleeve and passed him a small envelope. He peeped at the girl's photos just as the lights dimmed.

A heavily made-up young woman in a gold dress topped by a large flower on her heart was on the stage. The crowd stilled. She announced the first act in sing-song Chinese and the stage filled with tumblers, centered on a couple joined sequentially by poles of many sizes, one end on his head, the other on his partner high in the roof above no net.

Daley wriggled in his seat. His neck still had a crick from the bus and his calf ached.

Now a flamboyant mandarin painted wide orange strokes on a flip-chart, tore off the sheet, shook it and chuted transmuted goldfish off the blank paper into a large tank. He then waved two empty nets above the audience, filling them with flashing fish. Finally a long rod held far into the gloom over Daley's head, hooked a foot long fish from thin air.

A girl executed contortions on the floor and in the air, six soup bowls positioned on her head or in her foot. A cowboy spun rope, skipped in and out of it, and cracked whips, blindfolded, at the hands and mouth of a vacant, smiling helper.

The lights came up. Daley glanced at his watch. 9.00. Time had flown.

Ane nodded towards the aisle. He stood up and she wriggled past. All round him people stood, pushed in and out, and talked, or rather shouted.

She returned, obviously agitated. He leaned to her as she sat down. "Ladies a problem?"

She shook her head. "Place is crawling with army!"

"Everywhere. Always is!"

"Not this much. Besides, it's not that. They're checking everyone going in the Ladies. A civilian is ordering 'em about. I noticed him, queuing for the toilet."

"He was queuing?"

"No. Me, not him. Me. He has a gammy leg. Wouldn't have noticed 'cept that brother was with him."

"What brother? Look, you're making no sense, and why we whispering anyway? Nobody can hear in this lot."

"Cos I want to. Listen. The brother of the girl with a husband in Montreal. Remember? He wanted help with her visa?"

"Him. Well, so what? It's a free country, leastways for going to the theatre anyway."

"So they're watching the Ladies. None outside the Gents. Caught 'em looking at me for a long time. They're searching for a woman, if you ask me."

"Well, you look nice tonight. You think they're looking for her, don't you?"

"It crossed my mind."

"Bugger! Why look for her. She's easy to find."

"Maybe not, you know. Think about it. I did, standing out there."

"What d'you mean?"

"Well, she doesn't live at home. We met her secretly on that bus. Maybe she's hiding."

"She was pretty conspicuous traveling to Xian."

"Yes, but don't you see, she was *with us*."

"An' you think we're magic."

"No. Just good cover. Visas, remember."

"Oh, for God's sakes. S'that conspiracy thing again, isn't it?"

"Hell, I don't know. Maybe swotting will-o'-the-wisps."

"Why look for her, for God's sakes?"

"Who knows why they do things," she replied lamely.

A woman pushed past forcing them to stand.

As they slumped back down, he said: "Look, let's assume you're right. I'm not admitting it, and they are after her. We'll have to get her out somehow, won't we?"

She stared at him as the lights dimmed.

In the middle of the dark stage now stood a demure, black-silk and gold brocaded lady. Around her in the rising glow, stood empty vases and she glided to each, touching, spilling flowers.

Daley watched moodily, preoccupied with the problem of leaving the theatre. Should never have got involved, he thought despondently. Already they're onto us and we haven't even started. He was mad with himself. She'd only come because he told her to.

The tips of the tiny fingers of the smiling beauty above him conjured a flower from nowhere, then another, and another. They grew on and on till the stage round her feet was deep with flowers from nowhere.

Noise rose like an approaching tide.

Here and there an involuntary clap, a breath sharply caught. Now the flowers became cards. all the time she stood alone, near nothing, saying nothing, a small brocaded body with deep smiling eyes. First one card from her upstretched right hand, then one from her left. Another from the right, now a card fan from the left. Then she seemed to run out, flicking an empty hand at the hush. A few more materialised.

Nothing special so far, he thought skeptically. He was absentmindedly playing with the epaulet of his coat, now on his knee to make room for his feet. Wait. He wrestled the problem. Maybe. He shifted uncomfortably.

Now a positive deluge!

Cards spun after each another, from the one hand then the other, thick, furious, fast. He counted two hundred before speed rendered resolution impossible. Kings, Queens, Aces, and their courtiers fluttered to the floor in higgledy-piggledy pile, flicking, spinning to the far left and far right from nowhere, they covered the stage like large flakes of technicolour snow.

The tiny figure finished with a flourish. Without realizing, he rose in his seat with standing neighbours, clapping and shouting. Cards fountained from her upstretched hands, and covered the brightly coloured flowers bunched round her feet.

The stage was now full.

His eyes pooled with unexpected tears, chest tight, throat jammed so his nose had to drag breath, tingles ran his back to his scalp. Never since that little woman sang "Memories" ragged, alone, in the dark of Hamilton Place, chord softly rolling in the din of "Cats." First word transfixed. Like Pavarotti's triumphant "Vincera."

A rising roar, propelled by hands way above heads, washed over her as she bowed deep and ran from the stage. There was an eruption of applause, and she took three bows.

The lights came up. Daley was stiff, his limbs ached, especially his calf, with all that rushing about. He tentatively stretched and shuffled slowly out the row. Normally he would have waited but the crowd was their only friend. Had to join it. Maybe it'd work! Had to try anyways.

He bent to his wife's ear. "Listen. Don't look at me. Just do as I ask. Please. Take her scarf, tie it on. Don't say why, just do it, before we get too squashed. Oh, and swap coats."

In the aisle order dissolved to chaos. Stalls emptied quickly and people were caught in a crush.

Ane was right. Standing as he did, head above the crowd, Daley could see the starred caps of military around the exit.

Suddenly he realized he was being propelled out of control, struggle was useless.

Shit! His shoulder rammed the wall.

The crowd was bobbing violently. He looked around urgently. The other side of the sea of black was squeezing in and out the row ends. He had to wriggle across.

He pushed.

Not possible, absolutely im-bloody-possible. He squinted to see.

A cylinder was going to smear him.

Christ, the extinguisher!

Inexorable, unavoidable, he watched, mesmerized. Down – *must get down.* He worked his arms vigorously. No way! Pinned like a strait-jacket.

One thing to be done. Lift bugger! Carry it, for Chris' sakes! Otherwise it's going to tear me face off!

He struggled his arms out, stretching like a relay-runner awaiting the baton.

It moved on its anchors.

A convulsion. He gripped it, tensed to lift.

Heavy! Christ, was it heavy!

It gave a little, then jammed, a metal pin through its bracket. Hug it. Lift it. Lift like a sumo wrestler. *Concentrate*. Ram a finger in the pin loop and heave. Off the wall in a rush. Can't hang on. Shit! Slipping! Lost!

Crack. Fog. Hissing, fogging fog.

Panic. Lost footing. Mustn't fall. He covered his face, rolled the door jamb and squeezed into the foyer like toothpaste from a stepped-on tube.

People, army, hats, coats, light, cold, dank, sweat, foggy auras of high ceilinged lights.

The tide surged him into the street of surprised people.

"That was very clever," Ane giggled in the frosty light, Yen's bulky coat pulled tight. "That extinguisher. I was just picked up and carried, feet off the ground, like a ride at a feast!"

His teeth chattered. "I'd nowt to bloody do with it! I just grabbed bugger and bloody dropped it."

He took a deep breath and blew it out like the first pull on a cigarette. "By the way, you look funny in that big coat and tight scarf."

A group of soldiers emerged at the top of the steps, back to them, checking the crowd coming out. He grabbed the girl standing behind Ane.

"Listen. Go! Quickly! Now! Be in the street at the back of the Friendship Hotel in about an hour." He cocked his watch at the single street lamp. "Midnight. At midnight."

"Don't worry, Yen. Just go. He's thought of something. Just go."

"Be there. Whatever else, be there!"

"We'd better find Ny before we freeze, Ane."

"You didn't plan that business with the extinguisher?"

He shook his head. "Don't want to talk about it. Too bloody cold. Can you see Ny?"

They stood under a street lamp, noses full of sulphur. She sought his hand in his pocket. "Hand's cold love, should've brought gloves."

"Who'd have thought we'd need em?" she said with a shiver as a car drew up behind.

The door swung open, erupting a soldier *straight at them*.

She felt him tense and began to turn as a gun cross-checked him in the back, throwing him forward with a gasp, jerking her sideways and ripping her hand out of his. Another soldier spun her, pinning her arms. The scarf was roughly jerked from her head.

"What the hell!" swore Daley, a spasm seizing his back as he started at the soldier crimping her. One blocked his way, gun across stomach like a staff, smell of unwashed shit and stale cigarettes overcoming the sulphur. Regiment number 8314.

A tall civilian, cupped her chin and forced her face to the light. A scowl flitted the haughty face as he let go with an impatient tweak, said something curtly to the soldier holding her, took the scarf and handed it to her with a penitent smile. "So sorry. A mistake, you understand, a simple mistake. Thought you were someone else. Sorry."

He murmured into a hand walkie-talkie and waved to the soldiers at the top of the steps, ignoring Ane shouting at him. Daley rushed to cover her mouth. "Kill it, love! S'over. You all right?" She nodded.

"S'him. That bureaucrat. Sweet aftershave. Didn't you smell it? God! Makes me feel sick. Bastards! Pig bastards!" She fisted her hand at them.

"Okay, love. Let's leave it. You're shaken is all."

"What was that all about anyway? How are *you*? You were really clouted."

He rubbed his back. "I'll be okay. Really getting knocked about in this caper, aren't I?"

The army had moved on, so he took her elbow, steered her from the light and bent to her ear.

"They mistook you, I think. You know, the scarf, an' all. Thought you were her. Really out to get her, aren't they? Now will you tell me why!"

"Thank God she left when she did."

"Okay. Have it your own way. You're right. Close call. Don't know about this bloody army though. Seems to have only one regiment, leastways we keep running into it." He nodded at the clump of soldiers jerking the steps led by a stocky figure and a civilian with a cane. The stocky man flicked a glowing stub that arched, bounced off the coat of a hurrying woman with a spray of sparks and came to rest on the edge of a step. The bloody sergeant!

The squad fanned out, searching.

"Where the hell's Ny? Could have been thrown into that bloody car and whisked off without bugger even knowing!" He rubbed his back so hard she had to stay his hand.

The cripple reached the car and was exchanging words with the bureaucrat holding the door. Ane was right. A trap. They were after the girl.

He leaned on the wall of the esplanade, Ane hanging on his arm, eyeing him anxiously. "You okay?"

"It's just bloody dawned on me. 'Long John,' I mean. Don't think it's whisky at all. It's Long John bloody Silver. *Treasure Island*? The pirate with the gammy leg."

"What you talking about?"

"The FAX message. Probably meant him. He nodded at the black limousine pulling away in the clammy night. "Leastways part of it."

Daley watched the knots of soldiers. Still not prepared to admit an organized conspiracy, just couldn't see how a girl, one girl, warranted all the fuss.

But she knew, and was convinced something was all round them but, she knew just as surely, he would panic if she told him.

He jumped as a hand came down on his shoulder.

"I go fora driver." Ny waved at the university taxi across the street.

The car pulled away slowly, scattering pedestrians like startled birds.

"You hava Wen's coat on?"

"She wanted to try mine, so we swapped," extemporized Ane.

Daley ruminated on the cryptic message. Still made no sense. Boadicea, for Christ's sakes. He fidgeted – forgotten all about the damn FAX. Was it the key to all this? He looked past Ny at the flashing parade in front of them. And what about Ny? Needed his help. In Canada he had been totally reliable but here, in China, maybe things were different. This was a no-mistake gamble. Daren't think of it.

He analyzed Ny's behaviour since Bojai. Had really wanted to leave his daughter there. Seemed concerned by her forced return but something was out of kilter. Hadn't asked about her just now when he picked them up; still, that was reasonable. She didn't live at home. Probably assumed she'd gone to her own place.

He tried to keep the "whys" still enough to analyze, as they bumped through empty streets.

There was a sick aunt that wasn't, a rape that maybe wasn't, Ny's hostility to DHS though he didn't know about the river-bank and, to crown it all, the bus interview. Worst was Ane didn't want *him* to know. They shared *everything*! Must be something horrendous.

As they entered the gate of the Friendship, he leaned forward to his friend. "Ny, we leave tomorrow. How about coming up for a drink?"

"Okay, but we can't stay long."

Daley sat back, grim smile on his face and glanced at his watch: 11.15.

He introduced the Ny's to the concierge on their floor and a cascade of Chinese accompanied the passing of the key.

Daley sought the lock of forty seven in the poor light but once inside, he rummaged for the bottle opener, pulled the cork of the "Great Wall," cooling in the window, filled the small plastic glasses and offered them round.

"Look, Ny, you're gonna be upset but we've decided to help that woman get to Montreal. You remember, the one that came to see us with her brother?"

Ny's smile faded. "You cannota, too dangerous."

"We think there's a way that's not dangerous. Only I'll need your help." He raised his palm to silence Ny's objection. "No, hear me out. I promise you'll not be involved."

"Nota that! This is nota Canada. Police listen. Prison, no discussion!" He drew his hand across his throat.

Daley eyed him for a minute. "You're right but it's not dangerous. We found the missing passport, you know, the one we reported stolen. Well, it could still be lost. All we have to do is give it to her. She could have got it from the thieves. She'll have to change the name and photo but that's her problem. Maybe her brother will help her. Will you help us?"

"You found it? Could stilla be lost."

Daley drained a mouthful of wine and nodded.

"Okay. Whata you want?"

Daley glanced at him. Just like that? He'd agreed just like that. Had expected more of a fight.

"You're tooa kind, Doc. It's dangerous but you determined. I help. You werea kind to me in Canada."

Daley searched the weather-beaten face. He looked tired. Not surprising. It was late. He extracted the passports and pushed his and Beth's, flat on the table.

"It's a Canadian passport so we must Xerox this page," he identified his visa with a finger, "onto this one." He indicated the blank page of Beth's document. "You see, the seal is pink so it'll come up faint grey. I'll tone it afterwards, okay?"

He sat back. The passports slowly closed on their own.

"That copying machine at the university. You know how to use it ?"

His friend nodded.

"It's an old unit so it's simple. Open the top and see if you can follow the paper path. Push down the feed roller and introduce this passport." He picked up Beth's. "Now it'll feed. Close the top," he added, picking up his own, "and put this one visa face-down on the glass, flush with the bottom corner and copy."

"Don't worry, Doc. Machina always breaking down, everyone know how fix!"

"Practise a few times and don't worry if it's off a little. It's more realistic. Oh, and while you're at it, get me a good copy of the visa on a white sheet, will you, please."

He passed the slight blue books over. Ny flicked the pages.

He felt a quixotic flush of warmth. Saw his friend shinning the pine at the Christmas tree farm to find the lost group members, all that time ago. "Oh, and Ny, one more thing. Get me a copy of this, will you, on these." He handed him the Money Form doctored with Post-It sticky strips to cover the writing and extracted four tissues from the box of transparencies. "Be careful! I must get a good copy on this paper and it's fragile. Machine'll eat it, so be careful. Oh, we leave tomorrow, so can you bring all the copies back tonight?"

Ny nodded, pocketed the passports, picked up his coat, struggled it on, changing hands to keep hold of the file as if putting it down would leave it behind.

He saw them to the door. "Ny, thanks. Thanks for helping."

His friend's smile widened briefly as he closed the door behind them.

Went well, very well, in fact. Better than he'd hoped! He took a look at his watch: 11.55.

VI
BEIJING AIRPORT

"Don't worry. She'll be there, Peter. Take your shirt off, let me see your back"

He did so and as she rubbed he winced. "Ugly. Badly bruised but skin's not broken. I'll put some of Nan's Tincture of Arnica on it. Magic, that stuff. Absorbs bruises."

She spread the liquid over the discoloured area and, when she finished, playfully knuckled his bum.

He walked to the window and lifted the curtain, fingers drumming the ledge.

She watched. He was worried, more restless than usual. Had worked with him for years, caught the chaff, dealt with the humdrum so he could concentrate on the important. She never sought to influence only to suggest tactfully, if there was a better way.

This task *he* must do; it was hard not to tell him why, but she was absolutely sure he mustn't know.

She stood up and returned the tincture to the bathroom; it was going to be a long night.

12.10.

A crisp moon with a wide ring hung in the sky as in a still lake.

Nothing moved.

A condensation of breath spread across the window and he

fingered his initials into it. Funny, people do that on misty windows, cave walls. Reassurance of existence maybe.

He shook his head. Looked really cold.

He dropped the curtain, picked up his coat and smiled quickly at Ane as she came out of the bathroom. He then closed the door quietly behind him.

One distant bulb illuminated the corridor. There was a faint smell of cooked cabbage.

He called both elevators and stepped into the first to arrive.

The lobby was empty, even the desk. He crossed the corridor to go down stairs to the basement but, as he opened the door, a movement caught his eye corner.

Someone was outside on the steps.

He crept past the desk taking care to stay in the shadows, stood sideways behind a pillar and peered round its edge.

DHS!

The bugger's watching.

Good job she's coming to the back!

He was talking to somebody. Daley leaned out as far as he dared. Still couldn't see the other person. Have to risk it.

Why? Why bother, a voice counseled. He ignored it; *had* to know.

Ny!

He was talking to Ny!

Ny, for Christ's sakes. Daley was stunned, shaking, images avalanching. A sudden chill hit like snow from an overhead branch, *passports! His passport! Out there! God! Stuck forever in this shitdump!*

He stood back quickly, leg giving way. As he bent to rub it his back screamed.

What a mess!

He leaned on the pillar and, as if mesmerized, watched the man. In cahoots with the army. How could he have been so stupid. He scoured his head for clues that should have tipped him. None. Hell, the reverse if anything.

And you thought you were being so damn clever. Amateur,

bloody amateur, dragged by your dick, you silly old sod!

He was desperately disappointed: he liked Ny, had only come to China because he'd insisted. Now there he was, plotting with the enemy. Bit melodramatic. He wrinkled his nose as if in malodorous air.

He looked back. They were gone.

Maybe he was there when Ny came out and started talking. Hell, for sure the bugger liked to talk. Ny'd sent his wife ahead to the taxi and was sharing banalities with him. Too long!

Maybe they'd some kind of a hold over Ny. Maybe that was why DHS attacked the girl with impunity. Knew he'd get away with it. Come to think of it, could swear she'd been giving in when close enough to see.

No way. After all, she'd been devastated.

Maybe she knew her dad couldn't cause trouble, knew she'd have to give in anyway. He realized he was gripping the hotel desk so hard his fingers hurt. They'd gone, better get on.

The clock above his head was thudding. 12.25.

Hell! She'd been there for twenty-five minutes!

He went briskly to the basement door and opened it. The smell of cooking oil and garbage was so strong he could taste it. He descended; holding his nose; another world. Cracked concrete walls stretched to naked wire-dangling bulbs in the roof and powder worms of efflorescence traced cracks in the steps. He pushed open the basement door and peered out.

Silence. A distant dripping tap, monotonous ping magnified.

A bulb dangled from the roof and he angled his watch at it. 12.30. He walked the dim corridor. Should have worn slippers.

He reached a side passage and, squinting hard, could make out the elevator.

So far, so good. Hope she waited. He quickly clicked the corridor, grabbed the lever, lifting at the same time. The sickening stench of rotting fish threw his head back, and he let go. The door began down. Catching it at knee level, one hand quenching his nose, he lifted again, entered and clashed the doors shut.

The elevator was a cavern without sides or roof, just floor with control cables snaking the dark. Craning backwards, he could see the dim line of the street. Controls were mounted on a corner post: manual buttons with Chinese instructions and arrows indicating direction. The machine awoke with a strident whine.

The floor slowly lifted. He anxiously watched the roof doors as he jerked towards them.

With a sudden click, the roof doors opened. He relaxed a notch as the night rushed in.

He pulled his jacket close. The floor was now the road, vertical doors over him like the jaws of a giant crocodile.

He squinted around. His breath blew dim ghosts coning the single street light. Nothing except mournful shadows, black on black. He blew through his fists and stamped his feet.

It was quiet, deep country quiet.

"Yen," he whispered hoarsely.

Nothing. She'd gone.

Wait.

Something. His heart rolled a throat beat. Did a shadow move?

Disembodied white patches bobbed in the meager light.

"Yen?"

A little sound and the wool coat materialized.

She reached him, hair still unscarfed, breath steaming the air.

She found his hand. He hopped her onto the platform and fumbled the descend button, floating, floating on her fingers.

He pushed the button to hurting. The floor jerked, then slowly moved downwards. She cringed. He squeezed her hand reassuringingly.

He felt her shiver as she covered her nose against the fish and realized that though he'd relaxed his grip, she'd not removed her hand.

Not a word was said.

When the descent stopped, he pushed the door lever firmly

up and stepped into the corridor, motioning her to stay.

Still empty.

She reclaimed his hand. He squeezed it and nodded her off.

They stood close, listening.

He'd decided to jump back, close the doors, and go to the street if it was anything but dead.

The comfortable far drip.

He pulled the strap, easing the half doors to a kiss, then quickly led her to the stairs and up to the foyer.

Nobody.

An elevator arrived like a train in a 3:00 station. He glanced at her quickly in the light. Pale, looking down, looking away.

Scared, he decided. Who wouldn't be? Life in the hands of total strangers. Like being operated-on wide awake.

The floor desk was empty. He'd forgotten to hand in the key. Little things'll get you.

12:40 a.m.

Ane rose from the bed and, taking the girl's hands, drew her to a squeeze.

"Let's get started," she said, helping the girl from the wool coat. "Hair first."

"Whatever it is, better do it in the bathroom. Ny'll be back an' he thinks she's the sister, remember? Best out of sight and, oh, Ane, remind her to clean her teeth and use mouthwash, will you? And make sure she washes there and behind. Close up Chinese smell. Got to be thorough."

She made to say something but thought better of it, picked up the brown bag and the Indian dress and, taking the girl's elbow, guided her to the bathroom. She closed the door behind them with her foot and soon the muffled sound of giggles and chitchat diffused the door.

He sat at the table, waiting, back aching. He rubbed it. Bloody gun had caught just above the left arse. Sharp. Probably the stock.

He drummed his fingers. Nothing to do but wait.

A glass of wine? Why not!

Holding the stem, he swished the liquid round, watching it sparkle.

Better not tell Ane about Ny.

Only upset her.

Ny knew a lot: the visa, the money form, the passport. Everything! Could have passed on everything!

Well, no. Not everything. Didn't know *who*. He felt a buzz. The passport even had Beth's photo in it.

He yawned. In the tired cold, it looked awfully thin.

A two-stroke motorbike pop-popped in the distance. Then silence.

The ill-aimed heel of his glass hit the table and wine dribbled on the cloth. He forced himself into the sketchy corners of the scheme, looking at everything.

What else didn't Ny know? Not about the bus meeting, the visit of his daughter tonight, the muffled preparations in the bathroom. Didn't know whose picture would really be in the passport and wouldn't know if they didn't meet before the X-ray machine at the airport.

That's it!

Don't meet her till *after* that barrier then he'd never know!

He sat back smirking. The "don't-knows" still seemed tenuous but it was becoming possible. More wine.

His head drooped...

Jerked up suddenly, he looked round, disoriented. Nothing. Murmurs from the bathroom.

He glanced at his watch. 1.10. He stared at the hall door. Had something woken him suddenly? No.

Where the hell's Ny?

The morning breeze sparkled the sun on the lake into silver butterflies. The Indian fishing boat put-putted in the distance, slowly gathering the net and working towards him. Now it was close enough to make out the fishermen – *DHS and Ny!*

He sat up with a start, tipping the loosely held glass in his hand, spreading more wine on the cloth. He glanced at his watch. Dozed for ten minutes. Ten minutes seemed like hours!

A headache was gathering. Wine? Maybe a mistake. He pushed the glass away, stretching stiffly, legs straight out in front, wincing as his calf tightened and his back objected. He picked up the wine bottle and quickly put it down. Need a clear head. Need to keep awake.

He stood and inspected the potato halves on the radiator, crawling his cold fingers into the cast-iron grooves for warmth. A dull sheen of moisture on the cut faces. Just right, won't smudge.

He sat down with a sigh.

The still, the cool. Swishing tall pines on skis in snow silence.

A knock?

He surveyed the room in quick panic. Nan's alarm said it was 1:40.

Half an hour this time.

Again...more urgent.

He stood up too quickly, grabbing a chair-back against dizziness then walked to the door, drumming a warning on the bathroom as he passed.

Ny was there, all smiles, wagging the transparency box. "I hava them good, Doc. Hava them good."

Daley, still bleary, forced a smile, then opened the box to extract the passports, thumbing Beth's to the visa.

Perfect. Perfect. Bloody perfect!

He compared it with the others. Realistically smudgy, faint, a black rather than red seal. He was surprised. Frankly, not thought it possible. How the hell had Ny done it? Even copiers in Canada and Word Processing experts couldn't have done better.

For an instant he recalled Ny on the steps and shivered. Just what the hell is your game? He searched the Chinaman's open face smiling a wide smile.

"Great, Ny. Bloody ace job."

He placed a concerned hand on his shoulder. "Time you got back to your wife, Ny. It's late and we both have a busy day tomorrow – today!" He laughed histrionically, trying not to give the impression of hurrying him. "Besides I'm expecting that girl and you'd better not be here when she comes, had you?"

Ny gave him a startled glance.

"Saya good night Mrs Daley fora me." He assured him he would.

Slow down. Rushing'll make mistakes.

The bathroom door opened. "We were listening. Waited till he left."

She turned and, with a flourish, presented the girl. "What'd'you think?"

His jaw slacked. A knee-collapsing thump dropped him onto the bed as goose bumps rippled his back.

The mirage minced past in a waft of Coty and stood by the lamp.

Tiredness, tomorrow; daft things – floating butterflies, bursting abacus, kitten's eyes opening – chattered in.

He tried to recall "befores" but there really were none, although perhaps his first E-Type, basking in German appreciation curbside in Koln; or perhaps the wandered-into mass at Notre Dame sung by a Pavarotti priest; the magnificent A-3 locomotive, steaming, ready, shimmering unexpectedly outside York's Railway Museum. Close? No, nothing came close. Nothing.

Young girl was sophisticated woman with brash beauty, subtly softened. The light cast a gleam on her now auburn hair.

"Sorry. What? What d'you say?"

Ane clucked. "You heard me!"

There was a stupid grin on his face and her heart sank. How can I fight when I tart her up?

Full red lips, wide smile, lined eyes fluttering. A star had entered his sky.

"Oh...er...yes. Jes, she looks good." He nodded too often. "'Specially the hair. Auburn. Told you wouldn't be red," he rushed nervously. "Different from black, isn't it? Clever those bangs, Ane. Everybody's used to her high forehead, scarf an' all. Bangs. Wonderful. Totally different."

"We're not just a pretty face, you know," Ane said petulantly.

The girl was pirouetting, dancing for him.

As he watched, a quixotic thought slipped in. Maybe he did prefer white socks and innocence.

She stopped at the TV and pinched off its cover, clicking the switch with a swoop of her other hand. Shaky music in the room as, salacious eyes smouldering and momentum gathering, she spun again and again, eyes now on him only.

Thongs swished, beads chattered, skirt rose, eyes flashed. He looked away but her eyes stayed and he knew it.

Must see her through official eyes! He cleared his throat and looked at her.

His first impression had been right. The disguise was good, very good. He searched for the young girl. Gone. *All* trace of drab, of innocence, gone! Exasperating, a fragment of a movie with an irretrievable title.

Now she was whirling: hands clapping, heels stamping, flamenco without castanets. He was mesmerized by the flicker of black-seamed stocking tops and the delicious white flashes.

On purpose; doing it on purpose. His chair was low, bloody floor chairs of China, she must know.

Suddenly she stopped, breathless, leaning on Ane, flushed, back to him.

"I can *see* what *you*'re thinking," Ane accused him acidly, over the girl's shoulder. "Forget that. Does she look western?"

"Oh, my God, yes!" he assured her. She pushed up her sleeves and knelt in front of the girl, fussing around the hem with needle and thread from a Tokyo President Hotel kit. "Good, it's got a deep hem. She's a deal taller than me."

A terrible tiredness suddenly gripped him. Late, overwrought, aroused.

Get a grip, not even bloody started yet!

"Got your doodads on, you know, under - under that?" He waved at the skirt of the Indian dress.

"Don't worry, you saw *everything*! Even the Pantyliners. Thin, sticky back, build breasts like Lego. Brainwave that."

He smiled and stared at the flickering TV. Like any other teenager – noise, noise all the time. A pretty announcer was waving her hands in front of a map of China, gesticulating at a swirl off the south coast and speaking in a sing-song. Ane sat back on her heels, needle in teeth, cotton end spinning. It was done.

He sat before the girl. "Now, Yen, we must talk and you *must* listen. I mean it, *really listen*." She poked curls behind her ears, palmed the dress under her and settled to the floor, popping off her shoes.

"You *are* my, er, our daughter – Beth. We call her Beth, remember that. Short for 'Elizabeth.' You look the part, no problem. Trouble is Beth doesn't understand Chinese, so *you -don't- understand-Chinese, no-matter-what!* No matter what's said, no matter what you hear, you *don't* understand! Be on guard *all the time*. One accidental slip and we're gone. From now on, speak *only* English."

She was staring the only-for-only-you stare. He looked away.

How the hell could he concentrate?

He turned to Ane. "God help us! This...this bloody thing is as full of bloody holes as a whore's knickers!"

She smiled silently and leaned to squeeze his hand. She knew what the girl was doing to him but would sort it out later.

The girl cleared her throat and he glanced up, startled – DHS's cough. She was smiling sweetly.

It's a game to her, a silly bloody game. His ire broke through: "Look, Yen. This is bloody life and death. We've got to get with the program!"

"You're too terribly serious. You'd make a good Chinaman."

"Listen to me. We must think of things that'll stamp you 'western.' You know what I mean. Something a western girl'd do that no Chinese girl ever would. You've gotta help. I've noticed Chinese women like lavender, for example. Seem to drown in it, so wear something else. Something different."

"'Je Reviens' is different. She can borrow mine. Can change her lipstick too, you know, to the deep red 'tart' one you like. Chinese women don't seem to wear any."

"'Every little 'elps,' old lady said, peeing in the sea."

"That's Nan's saying, Peter."

"I know. There's other things too. Obvious things like brown hair. Lucky for us you always wear a scarf. *Don't* wear it tomorrow. I mean, today. Makeup, dress, stockings, high-heels, boobs. All obvious. Oh, don't get me wrong. They're important. It's just we have to find subtle things." He paused as something occurred to him. "Don't fight."

The girl's eyebrows rose.

"Don't push. Stand back, let the crowd have what's going. A westerner'd be confused by the rush, would find it – well - distasteful. That's subtle. Must be more like that. Something only a western girl'd do, a Chinese girl never."

"Insist on knives and forks," offered the girl with a grin.

"That's good but we may not be eating. That's the sort of thing, though. There's two ways to get out: merge with the background and hope, or draw attention and totally mislead. And I mean *totally*. Not even the slightest doubt. Ray Jenkins' wheelbarrows."

"She could use foreigner's money, Peter. The coloured stuff. Wouldn't have that if she was Chinese. Give her some."

"Not strictly true. They don't use it but prefer to. SHL used our money, but it'll certainly help." He struggled the wallet out of his pocket and passed her some notes.

She rolled them tight, end peeping from her clenched fist.

"We've got to think of something that stamps her unequivocally Western. I'm sure Chinese men fantasize about glamorous western women. Be one, but don't overdo it!"

"Tip."

He glanced at Ane. "What?"

"Tip, you know. Tip lavishly. No Chinese *ever* does. They're mean tippers!"

He sat forward, more awake. "You sure?"

"Course I'm sure."

"Jes. Come to think of it, you're right. Usually don't give anything. Explains why they're so surly in shops!"

"Nothin's ever *given* away in China."

"Be careful though. Don't give so much. It's taken for a bribe."

"Oh, don't be silly, Peter. She knows how much to give. She lives here!"

He eyed her diffidently then remembered his plan for fooling Ny. "You'll have to buy your *own* ticket. Your dad'll be with us, so we'll have to meet *after* he's gone. I just hope he doesn't hang around is all, to see us off. You understand? You'll be on your own till then." He enunciated the words slowly, as if talking to a child. Tiredness tempted unleashing the words to slur and pile into each other.

Consternation curved Ane's face – the Daley subterfuge– the turn-away-don't-look game? No. This time just good sense.

"Don't worry. First thing I'll do when we get there is go to the Ladies to meet you. You'll see me so you'll know we're there. I'll give you the papers, freshen your face and hair. Then I'll leave and you can follow soon after. Just remember, we're there watching– there for you."

The girl smiled gratefully. "I'll be all right. 'T'll be easy with your money. This money. Foreigner's money."

"Yen, what I'm going to say may sound hard, but it must be said, you understand. God knows I – we - pray it'll never happen and are striving hard to make sure it doesn't, but if they arrest you, we can't help. You're really are on your own. *Can't* be implicated, you see. In fact, when we leave this hotel tomorrow morning, I'm going to report the dress stolen whilst we were at the theatre. Just in case. The passport's already reported stolen so that's covered. So, though we have a plan and it's goin' well, we *must* face reality. Just got to be sure you understand it's not a game, s'not an adventure you can escape by closing the book."

"I'll be fine. One westerner speaking English, a porter helping, buying a ticket wid western money and the army busy. No trouble. No trouble at all. I'll be all right."

"Good." He stretched a hand towards her shoulder but did not reach it. "Right," he said, studiously picking at lint on the duvet. "That's what we need more than anything. Optimism."

He pointed at the tight roll of cash in her hand. "Flash that around as much as you can, but surreptitiously, mind you. Be western but refined. Goes with the outfit!"

He went pulled a few sheets of hotel paper from a folder. "I'm going to write out everything I can remember about Beth. - with your help, Ane. When I'm finished, I want you to memorize it." He took a deep breath. "It'll be sparse but it'll help."

Ane switched off the TV and the silence amplified his scribbling.

Finally he stood up and stretched, wincing with woken aches.

"That's enough to be going on with. If we think of anything else, we can add it later. Go to the bathroom, stand in front of the mirror and read it out loud to yourself, twenty times. Watch yourself, all the time. Be western. Be her. Be Beth. Be her, no matter what!"

"What d'you think, Ane?"

"Looks okay, but that's only the half of it. Think she'll make it but it's you I'm worried about. It's late. How you going to get finished?"

He squatted down beside her. "You know, we have one thing goin' for us, the most important thing of all – people. People hate to upset the *status quo*. Anything for a quiet life. Be the same here for sure."

"You've not answered my question. What about you?"

"Don't worry about me. Once she's gone, I'll get going. No, really, what d'you think? Can she carry it off?"

"Think so. She's right about the army. Chaos'll keep them occupied. Besides, her life depends on it. I'm sure it's a serious offence to use false documents. Shame, though, you had to tell her about reporting the clothes an' all. Did she really need to know?"

"I won't report them, of course, but she won't know. S'important she realize she'll be on her own, really *on her own* - at least till we get to the gate."

"But she's supposed to be, Beth. Wouldn't she be with us?"

"In the best of worlds, yes, but we have to be separate when she's buying her ticket. Understand that, don't you? I mean Ny'll be with us and he thinks we're helping the bureaucrat's sister. We wouldn't buy her ticket, would we? No, he would, the brother. So it adds up okay."

"Suppose you're right. We'll be close by anyway."

The girl emerged from the bathroom, glass for water in her hand. As she filled it from the thermos, he stood up, squared the muddle of writing paper on the table, held out a pen to her and told her to sit and practise Beth's signature from her driving licence by tracing it through tissue paper.

Time's a wasting. He smiled at the Dixieland tune. There was so much to do. Had to get her off.

He stilled her scratching "That's enough. I think we should reminisce now, *Beth*." He stressed the name. "Get used to it. Today you must *be* Beth. Concentrate, watch for it. Turn when it's said."

Ane read his watch. *3.05..*

They sat in a circle on the floor, speaking English, speaking of the Beth she didn't know.

Finally he checked the time. "God! You'd better go. "

He stood up staggering a little as the blood rushed back into his crimped legs. "We've done all we can, I'll take you down to the road. Will you be all right from there?"

She nodded, rising to her feet with a crackle of beads, and pulled on her own voluminous coat.

They crept to the elevator. Please, just a few minutes. Through the basement door and it's over.

The elevator arrived and just as they entered, Ane came running up. "You forgot this!" she said urgently, holding out a brown paper bag. "High heels, perfume, lipstick, and – well - everything."

God, the little things. Get a grip. He blew a long breath; pay attention! So you're tired, so what? Pay attention or *you're dead*!

"If you drink, don't drive," warned the Canadian booze bag in Ane's hand. He smirked. Maybe a good omen.

"Thanks." He waved the bag like a chicken."Not be long."

He turned, pushed the girl into the open elevator, and pressed the button. She took his hand like a child.

The doors shook open at the first floor.

Nothing. Empty as the graveyard watch in a cemetery.

The basement door released the same gagging stench and he squeezed her hand reassuringly as they edged quickly down the stairs, taking care his shoes did not clack against the concrete.

The basement door.

Nobody.

So far so good. They flitted silently to the street elevator. He lifted the lever, heaved up the door, walked her in, and pulled down the strap, all in one fluid action.

The primordial jaws slowly opened and he stepped into the street, breath ghosting in the single light.

He felt her shiver as he looked around. Quiet. Wee hours quiet. Cold.

"Now don't forget. Take a taxi to the airport, tip the driver generously. Make a fuss." His teeth were chattering. "Have him find you a porter. Talk loud English. Tip the porter when he leaves, or, better, tip him to watch your luggage whilst you go to the Ladies. Ane'll meet you, fix your hair, makeup an' that, and give you your papers."

He smiled and let go her soft hands. "Sorry. I go on so. Nerves. Just nerves. Forgive me."

She smiled, rose on her toes, gave him a kiss on the forehead, longer this time, turned and walked off quickly.

He retrieved the ice and seal molds from the freezer, and stretched numb fingers into the radiator to revive them. His watch got stuck. He wriggled it out: *3:30.*

As he extracted the photograph from his inside pocket, his heart bumped: her big eyes shone at him.

No scarf, thank God! He walked to the bathroom and, leaning over his wife's shoulder, took the tooth glass from the narrow shelf over the sink. "Went well, Ane. If you could stay awake with me, I'd appreciate it. Can't risk falling asleep."

"I'll try."

He looks so tired, she thought, big rings round his eyes, face pale, like when he's sick. Must try stay with him. It's only a few hours after all.

She puffed up the pillows, piled them against the headrest and sat to watch.

He turned on the radio, decanted water from the thermos into the glass, lifted Beth's photo from the passport, placed it on top of Yen's and trimmed it to size with the tiny scissors from his knife. He chuckled without looking up: "Me Swiss army 'wife'! No man should be without one."

He placed Beth's picture in the mold and inscribed grooves in the wax around its edge with the razor, humming to the Sousa march as he did so.

Chaplin's "Theme from *Limelight*" floated into the room. God, some time since I heard that, he sighed, humming a few bars as he carefully fitted her photograph into the wax, aligning it with the scribes.

He adjusted the picture, carefully paring slivers until it fit snugly. He sat back.

"Look, Peter. You're too tired. Why not get a couple of hours sleep, then get up early and finish it? You'll make mistakes like this."

It was tempting. "Better not. Probably feel worse. Make me a strong cup of coffee, love, good an' sweet, then wake me if I nod."

"Put in your own sugar."

"It's in my jacket pocket. Get it please, will you. I've got to keep hold of this."

He sipped the cup edge, realized it wasn't hot and took a

deep gulp. "Good, love. Well, not bad."

The edges of the picture were too stiff so he dropped it back in the water, lifted it out, tissued the surface, placed it on the male mold of the seal slice – edges to grooves – and fitted the female on top. This was followed by the thermos for weight. He sat back, humming. The slice of seal was now impressing into the softened print.

She hated his humming and was about to chide him when he took a deep draught of coffee, tested the stability of the press then asked she pass the potato halves.

"On and off this bloody bed like a yoyo!"

"Like a well oiled whore."

"You're awful," she said with pretend disgust.

He pared peel from the edge of one half, to avoid the brown ring, then watched as moisture crept back to the cream surface. The xeroxed, visa seal was pressed on and, after ten seconds he turned the potato half over. Enough thermoset remained to discern the Chinese stamp.

He bunched his finger ends into his mouth and blew. "It's getting cold." He splayed his hands into the radiator, looking out the window.

"Always coldest, three in the morning. I remember from night-duty on the ward. Hated this time. Most deaths occur."

He steadied the slide-viewing lens and cut into the trace of the seal with the razor point.

"You'll bite it off if you're not careful. Your tongue's out again. You don't know, do you?"

After much irritable finger combing of hair from his eyes, he finished practising and started the other potato half, the final version.

The idea was to leave an impression rather than detailed wreath and stars. Intermittently he dipped the potato into the thin pink water and pressed it onto the white page of practice visas Ny had made.

Slowly the image emerged, like the shape of a sculptor's stone. He took a deep pull at the cold coffee and looked at his watch: *4.10.*

Gentle snores from the bed, Ane was curled in fetal position.

Suddenly he felt exhausted. Concentration had developed a fatigue that tempted shortcuts, make-do's. His hand was shaking so he rose, disassembled the seal pile, and extracted the photograph. His chair scrape had awakened Ane.

"Good," she said thickly.

He gazed at the picture.

A perfect seal slice was embossed into the still-damp print. For the first time, he began to think they might make it.

He gave Ane a squeeze, wondering if the secret agents of fiction might be proud. It had worked.

Then the smugness blew away. How was he going to stick it on the page?

He went back to the unfinished potato. He teased the final touches of leaf braids by cutting close parallel lines and popping the flesh with the razor tip. He sat back. Not done this since a kid.

God, he longed for the comfortable, idleness of then. Before killjoys and responsibilities, before the world intruded. Breezes surfed treetops, rippled ripe-wheat like sunny lakes, stirred the hair of the girl giggling beside in the long graveyard grass, old church frowning, silent. He remembered the symmetry. Forwarding life in the arms of death.

The potato-half slipped to the floor. He jerked awake, wiping cold sweat from his forehead, heart racing *"Keep awake!"* He banged his knee so hard with his fist, they both hurt.

He cut a narrow "v" to one of the side flats of the rescued potato for alignment with the two faint pencil lines on the visa itself.

The stamp was ready.

He dipped it in the "ink."

This was it!

He pressed it lightly on the practice sheet to remove excess, then firmly onto the passport page.

The pink and faint black blended, blurred enough to be real. He held it out to Ane. To stay awake, she was teasing her cuticles with nail polish remover. Acetone was in the air. She mustered a smile and nodded encouragement.

He was still worrying at the unsolved glue problem, dawdling with the scotch-tape dispenser, finger-thumb creasing his bottom lip, wondering if the tape could be bent to hold the photo snug to the page. Never worked that. The "u's" of tape always loosened.

The smell of nail polish remover was making him feel dizzy. He wondered about opening the window – if it would open – but quickly dismissed the idea. Too cold.

He was turning to ask her to stop when he remembered something from long, long ago, from his graduate days, a technique they'd used to image ceramic microstructures for electron microscopy. The acid-etched ceramic would be pressed into scotch-tape, leaving the surface detail therein. The tape was then peeled off and floated on acetone. The solvent dissolved the plastic and left the gum *with its information* floating on top.

Maybe.

"Can I borrow a Q-tip?"

"What'd you want with that?"

"We'll see. I've got an idea."

He applied vaporous wet cotton to a strip of tape stuck on the back of Beth's photo. Sure enough the plastic softened and could be lifted off with tweezers, leaving the gum behind.

Eureka!

Solved – bloody solved!

He had to have air, so stood up and went to the window.

It'd work. His tired elation was dangerously close to euphoria.

Wide awake now. Second wind.

He decanted nail-polish remover into the cup.

"How many times have I told you not to do that! We drink from that."

"Not now, love."

"No. Always the same. You never listen. How many times

have you used tupperware for weedkiller? You just don't care."

"Okay, Okay. Leave it for now."

She hrumphed and leaned back against the pillows, arms folded tight. It'd worked, her petty objection had woken them up!

He glanced but she was looking away.

He stretched tape along the back edges of the girl's photograph and massaged away its plastic carrier with the Q-tip. Holding the photo edges, he lined up its seal slice with the one on the page, nodding to himself. No worries: the impression was self-centering as the page already held the complete original seal. He pressed down for a moment to make sure and looked up.

Snow moths meandered the window.

Just what we need, snow to shut the airport, to make the roads dangerous. No worries these buggers'll drive and fly right through it!

The photo stuck perfectly, the continuous emboss circling unbroken. The girl's confident, trusting face stared back as if it belonged.

He took out his wallet and spread Canadian dollars on the table, split off forty and slipped them into the passport. Then he took one of the Money Forms and filled in the blanks with "forty dollars," and the ring Ane had worked off her finger. He folded the sheet unevenly, squeezed the creases, reopened it, stapled a corner into the passport and refolded it inside.

He sat back. It was finished! *5.00.*.

His legs ached. Everything ached!

Fatigue suddenly loosed and the room spun. Ane reached and put a blanket over him. He smiled, eyes tightly shut, pulling the welcome warmth to his chin. She sat beside him for a moment, stroking the cover. Gone, dead to the world. She brushed the hair from his eyes, lifted the blanket, and spooned into him, arm over his neck.

The sun was bright in his eyes. He cringed and moved. Funny how you ache; think rest'll bring relief. God it's a pain getting old.

Inside felt the same, but joints he'd never had objected. Suddenly a locomotive hit. Today's *the* day!

Frantic maybes gripped. How could they be so stupid. A growl rose in his throat – more danger than you could shake a stick at! Coffee – must have a coffee to soften the sharp, make things look better.

He tottered with momentary nausea, steadied, picked up the mug, spooned in the powder and poured tepid water from the thermos.

The skiffle of overnight snow hurt his eyes.

Ane was washing her hair in the bathroom.

He stood before the mirror, pouches under his eyes like hanging bruises. Look like shit! He took a second gulp of coffee and scratched his beard, suddenly full of itches.

She sat back, pummeled her hair, and asked: "How'd you feel?"

"Okay till bobby cops me." He splashed cold water on his face.

He stood up too quickly, holding the shelf with dizziness. The suddenly nudged coffee teetered and he grabbed at it, almost causing it to fall.

"Funny isn't it, Peter, how your belly disappears in the morning, when you get up, I mean. Wish it'd stay that way."

"Gravity."

She held out a Mars Bar. "Better have one of these. Ny'll be here in a few minutes so there's no time for breakfast, and God knows when we'll eat."

He sat on the corner of the bed peeling the wrapper. Chocolate suddenly seemed inedible. He drew a deep breath and looked out the window. The sun had turned the snow to puddles. Terrified and excited at the same time, maybe because we're going home. Always got delicious collywobbles before a long journey or maybe, he shook his head, because he was helping *her*. He chomped the compliant chocolate.

No! S'going home, light at the end of the tunnel, through the day and we're free. He slid on the Harris Tweed, patting the pocket of passports for luck.

He scanned the room. Ane had cut up the potatoes and flushed them down the toilet. The wax mold had been broken into tiny pieces and remelted. She had scrunched the practice sheets, burned them in the sink and swirled the ashes down the drain – all while he slept.

She knew he'd want her to attend to the little things. A surge of warmth rose. Together, they could do this thing.

8:30. The clock in the foyer.

The chill breeze canceled the sun, spun a wizened leaf in the puddle at the bottom of the steps, and greeted them, lifting Ane's hair as it passed.

Their flight was 11:30. She bent to pick something up,

"See a penny pick it up. All the day you'll have good luck."

"Hope you're right. Goin' to need it. Luck!"

Ny manhandled the luggage into the Nissan official flag flapping on its antenna. Wish we could take that with us.

They drove in silence, he mulling the scheme, Ane mulling him.

What if this...what if that...so many pitfalls only authority's credulity would help. Amateurs could beat masters - at first.

The car stopped on the windswept concourse. The automatic doors were still open. Inside, people anted around the green plywood partitions of the X-ray machines.

The floor was wet. Daley cursed. The suitcase had fallen off its tiny wheels for the third time.

Ny handed their passports and tickets to the pert check-in girl and she tore a page from each and passed them back with bright Chinese, "Have a good flight."

"Cannota stay, Doc. Sorry. Taxi cannota stand in a way."

Daley forced the documents into his pocket and pumped Ny's

outstretched hand. "Thanks for everything, Ny. S'been a real experience. Thanks for organizing it all. We'll be back." *Not-bloody-likely. Enough already of disorganization, eager people, dust, and damp.*

"We're off. Stroke of luck, Ny leaving. He'd have been expecting that woman for Montreal. Wonder what would've happened if he'd met his daughter."

"Well, he wouldn't have, would he?"

"Let's hope it continues, luck. Listen, Ane, you'd better - "

"I'd better," she began simultaneouly, "go to the Ladies. Get this show on the road." They laughed together.

She turned to go. "Just a minute, you'll need this." He held out the passport.

"Thanks. I'm as nervous as a kitten."

"Me too. Don't worry. S'natural. Oh, you'll need these too." He gave her the Ryerson meal tickets and the boyfriend's picture. He glanced at their boarding-passes. "Thirty-three A and B. Our seat numbers. Tell her get as close as she can. Should be okay on the plane, if we get that far!"

"Thirty three A and B."

"Just remember the threes and there's *three* of us. I'll be over there, the bench we sat on before...all those *years* ago."

She smiled and walked briskly away past the untidy gift counter.

Cold as bloody ever. He pulled his coat tighter, rolling the smooth stone but not noticing.

Down the hall, the crowd noisily milled. *How the hell do they ever get 'em through? Buggers pile like leaves.*

It was quiet round him. Occasional travelers squelched by. His eyelids weighed a ton.

His falling head woke him with a jerk, just as a mud-splashed Mercedes pulled up outside. The driver hopped out, closing the door with a distant clump. *The bureaucrat* !

Christ, almost missed him. He shivered with the cold of day sleep. *Shabby clothes, overcoat like it's been slept in, jeans, sneakers: definitely not Brooks Brothers today. Same smooth smile.*

Daley slid up the bench out of line-of-sight. What's he doing here, dressed like shit. Think. Likely to see Ane. Well, so what? He let her go last night.

Oh, bloody-hell! Last night!

Bugger'd thought he had Yen, fooled by the scarf and huge coat. He squeezed the stone so hard it popped his fingers.

Yen's coat.

A bloody flag!

Bugger couldn't miss her!

A shiver ran him and he jumped as Ane touched his shoulder.

He blurted at her: "What's she wearing? I mean what coat."

"What? Who?"

"Yen."

"That big one."

"Get it off her! Throw it *away*."

She paled as though struck. "What's happened?"

"Just go! Go before she bloody gets out here. Tell her just wear the dress."

She opened her mouth to speak.

"That brother's here!"

She was awestruck.

The girl was just emerging, clicking uncertainly on the high heels. Ane rushed to march her back to the toilet. Her heel went over but they did not stop. She bent to pick up the shoe and hopped behind Ane, all poise gone.

Maybe his day off, but why spend it here? His sister?

Maybe she'd got a passport and he'd come to see her off. Dressed like that! No way. Maybe to blend into the crowd. But why? Maybe to *watch them* unnoticed.

Take the initiative. Go over, greet him, invite him upstairs for tea while Yen buys her ticket and goes into the boarding area. Might work. No. Make him suspicious, 'specially after last night. He slid back up the bench.

Gone! Bugger'd gone!

He scanned the concourse with alarm. Nowhere. A distant

jet wound up, whistled beyond audible then slid to a drone.

Wait, that's him! The crowd gave way as he walked past the arch of the X-ray machine into the boarding area.

Taken himself right out! Right bloody out!

Daley wondered if someone was watching out for them. He was shaking and he yawned with fatigue.

Probably seeing his sister off.

Ane sat down, pulling the wool coat over her knees.

"Sorry about that. Bugger's gone. Walked right through X-ray as though he owned it! Probably seeing his sister off."

She sighed. "God! What next?"

The public address system sang out.

"You gave me such a fright. I hate that man!"

He rolled his thumbs in agitation. She squeezed them still.

"Funny we keep running into him though, isn't it? Dressed like shit, this time. Like a bloody navvie!"

"You're kidding. Why, d'you think? Probably knows our itinerary. Maybe he expected to see us here. Thought of that?"

He nodded. "Lucky we're up here out if it. The Information shack guy probable saw us. He checked with him when he came in. When we weren't around he likely assumed we'd gone through. Anyway, we know he's here and he doesn't know where we are."

The girl sashayed by.

At first she didn't register. A woman, tall, straight, swishing like a model on a fashion runway. A swift smile. The dress fit like a glove, Ane's necklace swayed on her neck.

"God!" he croaked, adding quickly: "You've done well, I must say. Hundred percent western, even to the swish of her bum."

He could not take his eyes off her.

Ane elbowed his ribs.

"Sorry, what I was saying…"

"That bureaucrat," she reminded him tartly.

"Oh, yes. Just pushed straight through the X-ray booth."

"You said that already."

"Well, that's all there is."

He glanced at his watch – 9.45 – then realized he was sitting on the edge of the seat and sat back to watch more comfortably.

The girl stopped by a Redcap with a barrow. He accompanied her to the check-in.

She tried.

Daley imagined her slow Irish-English. The porter pushed her aside and took her documents.

Here we go. Battle is joined.

"Let's go, Ane. Aim for the nearest security machine, that way we'll be furthest from her. Did you tell her our seat numbers?"

"She wrote them on her hand."

He nodded approval. "Best keep away from her, at least till the aircraft."

They joined the jostle in front of an X-ray arch.

"What if she comes to us?"

"You did tell her didn't you. About him."

"Yes, but I'm not sure she understood. So excited. Besides, we didn't tell her about last night, did we?"

"Didn't want to alarm her then."

"We'll have to shoo her off somehow," he shouted over the racket of Chinese and creaking bamboo trunks.

"She'll be frightened."

"Who wouldn't be? Look, I empathize but we must keep apart in case he is looking for us. She'll understand."

Ane looked at the floor, drawing figures-of-eight with the toe of her shoe. "There is something I can do, you know," she said pulling a blue and gold cloth from her pocket. "I can wear this. She'll know something's wrong if she sees me with this on. After all, I wore it last night."

A grin spread his face. "Like it. It's neat. Put it on. You're a blood-alley, you know. Ever told you?"

She shook out the golden dragon on the blue square, deftly wound the silk round her hair, rolled it tight on her forehead then tucked in recalcitrant strands. "There. How do I look?"

"Like her. Don't think he'll bother you again, do you?"

"After last night? No way. Lost a lot of face last night."

At the security booth, Daley was pushed from behind. He whipped round angrily. A small boy was eyeing him with unblinking eyes.

Ane fed the case into the squat X-ray machine and they followed the higgledy-piggledy line through a double door guarded by two soldiers, stens leaning against the wall beside them. One inspected the boarding passes and waved them into a large room with corrugated glass at the end and a boarded floor that squeaked like the bird-singing floor of the Kyoto palace, specially designed to warn of intruders.

The floor had been washed and the air was full of wet wood.

Looks pale, she thought. Got that bloodhound look of lost sleep. Wrestling with problems, even imaginary ones. No point offering help. Least not yet.

The line divided, each meandering to a doorway in the long wall. Curly figures were discernible through the frosted glass: one seated, one standing, sten on hip.

Thin muzak walked the air above the crowd noise. It was difficult to talk.

Daley looked back. He scanned the room for the bureaucrat. No sign.

"Must have a lot of clout, that bureaucrat. Pushed through security and nobody got pissed. Like he owned the place."

"You said that before. Not surprising: had the army with him last night, remember. Anyway, quit worrying; so far we're getting all the breaks."

"Yes but - "

"Piss off with your 'yes-buts.' Always analyzing. You'd analyze stamps off envelopes, you would."

She pushed her arm through his and jiggled him.

Then he saw him, back to them. Tall, three lines over, talking to a woman. The sister? They were next into inspection.

He watched. Suddenly the man turned and made his way back.

Daley ducked.

"What's up?"

"Him. He's just leaving." He glanced to his left.

"Bloody good riddance."

"God! Could run into Yen. Could run right into her."

"In this! Nah. Too many people. Besides, don't think he'd recognize her. Bit different from a Chinese schoolgirl!"

"I don't know," he said, pulling his leg out of the way of a huge, bamboo container.

The girl appeared in the doorway, causing his heart to heave into his throat. Perfectly poised, she slowly scanned the room. God, she is handsome! Pull it off if anyone could.

She saw them, waved, and sashayed up, ignoring the line.

"You've got me scarf on?" She giggled.

So much for the warning signal.

"So you'd see us." Ane pulled it off and shook her hair.

The girl stood close, tawny tassels bobbing. Her eyes held his for an instant. "Look nice," he stumbled then looked away.

"You think so?" She smoothed her bangs with wetted fingers.

"Er, yes."

She touched the girl's arm. "Any problems with the inspection?"

"T'was easiness itself! Clockwork. Like clockwork. This money works wonders." She opened her hand. "Thirty three C."

"What?"

"Me seat. Thirty tree C. Next to you."

"Across the aisle."

The girl looked at her blankly.

"Your seat. Across the aisle from us?"

"Didn't use much money."

Ane squeezed the bag shut. "Keep it in there."

"Count it and fill in your money form," Daley told her, holding out his pen.

"Tell me," he asked. "Anyone talk to you?"

"No, nobody. Wait! There was a man. Seemed to be talkin' to everybody."

Daley controlled his voice. "What was he after?"

"People travellin' to Hong Kong, to watch for his sister. She's afraid of flying. I wrote down her seat number."

She inspected her other palm.

"'Eleven G.' Not far from us is she?"

"Some people are scared of flying," said Ane

Daley was alarmed. "Did he speak English, the man?"

"To me. Oh, yes. Took me for a westerner."

"Didn't try Chinese?"

She shook her head.

"What sort of English was it?"

"What d'you mean?"

"Well, Chinese-English? English-English? What?"

"Oh, good English, very good. Why? What's the matter?"

He grinned weakly. "No. Nothing." There was an empty sensation in the pit of his stomach.

"Peter. Why the third degree?"

"No reason, just interested. Must look western, mustn't she?"

The girl stared at him. "There's somethin' wrong, isn't there?"

They said nothing.

The girl took a deep breath. "Well, if you must know, I saw *him* first. In the door, comin' backwards, talking, when a huge basket pushed by this tiny old woman, hit him. Boy did she blarney him. 'Be off wid yer,' she said after him."

"I see. He really was talking to people?"

"I remember thinking, if he hadn't been so busy talking, he might have seen the basket."

"Then what did he do?"

"Went out. Look, who is he? What's wrong?"

So the bugger had left. Maybe he hadn't been sure. Maybe he had gone for backup. After all, he wasn't dressed the part. No! The soldiers let him come and go as he pleased, so could have just had her arrested. Maybe he didn't want a ruckus round his sister. They were funny about citizens leaving for the West. Course it was possible he hadn't recognized her. After all, if she was to be believed, he'd been asking around before he saw her and, besides, she had never been present when they had met. Maybe last night he'd been told to watch for the scarf so grabbed Ane. Devious, bugger's devious. What if he spied Yen – she was striking – *then* turned to talk to people round him, planning to include her "accidentally." Wouldn't put it past him.

Their air was kerosene, cigarette smoke, and wet boards. The harassed mother and her children – somehow now in front – split apart as the boy rushed by, chasing his sister, catching her pigtail with a yank. Little sod! I'd lace his bloody arse.

Daley watched warily, weary of "what-iffing."

"Flight 606 to Xian now ready for boarding. Please proceed to Gate Seven," sang the tannoy.

He glanced automatically at the roof. English! Definitely. Funny how in babbles of everything one picks up one's own language. Westerners visiting the Emperor's army – on the ball. He felt the coal smoke tingle his nose.

A jet wound up tightening his stomach. "Yen, er, Beth, let me have your papers. You are our daughter. Might help, you know."

She glanced at him uncertainly.

"I'm sorry for the interrogation. Nervous, is all."

She passed him the passport, money and ticket. He returned the money with a grin, then stuffed the passport in his pocket. He noticed goose bumps on her arms. "Ane, my jumper, is it in here?"

She passed the garment and the girl slipped it over her head. He watched, fascinated. It reached below her hips and she spun with a giggle

He looked at his watch: *10:15.*

He could swear she was staring when he wasn't looking. He glanced quickly but she looked away.

At least two baby squalls echoed from the high roof, mingling with the muzak, the whistling jet and the floor creaks.

Ane smiled with a faraway wistful look. Lisa's urgent cries before her tired heart stilled. Funny how yesterdays stop by.

The Chinese mother lost control of her boy. He rushed the

parallel lines – head down, arms out – screaming like a diving jet. The pitch increased as he penetrated, arms swept backwards, body tilted. Daley rolled the stone – forefinger, thumb, middle finger, thumb, forefinger back –I'd kill him. He looked away; keep calm!

An old man in the next line, sticking rice from a bowl level with his mouth, never saw him. Swooping junior hit, the bowl flew, a chopstick up his nose.

An hour to the flight. Cold, damp. Late autumn not lyricised by poets.

The girl was playing with the young pilot.

The weak sun sneaked through a narrow skylight, burnishing her hair. Her tassels moved as she made as if to catch the rambunctious child. Daley drew a deep breath. A radiance forgotten: face full of eyes, excited and, God help him, trusting. He looked away. The glass wall now closer. How could he play this game with knees threatening to fold and concentration continually blown.

Then he saw *her* !

His heart lurched.

Ane grabbed his arm. "You all right? Here, sit. Sit on the bag."

She pushed him onto the broken zip and squatted, fluttering her hands in his face. "What? What is it? What? For God's sakes, Peter. Pain? Do you have a pain?"

His dry mouth was working, he was shaking as if to shed a shock of snow.

The woman! SHL – in uniform, *army uniform*, shoulder stars and all – had just *joined their* table, the one *they* were approaching! She had removed her hat. That had done it. No mistaking the tight hair. He fought panic, explanations avalanching impotently.

It was over!

His grip on Ane's arm tightened.

He felt sick.

Ane was mutely rubbing his brow, making little noises. He

was too tired to carry on. Something had scythed him away. I asked too much, she accused, heart going to her man.

He glanced around, close to panic. Soldiers now were pushing the line to single file.

He'd first seen her entering the partition two lines over but the peaked cap had fooled him. Wasn't till the hair!

There was a chance she'd not seen them yet!

So bloody what! There she was, bent over *their* table checking a list.

The interminable squeaking of the floor suddenly got on his nerves and he stood up.

Then it dawned; his jaw dropped. Ane felt him grip. "'Boadicea in Long John's army.'"

"Long bloody John, the one-legged pirate of Treasure Island, last night's nemesis, and the Warrior Queen. *Her*!"

Ane was staring wide eyed, silent, worried.

It spilled out like a confession: "SHL's here an' she's one of 'em! Devious sodding bitch's nailed us."

She gripped at his sleeve . "What? What'd you say?"

"At our table," he nodded at the partition. "Standing behind our table."

She glanced at the door and murmured under her breath. "What d'you mean she's one of 'em? Make's no sense. She was with the students, remember?"

"So *she* bloody said. God, don't you see! You've been right all the time. We were supposed to think that! It's no good. Saw her come in. Has two stars on her shoulders. Must have been *on* the damn bus not surrounding it!"

"Jes! Thought she was a friend."

"Aye, that's sad part, isn't it."

They were force-shuffled forward. The boards creaked.

SLH had sat down. All that bloody work, blown to buggery! She knows us, she knows *her*. Can't miss we're flying to Hong Kong with poorly forged documents to boot!

Maybe *they'd known* all the time.

The girl's hand circled his arm and she gazed at him. "You gave us a terrible turn. Are you all right?"

He smiled weakly. It was hard. Like slapping a kitten. His heart sank. Send her to another line? Let us off the hook. He immediately dismissed the option. Not on! Not bloody on. Just not, s'all!

SHL had been friendly; maybe she'd let them through. Nah, a frosty smile and a march away! S'funny, in the crunch one always reacts better than the movie's star. Well, here it is and he didn't! Bloody blowhard. Bloody obvious!

As they shuffled forward, desperation became despondency. Would the Canadians ever know of their arrest? If they did, what could they do? Chinese autocracy was absolute. In prison for years, friends'd never know what happened to them. Just disappeared!

His ascot was suddenly too tight. He ran a finger round, smiling sadly at Ane. Least they were together, but for how long? Sure to be separated. Couldn't stand that. God, what a mess! All for a bit of nookie!

Ane was pale. Probably thinking about separation too. She'd be confused. Depended on him, and he had brought them to the firing squad wall.

She found his hand and gave it a squeeze, smiling at him. There was love in that smile, forgiveness, years-of-together love. He blinked and glanced away, moodily switching to anger. The army were zealously tracking reactionaries, and SHL was army. They hanged them in windows for all to see!

Yen. Oh, Yen, he agonized, real pain twisting.

She had returned to playing with the junior pilot, poking him in the belly with a stiff finger; each poke eliciting a giggle as he peek-a-booed in and out of his mother's scarf.

Daley took a deep breath. If only. God! Life was full of if-onlys.

They were almost to the door. So close he could count the lace-eyes in the boots of the seated soldier, sticking out under the table. He cursed Ny. This godforsaken country, its people, and his own bloody stupidity.

The mother herded the children to her and entered. The little pilot refused, so she cuffed him with a satisfying clump. He looked at her, startled eyes glazing, yowl gathering.

Maybe if Yen went farther back she'd stand a better chance. Coward!

The mother muddled to the table.

He felt sick. His head was pounding.

Next!

VII
Outside Beijing Airport

Time, time to think! The next line?
He bent, heaved the bag onto his shoulder and turned to leave with a grim face.
An upheaval three lines over.
Raised voices...milling people. Sods, pushing in!
He stopped. Ane banged into him.
The man!
THE MAN DHS! *He'd* bloody pushed in!
Slicked hair, Adam's apple like a chicken's, oversized jacket, flailing hands.
Daley waved his hand as Ane wound up to blast him. Her jaw dropped as she saw *the man* at the end of his point.
He shot a glance at the woman. She had turned.
He glanced back and forth like a tennis spectator. A briefcase appeared, then descended into the knot. He looked back. She was gone, image wobbling two partitions over.
A chance? *He'd* given 'em a chance. The silly, God- I-love-you bugger had given 'em a chance. More nerve than toothache. Sudden warmth welled. If he'd been there, he'd'a kissed him. He grabbed Ane's hand and pulled.
 The mother, daughter, and unruly son were still at the table. Little bugger was squatting the way women pee, playing with the seated sergeant's bootlaces, carefully lifting one lace over the other, the way children tie shoes.

A soldier pushed Daley's back.

They were in.

Daley gathered his women round him. Wellington, Waterloo, six-o-clock.

Smile. Keep smiling, jaw-aching-smile. He clenched his left wrist to stop it shaking. The girl stood, eyes on her shoes.

The bored soldier scanned their faces.

Suddenly the table rocked straight up at him!

Daley jumped back.

The sergeant, cap in hand, kept coming. Up, over table, telephone, papers, hurtling at them. The girl backed into the partition, hands to her turned-away face.

The sergeant dropped the passports. Daley scooped them up as the phone fell to the floor and the lamp went out. He grabbed them both and hustled into the dark!

The bag bounced but he muddled on, gripping Ane harder.

Forgotten the damn saluting nonsense!

The dimly lit tunnel became stone flags. Crowds, jets, tinny music, tannoys faded to collective breaths, rubbing coats, quick clicking shoes.

The girl kicked off the high-heels and held them in her hands.

A monumental cough was building. Stop or go down. He fell against the wall, heaving, hands on his knees, heart beating so vision moved in and out with it. A sweat drop gathered on his nose. He wiped it away roughly with his sleeve.

His face was grey. He fought for air. The women hovered.

They huddled; he heaved. Nobody came.

He slid across the wall.

His breath deepened. He straightened.

One thought spun like a leaf in a spider-web. DHS had pulled a diversion! For whatever reason, the gaunt Chinaman had made his move. But, God, *why*? Feet in boots, clinking! They turned to the wall. A huddle of soldiers hurried by, stens in fists, rattling their legs.

They slowly walked up the hill to the light.

DHS. Poor silly bugger. Hate dissolved. Daley took back all the shit he'd showered on him. Someday, maybe, he'd thank him.

They emerged into the familiar rosette of departure gates, sudden life, kids, pushing people, kerosene and winding jets. The area was full to heaving. The ceiling clock flicked the time. *10.40.*

A determined cleaner herded the crowd aside, wide mop shunting dust that assaulted the nose like chlorine.

A jet took off in a rumble of distant thunder.

Women in tow like children, Daley dropped the bag.

One more door.

"There's fifty minutes. Almost an hour! If SHL was expecting us, they'll soon come looking and we're damn vulnerable here."

Ane eyed him. "All so rushed.. DHS. I can't understand. What's going on?"

"He's an ejiot! Stupid article!"

Ane rounded on her. "No, he's not! Just saved your bacon, young lady!"

Daley ignored them. "Someday we may find out but now, we must go with the flow. Ane, you still have those Empress Cards?"

"Somewhere. Why?"

"I've an idea that's why. They're expecting three of us, so let's split up. Just for now," he added quickly to reassure the girl as her face fell. "After all, we have our seats. We'll meet on the aircraft."

"But where, Peter? Where can we go? No point in splitting up here."

"There!" He pointed at the empty lounge.

"You're joking! We'll be like a sore thumb in there!"

"Exactly! *We'll* stand out. *We two!*" He pushed two fingers at her in the victory sign.

The girl was wide-eyed with alarm.

"Don't worry, Yen," he said gently. "It'll help. Believe me. You'll be safer out here, really you will. Push into a sill. I'm sure they'll let you. Remember you're a westerner. Get your head down and keep it down. Never see you in this lot. Oh, and you'd better have this."

She took the passport reluctantly, turning it over as if unable to believe she had it back.

Ane was dubious. Was Daley ducking again? "But they're for Canadian Airlines, Peter, these Empress cards!"

"Doesn't matter. Depend on human nature. Bet that girl is bored out of her skull, love some business, something to do. Not give 'em a second look."

"Yes, but - "

"Let's try. Maybe CAC are hooked up with Canadian Airlines." He put his hand on the girl's arm. "We'll see you on the plane." She pulled away.

"Don't worry, you really will be safer out here. Believe me." She lifted her chin petulantly and flounced into the crowd.

His heel clicks disappeared in the deep pile of the deep blue carpet. The pretty hostess with a perfect smile greeted them in surprise. She took the silver cards, lavender wafting as she moved. She slowly wrote their names and numbers into the first and empty page of a thick ledger.

"Whicher flighter, sir?"

He handed her the boarding passes. "Willer call, sir."

He walked to a table in a corner near the window.

"I can't believe you did that, Peter. Left her out there! She's terrified! I'm going back to her."

He put a hand on her arm. "Ane, listen. I'd be terrified too, but it's our best shot. Here we're like sore thumbs. *Two*, not three. Don't forget SHL *never saw us*, she was behind frosted glass and we were far back. She went up two desks then over to DHS. Maybe she'll think Yen took off, got cold feet and left. Sitting here makes her job easy. She'll not bother struggling with the herd out there. Also, we have valid visas. She can do nothing to us. The girl has the bottle for it. Quite spunky. I understand how you feel, but, if you go out and join her, I'll have to come too and they'll catch us all!"

She twisted her fingers, lips working. "Suppose you're right. It's just that, well, she looked so forlorn."

He patted her fingers still. "I know, love, believe me, I do."

They threw their coats over seats. She sniffled.

"Bad, isn't it? Place is wick with lavender, even bloody carpet. We've got to try stay, somehow. I'll get you some tissue. Would a drink help?"

She nodded, eyes wet, handkerchief pinching her nose.

He padded to the window. A voyeur moon was peeping round daylight's door in the sky. Good luck? Keep an eye out for us.

The sideboard was mirrors, empty glasses, soft drinks, wine and booze.

He pushed his hair back, sizzled some ginger ale into a glass, poured himself a red wine and took them to the table.

Wine in hand, he felt pleased with himself. Apart from Ane's discomfort, it had gone well.

He looked round. Proved the Chinese could do it if they wanted to. The paneling was professional, plum and seamless, window caulking invisible, windows clean and curtains even. Dragon vases guarded each corner and exotic flowers sprayed on the centre table. No dust. The carpet was bright new, their footsteps still tracking the bent pile. It was quiet, except for the muzak.

He took a long pull of French Beaujolais. "Better broth, as Nan'd say. Now all I need is a Tueros cigar." He stretched his legs.

Ane still wasn't convinced.

He glanced at the clock. *11.00.*

Half an hour to boarding.

So far the passport and papers had held. Well? He had survived the beginnings. Soldier had been passing them back. SHL had taken herself out. The kid had tied the shoes. That's what really did it. Confusion.

A thought tacked in. "Ane, do you think that bugger told SHL when he went out?"

"Hope not. Doesn't bear thinking about. If he did, they've got us cold, a relay team."

He shrugged and carefully placed his wine glass on the table. "I don't think he did, if Yen's to be believed. If he suspected her, he'd have tried her with Chinese, to watch her reaction. Maybe he was genuinely worried about his sister. Dipo visas worked, didn't they? The knee-jerk response they get is, well, our ace-in-the-hole."

He sat forward, picked up his glass by the stem and swirled the wine slowly. "If we assume you're right about a hidden agenda and they stole the passport to stop us, it had no visa in it; so there *is* a chance they don't know we have them."

"Ny knew."

"Maybe he didn't tell." He was unwilling to abandon his theory. "Don't think he's part of it anyway. Do you? Well, at least, if he is, he's unwilling."

"What about DHS then?"

"That bugger's a puzzle."

"You think he pulled that stunt on purpose?"

"No doubt about it! Sad thing is the down side."

"What?"

"Well, SHL'll be really pissed and have got him. I keep expecting to hear trotting soldiers out there."

Suddenly he felt very tired. The doorway moved off the floor and wobbled mid-air though he tried hard to hold it still. He gave in, doesn't matter if it does move.

SHL and DHS danced a slow waltz, arms high, towards the girl. He stood between. Ane was waving through thick silent glass which suddenly fractured to opacity as the wine glass fell from his fingers. He started up and looked round confused, unsure where he was.

Ane was dozing.

The receptionist was still reading unconcernedly. He picked up the pieces of glass he could see, fed them into the ashtray, then sat back. A quick glance at the lounge clock. 11.10. Asleep ten minutes. Time to move!

His stomach tightened nervously as he shook Ane awake.

The PA system sang Chinese and the hostess slipped off her stool and minced over. "Flighter one-o-one leady for boarding sir."

Time for the bathroom? No, later. Out, back to the game!

He helped himself to sugar lumps as they passed the tea urn, wrapped them in tissue and popped them in his jacket pocket. "Grazing sugar," Stephen called it. He smiled, remembering his droll brother-in-law.

The little girl in blue smiled sadly as they passed.

Outside they joined the crush and pushed towards Gate 8.

The girl? No sign.

Probably gone in already. Probably sat near Gate 8.

A sudden surge threatened his balance. Craning as far as he could, he saw the reason. His stomach contracted as he saw a squad of soldiers with stens at their chests, forcing passage.

He'd known they would come. She better be through!

Well, you buggers, you're too bloody late. We're by ourselves and have every right to be here, boarding passes, visas, and all. Bit light headed. Good job they'd split up. He smiled grimly at the top of Ane's head. Not seen them. Best not tell her.

The woman with the children, spoke to the sergeant as she went through, children daisy-chained on her arm, fingers in mouths. Her hair was short and thick.

Ane broke into his reverie. "Peter." She had seen the soldiers. "Have they got her?"

"Don't think so. She wasn't here when we came out. Think she's gone through. Besides they'd take their bloody hook if they had."

"They'll search the aircraft for sure, won't they?"

"Suppose so, there's nothing we can do. She's on her own."

She squeezed his hand. "Don't worry, she's resourceful. Imagine the chaos on the plane. She'll think of something."

The line behind parted as a flight crew pushed through. The soldiers waved them through.

"The pilots are so young, Peter."

"Probably flew fighters against Taiwan. Don't worry. Only kidding. They flew the plane in, don't forget. Besides planes fly 'emselves these days."

A private was checking boarding passes, the sergeant standing behind.

He noticed the soldier was not really examining the documents at all. They were searching all right.

Daley passed them over with a smile.

The private turned the passes over and over, finger following the information with zealous attention. The uniform was primitive, stitches heavy and missed. The cord of his hat bristled and the edge of the neb was frayed through.

He shifted his glance to the sergeant whose behavior was strange. He dropped his cheroot stub, squashed it and deliberately looked everywhere but at them. The soldier glanced at him and received a nod. The sergeant's face was grim, thin nicotine-stained teeth protruding, eyes nearly shut. The soldier held out the passes and waved Daley and Ane through.

He looked back. The sergeant was gone. To report I bet. He quickened his step, urgency tightening his chest. *They hadn't got her yet, but he had to know.*

The tunnel narrowed and turned. The plane at the end was western. Thank God!

A last soldier stood at the entrance, clicking on passengers, sten leaning on the wall at his feet. Daley pushed the boarding passes at the smiling stewardess. She motioned to the near aisle.

No narrow Russian facsimile, this Boeing 767 was bright, colourful, roomy. He bumped down the seats, waiting with forced patience as passengers struggled bags into bins and disrobed onto seats. Numbers were hard to see, window seats offset behind centre ones. Thirty-one, thirty-three, three empty seats, two on the side, centre one offset backwards. A. B. C. Empty!

Empty!

He collapsed into 33 B, not knowing he had, stunned, held breath jolted from him.

Oh, Yen, Yen, Yen.

Chuntering Chinese pushed by.

Nowhere, nowhere. She was nowhere!

They should never have separated, never have left her like a pariah. He had ducked, that's what he'd done. Got her away, persuaded himself it was best, a sensible *ruse de guerre* – a runner, a stand-back, safe.

He craned past Ane to see out.

Nothing! No hurrying group heading for the terminal.

The day moon taunted.

He drew a deep breath. Why did it always work out like this? This time *required* involvement.

Ane leaned across and clicked his belt shut. She was confused. He was her rock, *her* rock. Why not be selfish? Because she wasn't. That simple. She wasn't selfish.

He looked up at her and said with the surety of years. "Sorry, love, about this I mean. We've lost her, I think." His voice broke. "Seems so impossible." He drew a deep breath and blew it out "So damn impossible."

"You did all you could."

"Shouldn't have left her."

"Look, we should. Had to. You were right. Together we were too obvious. I think you were right. Not at first, mind you, not at first. At first I was mad as hell but then saw it was the only way."

"You really think so?"

She nodded.

He looked away.

The aeroplane was pandemonium but he knew the door had shut.

The overhead TV screens snowed on with a series of loud crackles. He stood for a last urgent look round. Nothing. Must have come on the plane and marched her off before we even got close.

The stewardess was miming safety procedures to the TV.

Galloping panic ran him. He struggled up. Got to get out! Go! Go find her...

The seatbelt held him down. Stupid arsehole! God was he angry – with himself, with Ane for getting him into it, with the vicious, smelly arseholes of the God-awful muddle of a country that had beaten them, and with the girl for meaning much more than she should.

What had she done? Nothing! Trusted completely was all. Innocently done everything she was told.

Got to stop. Got to think.

If they had her, they had her passport, they had *Beth's* passport, they had the *wrong* photo in the passport. This plane better get the hell off!

Ane could feel him shaking. Got to get him away so I can help, away to cleanliness, softness, warm beds.

The wall beside her stirred as they rolled back from the gate. The engines wound up.

He bleakly watched out the far window, over her empty, accusing seat.

He fidgeted uncomfortably.

As the bumping smoothed, he glanced around the cabin.

Desperation. Nothing to be done.

The safety-features video was still playing, now in English. Wonder if they'll finish it before we take off? He was completely disgusted with the half-arsed organization.

Ane elbowed into his reverie. "Don't like aircraft with only two engines, do you? They're not as safe, are they?"

He studied her. She had said something but he had only got the end of it.

"Sorry?"

"Two engines. This plane. Only got two engines."

He smiled bleakly and patted her folded hands. "Don't worry, engines these days are reliable. This is a Boeing so ETOPS applies."

Her eyebrow arched quizzically.

"ETOPS, you know what Bill Stirup told us. Extended Twin Operation Passenger Service," he remembered. "Engines have to be reliable enough to fly the Pacific or Atlantic with only one." He smiled uncertainly as he remembered Bill's cynical translation: Engines Turn Or Passengers Swim!

The aircraft stopped. He looked at the grey, stubble fields as far as the eye could see. Folds of grey clouds stretched across the horizon like the page edges of a well-thumbed book. The moon was gone. Good job, he thought. He felt grey, numb. In the air was the rest of the world, warm, happy, bright, dampless, dustless, unmuddled, with no linger of urine.

"Sure, I thought I'd never get away."

He jerked round, wincing as his neck cricked. His mouth fell open.

The girl had sat down, was fastening her belt, was smiling at him.

He gasped, closed his eyes tight then looked again, heart pumping in his throat. Inside, he was singing like a pond in a spring wood. As the aircraft slewed and accelerated at the same time, he was pressed into the seat.

The plane clawed into the air.

As they leveled, she flicked her hair onto her shoulders and smiled at him. "You'll never believe it. Wasn't I almost taken? I can't believe. I felt so alone sittin' on that window ledge, like you said. Sort of brought you both closer it did, doing what you said. I couldn't see you. Couldn't see anything really, just people. The little boy found me but I didn't feel like playing, so he left. All I knew was I had to get on the plane first when the gate opened."

"Well, did you get on first?"

"Got on first all right. Least among the first. Found my seat and was putting my bag and sweater - your sweater - into that bin, when I saw the soldiers."

Shit! Should have checked the bin. Too obvious. Never think of the obvious. Least we'd have known she'd got on board. Still, wouldn't have known if she'd been dragged off.

"I didn't know what to do. They were asking people for papers and movin' towards me." A wild look briefly filled her eyes.

Ane was listening. She had slipped off her shoes.

"I got up and went to the back. The toilet was all I could think of. I knew they'd look but couldn't think of anywhere else to go. Well, there were these curtains so I pushed through into a cubby hole full of silver cupboards, red and green lights, dials, and things. A blue cloak and cap were hangin' in a corner so I put them on. They were there, so I put them on. Then I pushed a black button, turned a big red latch, and a cabinet rolled out, full of small tins. I could hear the soldiers so I opened an overhead cupboard. Stacks of plastic glasses fell on top of me!" She giggled. "I was stuffing 'em back when I had an idea. I split a roll, lined them on the counter and was just openin' the first can when this soldier looked in. I was shaking, holding a glass so tight its rim bent." Her fist closed. "He nodded and went away. Just nodded and went away."

There was a small silence. Daley and Ane waited.

"He just went away."

"Jes."

It was slowly dawning they'd done it. Absolutely God-damn done it! Away, up, up and away. He hummed the sixties tune as they broke into the sun. He could swear the now-visible moon wore a smile.

"Told you she was resourceful!" He surfaced. Impressive! Quick thinking. Maybe she'd noticed the soldiers ignored the crew. He felt deliciously warm.

Plain sailing now.

He hummed to himself. "S'Wonderful, S'Marvelous, You belong to me. 'S'Wonderful, S'Marvelous." Couldn't remember the rest of the second line. Ah, what the hell! Can't be bothered.

Beside him, Ane struggled up. Orange juice was coming.

Ane was intently watching the engine pod out the window.

"Can't see they're goin' anymore, can you Ane. Not like propellers."

"Worries me."

"Not always good, taking comfort from spinning propellers. Remember Bill Gronau flying back from Dortmund after a bombing raid. An engine got hot, I mean really hot, the shaft glowed bright red. They feathered it but suddenly the prop spun off and cartwheeled away *ahead of them*.! Pilot told them don parachutes and blow off the doors for easy exit but they managed to land, doors all gone, freezing to death! Can't always trust them, propellers."

"But that was war. S'not the same."

"Jets are much better. Besides, there *are* three on this plane."

She searched his face. He was playing with her.

"Pull t'other one, s'got bells on. There aren't. I looked.. Tail is normal."

"Aye, but there's one in there. It runs all these." He waved at the lamps and the seat arm with its audio system. "Called the APU, the auxiliary power unit. Weighs less than the paint, an engineer at Pratt told me. Boeing is always after them to reduce its weight."

He idly scanned round. Most passengers had slipped off their shoes under the seats. He yawned. God, he was tired! Like being ill - could hear his own breath. He pressed the seat button and closed his eyes as the back eased away. Darkness whirled in and he sat up quickly. Fatigue, like too much booze, makes your head spin.

"She's all right, the sister, the one I told you about." She showed him the number on the palm of her hand, 11G.

"You went to see her," he blurted, aghast.

"Why not? She was frightened when we took off. She's okay now."

He gripped her arm. "Does she have a baby with her?"

"No."

"So much for the husband seeing his son for the first time. Look, Yen, stay away from her, please. Stay away."

She shook her head petulantly and leaned to Ane. "Can we go shopping in Hong Kong?" She pleaded, standing on one foot then the other with excitement.

Shopping seemed the thing. Not for girlish things. For VCR's, microwaves, stereos.

He was piqued. She was unaffected by events that had broken around her. Then he realized *she didn't know*!

She didn't know about SHL, about DHS, didn't know about any of it. Had innocently enjoyed the symphony whilst the concert hall burned.

"You won't need those things," he assured her. He remembered how proud her father had been, showing appliances though they weren't plugged in. "Everyone has 'em where you're going."

As he said it, he realized, they had no idea *where* she was going!

Not given any thought to Hong Kong, just getting there. He wondered should he ask but decided against it. Not their business. Once out, she was out.

Daley looked out the window at the sun dancing the wing and the dark clouds below. Funny, it's early for evening! Besides we're not flying east? He tried to visualize the map of China but couldn't keep it still. After a while he gave up. Ane was right, he analysed too much.

An attendant rushed forward. A bump had sprung a bin and a set of collapsible luggage wheels had fallen on an unsuspecting pate. Blood was spurting. The passenger disappeared as more stewardesses brisked by.

He relaxed to consider scenarios for Hong Kong.

"Can't believe she's one of them, SHL, Peter. And DHS's on *our* side."

"Been wondering that myself," he lied. "Remember how she treated that Chinese officer on the road? We thought she was brave but maybe - "

"She was nice, though, specially when you were sick!"

"Maybe she knew but couldn't do anything then, I mean. Funny, every time I've underestimated things, the visas have saved us."

"But she didn't know about 'em."

"They seemed to know everything. Every time we turned round, there they were."

Frustration was replacing good humour." Suppose you're still not going to tell me what it's all about. It is nearly over now."

"Soon. You'll know, soon."

"I don't understand it. It's ridiculous. What the hell could she have done, for God's sakes? She's only a teenager."

"Not so loud. She'll hear you."

"Don't care. This whole secrecy thing pisses me off!"

He scratched his chest through his shirt. "DHS is baffling. He *did* try to rape her. Remember. She was scared of him too, but I can't help thinking she was *letting* him!"

"Oh, for God's sake! You men are all the same! Just horny." She turned away, disgusted.

"No, you know what I mean. When we were coming up to 'em. Could swear she pushed something white in her pocket. Pants, maybe?"

"What's wrong with a handkerchief?"

He shrugged.

Suddenly he sat forward. He had realized with a jolt, her passport had *no* Western *embarkation* stamp, nothing to prove she had *come from* the West *to* Beijing, wasn't just a refugee fleeing Beijing.

What ports of embarkation could she have used for Beijing anyway? Why not London? When they had flown British Airways to Bangkok, the authorities had not stamped their documents at Heathrow. Should work. Reasonable. There were British entry stamps on the passport. Beth had been in London. Neat!

The loudspeaker crackled. They were looking for a doctor *twenty minutes after* the wound had been inflicted! Stupid sods. Right on! The Daleys looked at each with the same smile.

It was getting bumpy.

The drinks cart hastily squeaked by as the cabin crew abandoned serving.

Daley looked out the window. Far below, keeping step, their shadow on the clouds, rainbow around. The clouds seemed to reach for them, touching, sometimes enveloping, hiding the engine pod.

"Goina get rough, I think."

The airframe creaked. The seatbelt and no-smoking signs flashed on. Ane gave him a small smile. A flutter of Chinese, a hasty scuffle to seats, a clicking of belts. He watched with misgiving. Many had not belted up for take-off!

Could clouds build to 32,000 feet? Either that or they were losing height. He glanced at his watch. 1:45. About two hours out of Hong Kong, so they were still over China.

He gripped the seat arms.

"Listen, if this gets worse, bend your head to your knees and cover it with your arms. Keep your knees together; in fact, put that pillow on your knee first."

He repeated the instructions to the girl.

It's a new plane, hasn't the flying hours yet for fatigue. But why descend into this crap? Had the buggers put two and two together, blown their pitiful smoke screen, reached into the clouds for them?

A man's voice on the PA. He glanced at Yen. She paled. Didn't speak Chinese, did she? Mustn't speak Chinese!

She gazed back, eyes wide, lips trembling.

Damn! Hoisted by my own petard.

As he watched, she quickly undid her belt and hurried forward. He grabbed at her but missed. A piss now? Ane just shrugged.

It was getting very bumpy. The plastic knife rattled on his tray. Could get hurt, he reflected, folding the tray and slipping the knife into the seat pocket.

The roof TV flickered on snow. Clear. *The safety video!*

Stewardesses quick-stepped, row to row, like sailors on wave-swept decks, hustling dilatory passengers.

One walked Yen back. The girl grabbed the seat in front of her's as the nose suddenly dipped.

She held on, swung into her seat and quickly belted up. He

turned to berate her but she shot him a brilliant smile. "Isn't this wonderful! I mean so free, so flying." Her eyes flashed naked pleasure.

"It's bloody dangerous," he shouted against the din. "For God's sake, stay put!"

The plane heaved and their heads collided. As they pulled back, she whispered: "Typhoon."

Angry clouds, buffeting air. Jesus Christ! *Typhoon* ! They were entering a typhoon, for God's sakes! And the bloody pilot's flying down into it!

Maybe he can't get above or around, so he's ducking it. What about telling us? What about papers, radio, TV? Oh, shit. TV!

He caught an involuntary breath. The smiling girl behind the pirouetting Yen, wagging fingers at a blue swirl on the map. They *did* tell us. Bloody ignored it. I bloody ignored it! He bit his lip. After everything, nature's scotched us!

The girl was prattling softly. "She'll be all right, the sister. I pulled her belt tight, like you said. Told her to do what you said."

Stupid bitch. He glared indignantly. No idea, no bloody idea! Like a fun-fair ride, for Chris' sakes!

It was now difficult to hear across the aisle. With every lurch, the noise increased. The engines powered up, fearful passengers quieted. Ane sought his hand. His was clammy, her's hot. He squeezed it.

He glanced out the window. Black–black as a tire fire–distorting rain sluicing the glass. He bent double to his knee, pulled Ane down then peeped sideways at the girl. She was watching him with a secret look, a ready to flick away look like a trembling bird.

The cabin lights flickered, went out, on again, then out for good. Two narrow lines of floor lamps stuttered on.

Sinister squeaks and thumps shuddered the inclined cabin as they entered the thunderheads.

An old woman across the aisle suddenly threw up.

A sudden drop like a stone.

He hated up-chucking. The fall stopped. They leveled, held. Oh, God, hold, he prayed, pushing hard with his feet.

A crash of crockery.

Of course, he would survive. Something would, something *must* intervene...

The aircraft gave a tremendous heave.

"He's losing it!" he shouted in his Ane's ear. She pulled him tightly.

Falling again – stomach in air.

Floored coffee pots clattered.

Hand luggage spilled into the aisles.

He covered his head, pillow tight to his ears.

A faint beep – almost missed – a methodical rumble, felt rather than heard deep in the innards. Wheels were going down.

He sat up risking a relieved breath and took a quick glance at his watch. 2.30. Ane felt him lift, swung across his lap, arms round his knees. He bent, leaning love into her, protecting. This woman, this mother, this buttress – I do love her. He squeezed tight.

Like a roller coaster, the plane abruptly plunged, wing up, window down. He piled onto her, she into the window, bent double by belts.

A chaos of bric-a-brac pelted them. Everything loose took to the air. The belt tore his midriff, the seat arm cut him in two and his back screamed. He tried to kick his stuck legs loose, stopping instantly as cramp threatened.

His nose shot a cold run. Black, shiny blood! Drops diffused her hair. God, no! Not a bloody nose bleed.

They weren't spinning yet! Nose down, wing down, shaking like a wet dog.

A cold drip hit his forehead. He rubbed it. Smelled his fingers. Water. He tasted it. No. Tea. Green tea, residue of lunch. He wiped his forehead with the retrieved cloth. Christ! Not tea but barf!

Barf, and he'd tasted it!

He shuddered, fumbled the cloth round his head, fighting a

heave, tied it with a tuck then bent and screamed in Ane's ear: "Hang on! Diving sideways. He's still got it though!"

She just gripped tighter. A blinding headache, black as the storm, was gathering behind her eyes.

He stiffened his right arm against the seat back. How could something the size of city block dive like this?

The girl hanging above him stretched for his shoulders.

She suddenly crossed herself.

He twisted, braced knees stiff against the seat-back tray, reached up and back, grasping her hand.

The roof, now wall, danced deep shadows like a lunatic house of horrors. A bag teetering the edge of the bin, slid and fell. It cracked his shoulder, bonked their fingers apart and, escaping his desperate grab, rolled over to the window corner in front of Ane. The noise was a maelstrom of screams, laboring engines, crashing luggage, torrential rain, scattershotting metal. Children screamed.

Daley bent over his wife. Faces flashed in his private darkness. Faces that hurt: mother abandoned, father scorned till too late, buried brother he had bullied, Eileen who loved but was not loved back. Photo flashes of people. Loved you all, he murmured into Ane's hair stiffening with congealing blood.

She was sobbing, visiting her little ones – always little – pulling at her knees, laughing as the kite caught the wind, a petticoat bird. Lisa, the lost little one, sobbed for Mama, Mama. Tired blue eyes that never understood.

Tears stung as he turned to squint out the "floor" window. A magazine hit his forehead and settled open. '"Does pink sand feel softer?" It could only be Bermuda', claimed the message before sliding into the window corner.

Were they levelling?

The floor wall seemed less steep. Was the belt easing? A pillow softed the back of his head.

The 767 was a leaf in the wind. Suddenly a white shaft wagged out, bright, ethereal, coning streaking rain, illuminating inundated control surfaces. The wing centre-panel shimmied like a loose shingle. Another light, like a battery of cameras, strobed on: navigation lights.

He breathed fervently. 'God bless the engineers of Seattle. Oh, absolutely. God bless the buggers'.

A bright orange balloon. Someone had inflated a life-vest. *If we don't level soon, we'll be buried in this crap*

There was a jarring thump as the pilot took advantage of the leveling to thump the giant to the ground. Everything loose re-took flight–a maelstrom of bric-a-brac in the rocking cacophony. The wingtip trailed sparks as they wobbled like a wing-clipped goose. The undercarriage hydraulics fought the dipping engine.

The floor lights blinked out.

Roaring blackness.

This was it, the crucial forever of a skidding bomb. His heart banged in his ears...urgent thumps.

Chaos. Jerking, slamming, yawing but down. He suddenly snickered deliriously – down, bloody down.

The aircraft careened like a derailed locomotive.

Fast! Too bloody fast.! Too bloody fast!

Slow down!

The roar of the reluctant reversers...the jerk of brakes.

Nose still up!

Runway must be running out. Knuckle–hurt. The seat arm dug his side. Turning, the mad sod's turning!

A tire burst. Skewing. Faster.

Now backwards, the jets screamed, the massive through-thrust-for-takeoff, out-bellowed the storm. Deep, deeper, pushed into the seat. The fuselage shuddered, their backwards motion slowed, slower, stopped, forward creep. The whines instantly unwound. Audible. Idle. Silence. Deafening silence.

Broken crockery clinked. Liquid dripped.

Dark!

Kerosene!

One, then another, then more, then all, including Daley, Ane and the girl, clapping – claps accelerating, clapping hands, claps of relief, claps through scattered debris. Claps for the captain hidden in his faraway cockpit.

The girl whispered in his ear: "Nanking! we've landed in Nanking!"

God! Still in China!

Outside, the concrete was intermittently illuminated by flashing thunderheads and swept by the gale yawing the aircraft, back and forth. The fuselage rattled, like hail on a bedroom window.

Apple juice circulated as Ane came back, smiling and refreshed, followed by a stewardess with a cup of coffee.

"She speaks English so I asked her," she announced with a flourish.

"Oh, God, thanks! What a wonderful surprise!"

He sipped it nervously. The unexpected stopover was bound to pique officialdom. *If we have to get off, we're dead!* A convoy of light beams swung in the gloom.

His stomach shrivelled.

A high lamp came on in the distance.

A tanker took station under the wing.

A second truck, carrying tires, disappeared round the front. A van disgorged a dozen figures who crouch-ran to the aircraft, dragging heavy ropes. They launched coils over the wing, quick wriggling snakes and, pulling both ends taut, wrapped them around anchors countersunk in the runway.

He tutted. "Battening down like a bloody ship."

"Don't care, Peter. We're down. Don't think I've ever been so scared."

They settled for a long night.

The girl had not said a word.

A long unused sense told him she was looking. He whipped a quick glance, but she looked away, stood up, opened a bin, pulled out his sweater and slipped it on with a quick smile. "Cold," she said, squeezing herself with folded arms and sitting down. He nodded with a smile.

He closed his eyes and wandered back the England of his youth, to Norma, the girl from Thorner. He had watched her secretly too, every morning as the bus bounced to Leeds. One day he had caught her watching him in the driver's mirror and pleased, he discreetly watched her watching, knowing she knew. Independently they adjusted buses to travel together.

Never a word, just eyes.

One day there was only one seat left when he huffed onto the bus.

He had to sit with her!

He had shuffled the aisle in wonderful shock and sat with a quick smile. Silence – hard working silence – considering, rejecting, embarrassing silence. Suddenly *she* was talking, a calm voice, a little unsure, looking directly at him – eyes of green hazel – wagging a cigarette, asking for a light. He'd fumbled out the Zippo bought in New York that summer, proudly flicking a flame.

A delicious shiver resurfaced.

He had told her of buildings so tall you couldn't see their tops, and noise beyond imagination. He had paused self-consciously but continued with her encouragement. After twelve miles they were friends.

Wasn't the same though. Never was the same again. Eyes had it. Pristine, magical. He had loved her perfume: Je Reviens.

His chin fell off his hand. He had bought Ane some but she didn't often wear it. Maybe she knows. Now the girl's wearing it. An unexpected breath. Maybe Norma was back.

The storm's temper subsided with the grey, uncertain dawn.

The tail engine hummed to life. He awoke to the smell of fresh coffee and cigarette smoke.

Refreshed stewardesses with repainted smiles circulated the coffee as Ane and the girl returned. She squatted beside him in the aisle as she chattered to Ane about the upcoming shopping.

He interrupted brusquely: "What's going to happen in Hong Kong anyway? I mean when we arrive. What you goin' to do?"

Her eyebrows lifted with surprise. "Stay wid you, of course."

"But we're only staying one night. What then?"

"I'll come wid you."

"We're going to Canada. Look, I'm sorry," he said more gently. "The future's almost here. Do you know anybody in Hong Kong?"

She didn't seem to hear.

He put his cup on Ane's tray.

"That was nasty," said Ane softly in his ear. "Not like you. Not like you at all."

He scratched his head. "We must face it. She just can't stay with us, can she. We'll get real bloody horns if we try to get her into Canada!"

"Could have been more gentle. She's only a child. In many ways anyway. Besides, I'm sure you'll think of something."

There it was again – that bloody trust. It was irritating. He'd absolutely no idea. No choice this time – just leave her in Hong Kong. Least she'll be with her own people. He was mad with Ny. Why doesn't he take more interest in his own damn daughter? Doesn't bloody know, does he? Doesn't bloody know she's left the country.

He glanced quickly at her. She was twining her fingers, looking out a far window. He stilled her fingers with a squeeze. "You've won, Yen. Won! Made it. You made it. Whatever else, you're free!"

He smiled. "By the way, you look lovely. That dress really suits you."

"Thank you." She smiled like sunrise.

Through the window, a small figure in a blue mac held tight against the wind with one hand, cap by the other, was slowly circulating the tethered machine.

The Captain.

"Kick the tires and light the fires," Daley murmured to Ane with a grin, recalling Stephen's saying about the Royal Air Force.

The Captain moved out of view.

It's over, he thought, as they shuffled through the flight tunnel into Kai Tak airport. As he hefted the briefcase Ny had always carried for him, he wondered how his friend would take it all. Probably never see his daughter again. Funny buggers, the Chinese. Still, if Beth goes to Australia or somewhere, I may never see her again either.

Ane and the girl entered a super-clean corridor with rubber walkways along the side and he followed. The girl had combed back her hair and reset her bangs. The auburn highlights danced as she skipped and chatted, swinging her bag, fingers fluttering like wings. Occasionally she'd slow. God, she walks proud! He admired her straight back and head held high.

He tripped onto the automatic belt and watched the ads on the walls.

It was warm.

A single violin soared. Vaughan Williams's lark was ascending all round them.

"These always stop short!" He grumbled as they stepped off the first belt. "Why can't they make 'em twice as long instead of installing another?"

"Oh, stop complaining. Just imagine you had to walk all of it; then you'd really have something to complain about!"

She looked away. Why'd I shout at him like that? Why do I always do exactly what I don't want to?

The girl's unsteady heels clicked on the marble floor in step with his.

Ane was sad. Was it all to end on this little island off the coast of China? Twenty-seven good years.

The suitcase fell off its wheels and she yanked it. I won't give up. Won't, she resolved, jerking so hard the bag wobbled over again. All those years must count for something!

The girl squeezed her arm and pointed at a dress on a very thin model. Thin, she tutted. Thin, thin, thin. What it is to be thin! What I'd give to be thin – immature – like this one.

He looked at his watch. 9.30. Wonder if it's another time zone? He looked round for a clock.

Ane was far away. Shibuya, Tokyo, the day they'd found "Little Black Sambo," her favourite childhood story. Now banned in the West, they had found it in a children's book store, whilst looking for the story of the dog, Hitchaco, whose small statue forever awaits his master at Shibuya station. It was good then; maybe if they went back...No, she sighed, revisits never rekindle.

Their turn.

Daley passed the three passports through the slide window.

Doesn't matter what country, he noted irritably, immigration officials work behind an eye-high barrier. Documents are inspected just out of sight, lists checked, names rolled on invisible screens. Insidious authority.

An older officer entered and the seated one passed him the passports. They huddled. The visitor came out, wafting a fan of the documents, motioning they follow.

They hastily gathered their luggage and fell in behind.

The Williams lark was faint strains in the lonely, upper air.

Daley was alarmed. Friendly soil and they've pulled us in?

What could they do to Canadians breaking the laws of China in the Colony of Hong Kong? Quite an embarrassment, boat-people from the Commonwealth!

He reluctantly admitted it was the girl he was worried for.

Why the hell were they in this mess? The soil beneath their feet was free and here they were, heading again for God-knows what.

He stared moodily at the back of the hat they were following.

Everywhere smelled of disinfectant – Jey's fluid – taunting, as though the entire airport had been done over to emphasize the dereliction of China, the China they'd left – the China they might be sent back to!

Suddenly his febrile mind stopped dead. Of course! The passport. Lost! They'd reported it lost, hadn't they? Well, leastways the hotel had. That's it! Hong Kong authorities would have entered it into their computers and now it had turned up. Ane was pulling at his arm. "Why'd you stop? You want to sit down a minute?"

He flashed her a smile. "It's all right. Think I know what's happened," he winked. "Don't worry."

He knew she would. Funny how useless it is to tell people not to.

He walked a little lighter. Always told his students to seek the simple solution. Well, he had, and he'd found it!

He remembered the simple test he used to hire a technician who arrives in the morning to find the equipment won't turn on. 'What d'you do?' he asked, and at least four candidates said they'd check the manual; one would even phone the manufacturer. Barbara had said she'd check it was plugged in, then check the fuse. She'd got the job. Always seek the simple solution!

He hurried after the official, happier, humming "Nothing but blue skies from now on."

Ane followed him, puzzled; Yen, at her side, was anxious.

They passed offices full of muffled conversation and clacking old typewriters.

For the first time he noticed a subtle scent in the air.

"Sandlewood," said Ane. An Indian student had given him a letter opener that smelled the same.

The black and white hat was carelessly swinging their passports in time with his step. Women whinnied with laughter in the distance. Two secretaries clucked outside a door like comfortable hens. Gone were naked bulbs on twisted wires; soft, hidden fluorescents illuminated the polished floor.

The official stopped outside a light oak door, motioned they wait and disappeared inside with their documents.

The last time he'd watched their passports disappear had been Russia but then they'd taken Ben's advice and had British papers as well – just in case. Not this time.

No documents!

Nobodies!

He smiled reassuringly at Ane. She was tired and it showed in her rounded shoulders and eye wrinkles.

"Think it's the passport. You remember, we reported it lost."

"Of course." She sighed in relief.

Suddenly things didn't seem so bad.

"T'is all my fault." The girl spoke for the first time. He looked at her. "I'll give meself up."

He chastised her: "Tha'll do nowt o' bloody sort! Tha'll not throw away all us efforts now. It's al'rite tha'no's. Don't worry thee'sen."

Her face smiled, liquid eyes blinking. She didn't understand but knew it was good.

"Spanish eyes, they glow in the candlelight," the line ran his head emerging as a hum. "Even a gringo knows it's wise to shade your eyes from the sun in Mexico."

The door opened. "Please to lenter," bowed the black and white hat, holding the door open, then walking away.

The room was small, dominated by a mahogany desk with a fan heater aimed at its leg cavity. A spiral light leaned over the centre, illuminating faint imprints of past writing on the blotter. Still uses a fountain pen, Daley noted as he tried to read the reversed, upside-down trace of a sentence.

An orchid stood in a corner, lighting the room.

They dropped their coats on the luggage. The women sat, Daley stood arkwardly between them. The girl looked up at him with a lopsided smile and made to talk but he put his finger to his lips and shook his head imperceptibly. They may be listening.

She sat, eyes down, hands carefully pressing the tassels of her dress flat.

He perched on the corner of the desk, one leg up, other toeing the floor. God, she looks good! As if reading his thoughts, she flashed him a smile.

He turned away, rolling his thumbs nervously. Ane leaned forward and squeezed them still.

He studied the orchid. Though it glowed in the space, it gave no scent. Orchids have none, Ane had told him. He glanced at his watch: 10.15.

A panel in the wall opened and a man in black uniform entered with a jug of water and splashed the flower liberally.

"Forglive," he smiled as he turned, placed the half empty jug on the desk, then sat, filling the close space with cheap cologne.

He studiedly lifted off his peaked hat, placed it inside–up on the desk then pulled their open passports from the squeeze of his arm. His grey hair was brush cut, face clean shaven to a polish and, under thin wire glasses, a persistent tic turned the corner of his right eye.

His uniform was black, creaseless with silver fluting. SS - Daley shuddered.

The bent head studied the passports in turn, delicately scratching a point in his hair with a rigid finger. He viewed them side by side in pairs, drum-rolling the fingers of his left hand.

Ane'll hate that. Daley was tired to aching but still confident.

The official stopped as if he'd made a decision and held out two passports, his right eye ticking lazily.

Daley leaned forward, assembling the explanation. Then he saw *it* ! Was clouted in the face by it!

Side by side was an all *pink* visa and one with a *black* stamp – Ny's copy of the Beijing *landing* overstamp – in the upper left corner.

Time stopped.

Daley stared blankly.

Sunk, sunk, sunk!

He took the offered passports, hand trembling, and the official carefully unhooked his glasses and cleaned them with his tie.

He had perhaps ten seconds.

The man cleared his throat. "Just want clear minor ploint." Tic. Tic. "Daughter Lizableth lentered Beijing same day as you but not same flight."

Daley pretended to study the documents.

"No," he replied slowly, switching to pidgeon. "She come London. We meet Beijing."

"Ah, London. Flavorite city." Tic. "Dlont understand his entry stamp." Tic, tic.

Daley looked at him, eyebrows rising. "Sorry. What's problem?"

Christ, I know the problem. How I could be so stupid? Chinese do everything in *pink*!

The man pointed at the offending stamp, raising his eyes to Daley's.

What was there to say? Brazen it out. I wish that bloody tic'd stop! Maybe the pink ink ran out.

The phone rang.

The officer jumped as though stung, carefully threaded on his glasses one leg at a time, and picked up before the next demanding ring.

Daley stole a glance at Ane. A pale smile lifted her cheeks; he liked the way her smile did that.

He turned back to the man. He was rigid in his chair. The glasses came off and on again.

He smirked to himself. Like the British in the department at Minster. Used them like extra fingers: off for emphasis, on again to propel pauses.

There was much fast, sing-songing Chinese. Then, with a clipped apology, the tic stood and left the room, closing the panel behind him. They looked at each other. Daley shrugged.

The girl made to speak but Ane touched her to silence.

A ploy, he thought flatly, gaze resting on the inverted imperial crown of the black and white cap. Funny, never been patriotic but the lion and crown gave him security, like the singing of "Jerusalem" on the radio in Russia.

The man returned, donned the cap, straightened his tie knot and, pushing his glasses up the bridge of his nose, held out his other hand with a slight bow,

"Welclome Hong Kong". Tic. "Hope stay lenjoyable," he said, still smiling and ticking.

They gathered the coats and cases and muddled out.

They stood round the luggage carousel in disarray.

Everywhere the smell of varnish, carbolic, and cigarette smoke. The shiny, naked metal sheets of the belt were still. No luggage yet.

"Don't understand. Someone must have said something. Must have. We were dead. Dead in the bloody water. He'd seen the seal an' all. A phone call, then bingo, bloody bingo!" He popped the "B's" like bubblegum. "Bingo. Nice as bloody pie."

"He seemed so nice. I mean, he smiled a lot, didn't he."

"Smiles of bloody triumph, Ane, an ace over a king! Till the phone call then bingo, bloody bingo."

"Not to worry. We're through, she's through. S'over. You did it. You fooled the lot of 'em *again*. Well, maybe not these people, but they don't matter anyway."

He gave her a quick smile. "Unsatisfactory though, isn't it? It's like you said: we've been manipulated. Even the phone call was part of it – must have been – why else? Feel a bit 'used.'"

"Know what you mean. But for all their plotting, you beat 'em. Go, find a cart." She had to get rid of him.

He was glad to go. The unthinkable was emerging and demanding attention.

Succeeding s'what matters. Everybody needs luck. Nan said it was better born lucky than rich. She was right.

She was with them and she was Beth, wasn't she? The passport said so! It'd pass into Canada. After all, it had fooled perhaps the most vicious regime in the world.

He whistled quietly to himself, "Keep the home fires burning till the boys come home." His *embouche* stretched, high, as high as his spirits.

She looked at the girl. "No matter what happens, you'll give me this dress back, won't you?" She rolled the soft hem between finger and thumb. "It's borrowed and Beth's sure to ask."

Liar – doesn't even like it.

The girl snapped the compact shut and nodded.

"He likes you in it."

"You said that."

There was a little silence then Ane whispered under her breath: "I think he'd like to be with you."

"Pardon."

"Peter."

"What did you say?"

Ane looked at her, testily stroking back her hair. "I've seen you watching him. Following his every move."

Nothing he'd like better than this young girl's legs clamped round him.

As Daley returned with a complicated cart, Ane quickly pulled at the girl's sleeve. "You will return the dress, won't you?"

The girl nodded silently.

"Look what I've found," he enthused.

"Why you smiling like the cat that stole the cream?"

"These little rubber wheels under the front. They're for descending escalators! Neat, eh?" He pulled the lever a few times.

"Canadian! Wait till I tell Claire you said 'eh'; after all you've said about, 'Horses eating it!' You're up to something aren't you? What is it?"

He ignored her and glanced at the girl who was watching the carousel belt as it clunked into motion. Their big bags came skewed on the belt. Ane and the girl heaved them onto the cart.

They followed as he headed for the exit, the girl's heels clicking in step with his.

He pushed with gusto, humming to himself. Young again.

The doors slid open to a babel. Not the same throng – better dressed – but still a throng. Waving badges, taxi-drivers hustled for passengers.

Suddenly they were through and alone.

He leaned his forehead on the cart handle. The struggle had worn him out but he felt good. Out – they were out. He savored the moment.

As he turned his head sideways to smile at his companions, two shoes, polished black like mirrors, appeared under him. Spit-and-polish, he noted, recalling Mick Lister spitting and rubbing his boots Sunday evenings before returning to RAF camp.

His smile shriveled. Army? Again!

He looked at the well-dressed Chinese: blue suit, red and blue paisley tie, white shirt, black hair, knife-parted and watered, eye-closing smile. He extended a hand from a starched cuff with a military link.

Daley took it without thinking. Funny how you do that, he reflected, shooting a quizzical look at the girl. Her jaw had dropped.

She took a step backwards, regathering composure. "My uncle," she managed.

The man pumped Daley's limp arm. "Splendid! Well done. I say well done, my boy," he enthused, bringing his other hand to Daley's elbow to reinforce the shake. "I say, I'll look after Yen from here, don't you know!" the clipped voice said as he dropped Daleys hand and firmly palmed her elbow, picking up her suitcase.

"Will you be okay?" Daley stuttered.

"Rather," the uncle answered. "Absolutely splendid, what!"

Her look of sadness for lost tomorrows would stay with Daley for years.

"You'd decided to take her to Canada, hadn't you?"

"No," he managed, avoiding her glare. "I'd not - I'd not really thought about it."

"Oh no! I know you too well. That's what you wanted to tell me, wasn't it. If you want to know, I'm glad she's gone. Did you ever think what *I* was going through?"

"Yes, love. All the time. You've no idea. All the time."

She hit his shoulders with the heels of her hands. "I don't believe you. I just don't believe you."

"Yes, love."

"Don't 'yes, love' me!"

"Yes, love."

She turned away, lips working, mad tears in her eyes.

They trudged in no particular direction.

"Doesn't look at all like Ny."

She shook her head.

"Could *swear* I've seen him before, Ane. Seem to do that a

lot these days, don't we? see people we've seen before."

"You have."

He stopped and stared at her. "What'd you mean?"

"Buying silk in that market."

"In Xian?"

"No, here. Hong Kong. Two weeks ago."

"Jes. The guy who followed us you mean? You sure?"

She nodded.

"You know what that means, don't you?"

She nodded. "A set-up, the whole thing – a set-up."

"I'd be surprised if Ny knew. *The whole* thing I mean."

"Well, must have arranged to have her met. How else would her uncle know to be here?"

"Don't think so. Ny knew nothing about her disguise, did he?"

"Look for two westerners with a Chinese girl that looks like a westerner."

"But she didn't look Chinese."

"They'd know."

He shuddered at the mass of the scheme.

"If you're right and it was him, here - I mean, maybe *he* scribbled on the FAX."

"Told you *then* something was going on. Solves one problem though, doesn't it? Don't have to worry about her anymore, do we?" Her resolve not to talk to him was melting.

He nodded glumly.

"Come on, better move." She took the cart handle and pushed it faster. She was in danger of feeling sorry for him.

He followed, walking without seeing. Everywhere was clean, full of french-fries. God, she was hungry.

She stole a glance at him and ran into another cart.

The Chinaman pushing the cart turned and the young pilot now in the basket swung a 747 balloon in his hand, back and forth with glee as if to launch it.

Ane apologized and the three adults smiled and sing-songed: "No ploblem."

As they went by, the boy stood and bonked Daley on the head with the jumbo-jet. A quick cuff on the ear by a relative and the balloon, released with shock and wail, floated to the floor. Daley bent, picked it up and gave it to the squalling pilot but he had lost interest.

They waited their turn at the automatic doors.

Ane moved over the rubber mat, thankful he was still there and the girl was not.

It had bitten hard. Hurts heal, Nan used to say, dreams never do.

They were staying at the Regent Hotel and would dine with Greg that evening. He had persuaded them to risk style – to be pampered by one of the world's most exotic hotels.

A tall Commissionaire with a welcoming smile cleared a path to the palatial Regent desk.

Their name was *there*.

A Rolls-Royce of prewar vintage was waved up and they were motioned in.

Gone! Again!

Ane sat silent. She took his hand.

Leather, walnut, peace, and Fauré's "Afternoon of a Faun" cocooned them. They went past piled shops, moored ships, and lingering lovers, along Princess Margaret Road, down Chatham to Salisbury. A Volkswagen muttered beside them at a light.

"Punch-buggy blue, no punchbacks." She playfully hit his arm in their children's game on seeing a "bug."

He smiled wanly as the Rolls turned up an imposing drive fringed with shrubs of red flowers and small trees with white Christmas lights.

They smoothed to a stop and three burgundy uniforms opened the doors, bowed and spirited away the bags.

In the lobby: thick Chinese rugs, marble floors, voices muffled by wall hangings. The harbour side was all glass: tall windows full of silently moving ships, dark water, and far-away buildings.

With no fuss a pretty girl in a red uniform eased off his coat and withdrew with a curtsey.

A discreet Grandfather clock chimed. Daley searched and found it, guarding deep chairs and glass tables in an intimate corner.

"Champagne, Sir? Madam?" A steward, white towel over his arm, silver tray of fizzing on his hand.

"Peter. Don't you think it's weird?"

"What?"

"Well, she was met and taken off."

"Didn't think you wanted to talk about it."

"I think she knew."

There was a little silence.

"He was very grand, her uncle."

Daley was very pale.

"Why don't you take one of Gypsum's pills – the ones for depression."

"And get a hard on?"

"Chance'd be fine thing. No, the other ones."

"Must be taken with food."

"Think they're serving tea over there. I've seen girls carrying silver trays in and out," she pointed out.

He followed her past a massive spray of dried flowers to the island of deep-piled green carpet, spindly gold chairs, tables with heavy linen cloths, and tall potted trees with leaves stretching for light towards the frescoed roof. Above in a hidden balcony, a small orchestra was playing, "We'll Gather Lilacs.".

They ordered Earl Grey and sat listening to a prewar medley.

A bellboy in a white uniform circulated the tables holding a chalk message board high.

They sat in silence.

"I don't understand," she said suddenly. "The way I see it, Ny's just a lowly Associate Professor. How does he rate such connections?"

"S'over now, love," he mumbled, licking his fingers.

"Really burns me, being used."

"Look. We went in, we came out," he said, unfolding his fingers one at a time, to propel his words. "You were convinced we should help, remember? So for whatever reason, now she's safe."

"You took a shine to her Peter, didn't you?"

"Who wouldn't? She's an old man's dream – an old man's dream."

The "room" was a suite. The bathroom opened to the right off the entrance hall and connected to the bedroom. It was opulent to decadence: white marble and gold sunken tub with peripheral countersunk seats and sidetables lined with tall bottles that matched the white marble floor.

"Sheepskin," he breathed, running his fingers through the toilet cover. "Sheepskin bloody everywhere!"

"Lambswool. See. Do it again." She ran her palm along the tight white curls. "Much softer."

"God, from pissing on stinking stones to pissing in lambswooled porcelain." He gave the golden lever a jerk and water whooshed contentedly.

"I could live in here. The hell with the rest!"

He turned the golden lion's-head taps of the bath and a waterfall cascaded from a black marble chute almost hidden in foliage.

She swished her hand in the water. "Makes me feel so dirty. Can't wait to get out of these clothes and sink into it. Feel as if I've had 'em on a month!"

They padded to the bedroom. Walk-in closets, shoe racks, sliding drawers, tie racks; all lined, hung and folded with their few effects. There was even an electric trouser press.

Wish I'd known, thought Ane, perusing her underclothes tidy in an open draw. I'd have made sure they were clean.

Shoes were shined, socks balled and shirts ironed.

"How'd they have time to do all this, Peter? We only had tea."

"S'pect they know everybody'll have champagne at least. Even if they don't, I suppose the desk can take enough time over registration. Impressive isn't it."

She nodded.

The sitting room was full of friendly furniture.

He felt an overwhelming urge, leg and back aching, to lie down. In a daze, he returned to the bedroom. "Gotta sleep," he managed as he collapsed on the bed and shuffled up to the pillow.

She gently removed his jacket then his shoes without bothering with the laces. He murmured objection but was out of it. She folded the counterpane over him and patted his bum. Rest well, my love.

Black. He closed his eyes and opened them again, still black but with faint lights shivering on the wall.

He unthreaded his legs. She must have done this, he reflected, dropping the down-filled comforter.

Through the open door, ghostly light danced.

Ane was in the shower singing above the rattling water.

A tall window stopped him dead at the door. Dusk, blooding the sky, was threaded with moving lights – with shadows – an everchanging firework display that never fell, just hung, wafting, twinkling across the bay from piles of flickering buildings on the far shore. Above, a comet tail oranged behind an aircraft in the dying sky.

Hong Kong! Hong Kong in the window like a colossal Christmas tree.

He fumbled a cigar from the Tueros box Ane had put out for him.

A moment promised. Through all the crap, he'd promised himself *this*.

Habit turned on the radio.

"See the pyramids along the Nile
 See the sunset on a tropic isle."

Jo Stafford.

"Just remember, darling, all the while
You belong to me."

He sang along under his breath, rolling the cigar in his fingers.

The cacophony of the world grumbled outside but the melody floated unaware.

A deep rumble shook the glass as he watched the back of a jumbo jet clawing into the sky above a winking-necklace freeway not a mile away.

Against the backdrop of neon signs - Foster's, Canon, Goldstar, Hitachi, Nikon, Coke, NEC and TDK – the shrouds of a darkened ship slowly swung, mid-channel. A tug chugged silently between, pulling house-backed barges laden with containers and spindley, double-gantry cranes. There were no seagulls. One large, black bird swooped the white debris between small and large ships as they were pulled and pushed. Daley watched the silent hustling world cramped on the toe of China.

"Quit for a minute, love, and sit." He puffed smoke into the air above her. "My, you look nice."

The suede suit with Scottish blouse looked smart.

"Shame you don't wear the Indian dress, Greg's never seen it."

"Don't have it anymore, do I?" She turned to the window, determined not to be impressed, but it wasn't possible. It was as if the night sky had fallen into the bay, a multicoloured twinkling carpet.

He bent and kissed the top of her head. "Let's not fight, love. The bloody nightmare's over. Let's enjoy. How you feeling?"

"Stiff."

"Wish I was," he said playfully.

"Bad sod," she pretend–scolded. "You'd not know what to do if it was!"

So they sat comfortably in silence.

"You know what I enjoyed most," she said suddenly. "The shower. I mean, you could feel the wet places to dry 'cos they were cold. Like home. Couldn't do that in China, you were cold all over!"

They chuckled together.

At the bottom of the daily polished stairs, a Laura Ashley receptionist guided them to a couch to wait while tasting canapés and sipping champagne. The heavy smell of exotic flowers and the far sounds of strings massaged their air. An ornate clock said 7:30. Greg was late, but there again, he always was.

When he did arrive with pink cheeks and puckish blue eyes, the orchestra was playing Grieg.

In the shush of Norwegian sea and aroma of jungle blooms, Greg told of his arrival.

"Close inspection of my documents. Revealed my reservation for the Prince Edward away from all this." He waved at the window. "So, I took a Regent room, on-spec. ' Four-hundred US dollars for a single, sir,' the neat, wool haired lady told me, not looking up, pecking her computer. I accepted, of course, and sat down, champagne in hand, to wait. In no time at all, a wonderful smile. ' I've upped you to a suite, sir – no extra charge – the Plaza Suite. Will that be satisfactory?' Well, " he sighed, "what could I say?"

Better born lucky than rich, Nan murmured in Daley's ear.

"I see you appreciate this," Greg motioned to the outside. "One fears its survival, I'm afraid. At the opening of a new nightclub, the Chinese Governor-General-In-Waiting assured everybody that dancing in public would be permitted. The term 'permitted' worries me. Portentous of Jesuitical tolerance!"

"Officialdom's always with us, Greg. Army, Immigration, Customs – in your face at every corner!"

"Ah, Customs. interesting Customs episodes."Greg put down his champagne glass so that it could be refilled immediately.

"I'm sure all travellers are replete with them. My arrival at Milan airport nine years ago – I know it was nine years for my son was two – takes the biscuit. I went two weeks ahead and my wife, knowing Italy, had me carry a large pack of diapers. The macho miniature Customs man wouldn't believe my claim. He spoke no English, so I mimed the adornment of a diaper to explain. This can be graphically achieved, let me say, overcoat high, hands sliding suggestively about. The line were entertained. They clapped and laughed, rendering the little man more adamant! 'Where's the baby?' he demanded in Italian, palms out, appealing to the gathering crowd and exaggeratedly peering into my bags and under the counters. 'With his mother! ' I answered, totally exasperated. 'Coming in two weeks!' Getting nowhere! Next, from thin air, he was hit by a handbag. A black shawled, tiny grandma was swinging at him repeatedly. ' Of course, he has a baby, you oaf!' she was shouting in Italian as she aimed blows at his head. She effectively deflated his bombast. I stood in shock, coat hoisted, before the delighted audience. After much arm waving and octave changing, he let me pass!"

Hors-d'oeuvres were served at whim then soup was ladled from a large silver tureen on a heated trolley and placed individually by the girl assigned to each guest.

"Don't we know that woman?" Daley asked Ane, looking up from his cream of squash with its float of mint and chrysant flower.

She followed his look.

"It's that President's wife,"she said with surprise. "You remember, that man in Beijing. I've a good memory for faces. It's her."

"What's she doing here?"

"Sending over a hostess, looks like."

A nubile girl swished up and whispered in Ane's ear.

She carefully folded her napkin and excused herself. Immediately an attendant pulled back her chair.

Daley watched her join the statuesque wife.

He half listened to Greg describing his China visit. He had insisted on staying at the Beijing Hotel and bought a knobbly wool sweater to fight the cold.

The wife didn't jibe, like a mourner at a wedding. Maybe she'd just noticed Ane; after all, they'd been thick as thieves at that dinner.

He was just launching into their adventures when Ane returned. She was pale and moving jerkily.

"You just won't believe it!" She passed him a small box spilling tissue from its open top. He pushed the paper aside. A glass apple, a glass apple with a horse painted inside, a glass apple swinging from a mahogany branch!

A live crab, hanging by its large claw, was dipped in the bubbling copper pot.

Daley couldn't watch.

White flesh, winkled perfectly, was dipped in Champagne, coated with lemon sauce, nested in watercress, and served on gold china.

"*Decies repetita placebit.* You know, there are still places in the world that do things *right!*" he declared with a quiet clap of his hands, savoring the epicurean precision.

Ane picked at her portion.

Odd, Daley thought. She loves crab, always chooses it when available.

"You okay, love?"

She smiled quickly, then looked down again.

Greg threw up his hands: "Ah, the wonders of *haute cuisine*! Delicious!"

Dinner culminated in fizzing champagne in very tall glasses as Hennesey flambéed generous Creme Caramels.

Well dined and relaxed, they reminisced of their world, watching the urgent ships of another, pacing the window in the exotic night.

Ane listened, silent.

The room smelled of stale cigar.

Daley's curiousity bested his desperation to pee. "What'd she say, love? I've never seen you so - "

"She thanked us for saving *her* daughter!"

VII
HONG KONG - CIRCLES CLOSE

"*H*er daughter?" He stammered, stunned. "You realise that means she's *his* daughter too, that arsehole!"

She nodded.

He couldn't believe it. The magnitude of it, the massive bloody magnitude of it! Jesus!

Ane hissed a can of hair spray into the air. "It's better! Should have known. Definitely wasn't a Ny, was she?"

He banged his fist on the table, rocking the radio. "Boy, were we set up!"

She felt guilty. She had insisted they help, had rough-shod his reluctance. If anything, *she'd* manipulated *him*. Made sense now - the banquet, the wife's worry about teenagers. She stood behind him, circling her arms round his neck. "She must have gone back to buy that apple in Bojai. No wonder it was gone."

He turned to the sizzle of champagne as she placed a glass beside him. She squeezed his hand. "Let's drink to home, love. To the kids, the dogs, Cape Croker next spring. By then this'll be a dream."

"There's so much I don't understand. Where's poor old Ny fit into all this?"

"Probably had to go along. After all, President's his boss?"

"When I look back, God, we must have been stupid, walking

round, eyes open, *blind*! Hell, she even looks like her mother."

"Look, we accepted what we were told. Everybody does. Too much trouble not to really! Can you imagine goin' through life, believing nothing's what it seems?"

He rocked the chair, cradling the glass in his lap. "Still, to tell the truth, should have smelled a rat when that 'aunt' in Bojai, turned out not to be ill, even warned you about the woman."

"Don't blame yourself. If we'd made a fuss we might still be there, in clink with the chinks!" She giggled. "She was in danger. Those soldiers were terrifying. They had real guns and would have used 'em. I don't know who was after her or why and don't really care now. You got her out in spite of 'em. You should be proud."

"Aye. A bloody elephant in a china shop, keeping 'em occupied trying to save the porcelain!"

He stayed, swaying in the rocking chair, glass fizzing contentedly on the table.

"Aren't you coming to bed?" He turned his watch to the window – 11.30.

"Not yet. Think I'll just sit."

Must be her uncle's brother. Couldn't be her mother's, she was an American Indian. They'd seen him in Hong Kong. Jes.

He'd probably been sent to spy on them. He must have written on the FAX, but why be so damned cryptic?

They must have been there too and had access.

He struggled the pieces together – forcing, failing, starting again. The FAX came from Montreal. That city had come in somewhere else. The bureaucrat. The smooth with the sister that didn't like flying and who had no baby.

He shook his head to clear it.

"Can't you at least turn the radio down?" Ane pleaded from the bed. He ignored her.

Her husband was in Montreal, they'd said. That was it! He'd probably sent it. But why the hell should he?

The girl had been too friendly for a stranger on the aircraft.

He'd been puzzled at the time.

Maybe the sister wasn't a stranger. So where's that get you? Bloody nowhere. The FAX was to put us *off* visiting. The girl needed *us* there.

Dead-end!

He stood for a minute before the window, not seeing its firefly swarm.

Who was he? SHL's boss? The bureaucrat's boss?

Must have had the passport stolen. Insurance, in case we ignored the FAX. Backfired when he got Beth's, didn't it? Still, they didn't know that. Must have thought he'd stymied us.

He sat down with a sigh. Better go back to Choi.

In the muddled office of the September afternoon, Choi'd warned him to watch for the President. Political animal, he'd said. That explained his hostility anyway. Couldn't be nice to a Canadian, could he, after the country had let all the Chinese students become refugees.

Concentrate.

The rocker squeaked. He braced against the floor to quiet it.

He'd also warned him to avoid people he didn't know. Not have people in the party that shouldn't be there. That was it!

That was why she was Ny's daughter, so there was no problem! Could travel with them, couldn't she? He would have objected if she'd just been parachuted in as a stranger! Of course. That's why they did it that way. Ny's daughter. What could be more natural!

God, talk about chalk and bloody cheese!

We noticed but accepted it anyway - like Ane says - too much trouble not to!

He watched the progress of a barge, squinting through the lines of bubbles in his glass – one spawning another, like threads of thought.

Ny *had* been surprised to see them. Made sense now. If the uncle had read the FAX. Must have. Wrote on it, didn't he? He'd have told the President we weren't coming.

Daley shivered as he remembered the long wait at Beijing

airport. Ny'd turned up in open shirt and sandals in spite of the cold, then taken them to a tomb.

They were not expected.

Back to Choi. Concentrate on Choi, hands behind his head, tilted back in his chair. He'd talked of how he couldn't go to China because he was *persona non grata*. He had warned about the President of the university. Not like the previous one, he'd said.

Wait.

They were daggers drawn, the President and his predecessor? He'd been a friend of Choi, the previous President, dethroned because of Tiananmen.

He had been hurt.

Daley was wide awake now.

The Vice President! He hated his successor. Had got hurt, Choi'd said. The limp...*the old man with the stick...Long John bloody Silver*!

He sat back, holding the wobbling image. Christ! The man in the Mercedes on the photograph, the man sticking down the theatre steps, directing the army. Been there every time, hadn't he? They just hadn't seen him.

But why'd he do it?

Face! Whenever you don't understand the Orient - try loss of face! Arrest the girl, *his* daughter, embarrass the shit out of *him*!

Excited, he half rose to go tell her, but gentle snores filled the dark so he sat down.

Let her sleep. God knows she needs it!

The girl came by again and he stared bleakly out the window till she receded.

Why'd she been so hell bent to get out? She loved Beijing, her friends, the excitement. Ane knew but wouldn't tell him. Just wouldn't tell him. Maybe a woman thing. He shook his head vigorously. Cheap shot. Heard his wife accusing, "Chauvinist!"

Her sunrise smile, eyes to drown in. Oh, you poor old fool. An old horse watching the young stride. Feeling forgotten muscles, recapturing delicious restlessness.

Old - that's what hurt. Known all the time, hadn't she? Must have, bloody must have. Sidelong looks, flashing smiles.

His nose wrinkled as if suddenly in sour air.

The moon was sitting on the shoulder of the hills. He had not noticed its arrival.

Was it possible she didn't know her father's plan? Nah. Not letting her off that lightly.

It was quiet; all that activity beyond the window and it was deathly still, except for murmuring radio violins.

Was it possible? Why'd she acquiesced to DHS on that cold river bank? Ane didn't think so, but he was sure.

Maybe she was enjoying it, he tortured himself.

He filled his empty glass.

The real pisser was that all the effort had been for the arsehole President!

Bubbles pricked his nose as he sipped the busy liquid. Like a chess problem. Wonder how you could have missed the obvious.

The moon closed its eye.

Sunday November 5

Ane had started packing.

She always reorganised everything they had before a long journey.

He shuffled to the gold and marble bathroom. "Hot water and it's past time!" He laughed.

He stared at the mirror: old eyes - grey-yellow, rheumy – eyes of an old man, overnight.

"Well, I don't know about you," she said, wiping her mouth of breakfast and piling the napkin onto her plate. "I'm going to finish my Custom's list and then go shopping. Got to find something for the kids. Must be some shops open, even on Sunday, and we do have a few hours, don't we?"

He nodded.

"You have a pen, Peter? This one won't write."

"Sure."

He clicked his four-colour pen and took it to her.

"This is green!"

"Doesn't matter, does it? I mean, it's only for you; s'not official."

"S'funny for this hotel."

"What?"

"Having a dud pen." He tried the ballpoint on his palm. "Everything's been so perfect. You'd think they'd check."

"Can't check everything," she murmured, head down.

He dropped the empty pen on the sidetable.

"Thought you wanted to go shopping."

"I'm almost finished. I'll pack when we get back. Let's go. Can't believe *you want* to go shopping," she laughed over her shoulder.

The Regent was attached to a mall of shops by overhead walkways. A window caught his eye and they entered to examine a porcelain: a boy riding a water-buffalo, hat round his neck, joyful arm up for balance. Laid out in another glass case were fifty-two copulating figurines in various stages of seventeenth century undress, rutting shamelessly. He turned away hastily as Ane came over from a Royal Doulton display.

"Nowt in here," he said, self-conciously. "Off to graze in there." He nodded at a tailor shop.

She tried a door - locked. Shirts with built-in back-packs had taken her fancy.

On her knees scrubbing, the proprietor of the next shop laughed: "That's a family business. Always opens late, Sundays."

He glanced at his watch – 9.50. "Well, that's that. Don't worry, we'll find something at the airport, we always do."

The flight was at one-o-clock and it was only ten.

Packing was still to do so she reluctantly accompanied him back.

Ane made space for the water-buffalo-riding boy in the open suitcase.

"Time is it now, Peter?"

"Twenty after ten."

"I'm off back to that shop. Maybe opened at ten-thirty. Finish this when I get back. I'll be quick. Promise. You'll be all right, won't you? Hour at the most. Oh," she chuckled, "better take me glasses this time."

He said nonchalantly: "I'm a big boy now. Think I'll laze in that opulent tub. May never get another chance. Promise I'll be good. Honest."

Home today. He tried to think about the dogs, walks in November fields, capaccino, Canada; but all roads led back to *her*. His throat constricted.

His leg and back slowly yielded to the warm stream in the shower as he stood, squeezing the tiny shampoo bottle and watching the contents dribble onto his palm He hummed to himself. Should've turned up the radio, he decided, straining to hear Judy Collins singing "Send in the Clowns." He mouthed the words with her.

"Isn't it queer? Are we a pair? You with your feet on the ground, me in mid air."

Another silly bugger he reflected, soaping his hair.

Another sound.

"Maybe next year..."

Again.

He stopped rubbing and listened. The song ceased.

Someone was knocking at the door. Cleaners, knocking to check before coming in.

He went back to the foam, washing it off.

Again, more persistent. Why don't they just come in? Must have a key. He felt for a towel, eyes tightly shut, leaned out, eyes open, and pulled the towel robe off the door. It fell to the ground.

"Shit!"

He stepped out, picked it up and struggled into it, inadvertently pushing the belt down its wide sleeve. Stop with the bloody door already!

He grabbed the knob and jerked it open. "You don't have to

keep knocking! Just come in..." His words trailed away.

In the dim hall stood the girl.

Breath was punched from his stomach. He stared speechless, gripping the door knob so hard it hurt.

"I came to return the dress," she said with a nervous smile as she held the brown paper bag.

"Ane's not here. Gone shopping."

She looked away, feet shuffling.

"You have it on, anyways, the dress."

She nodded, hands running her sides. "Like it. Like the feel of it. Wanted to wear it as long as possible."

She pirouetted slowly, flairing the skirt and lifting the little crucifix round her neck.

A distant ring. Insistent.

He turned. "Just a minute."

He walked in a trance and sat on the bed.

"Peter?"

"Greg. Oh, hi!"

"Just thought I'd wish you *bon voyage*. Back to the land of Mounties and mountains today, aren't you? Wasn't last night delicious?"

"Yes, wasn't it?" He replied vaguely "Just like you said."

"Indeed, indeed. Well. See you at the Gordon Conference next July?"

"Sure. Yes, see you there. Going back today too, aren't you?"

"Um..."

"Have a good trip. Don't drink too many free First Class drinks." What a bloody daft thing to say!

"You too. Regards to Ane. *Bon chance*."

"Thanks."

Click.

Christ, he'd left her standing at the door!

It was shut.

She'd gone!

The dress? He quickly scanned the closet beside the door. Nothing.

He groaned. Gone. She'd gone. Come back and gone. The rocker creaked.

He turned to find her sitting at the window.

"Wonderful, wonderful," she murmured to herself.

"Should see it at night."

"I can imagine. *Feng shui*."

"What?"

"*Feng shui* - designing with nature." She painted the air with flowing fingers. "'Wind and Water.' Building in concert with nature, mountains behind, water in front. This city was designed to feel right, still does. Chinese *feng shui* is very important here."

There was a small silence. He feverishly searched for something to say.

"I never expected to see you again," he said finally.

She smiled quickly and turned back to the window.

"Met your mother last night," he finally managed.

"You must think us awful."

"Don't think anything, really," he lied.

"I went to school here, you know."

"Hong Kong?"

"Stayed wid me uncle. Went to St. Patrick's. The nuns taught me."

"Really? Me too."

She glanced in surprise.

"Not - not here. In Ireland - and England, I mean. Used to be a Catholic."

"Me favourite was Sister Mary Winifred. She came from Ireland."

Whispers and giggles flashed into his head from nowhere.

"Pavlova."

She paled. "What you say?"

"Oh, nothing. Something I overheard is all."

"They called me that at the convent school. Awful girls. Just jealous. One time, I thought I'd be a nun. So clean. Such a simple life."

Pears and the brogue, he sighed to himself.

"She was always talking about going back. Sister Mary Winifred. They all did."

"The Irish always do."

"She taught me English. Very kind, Sister Mary Winifred. Gave me sweets when I did well. My favourites were fruit gums."

He grinned. "I noticed. Would you like a coffee? Sorry, cup's not clean. S'only had coffee in it though. Lukewarm I'm afraid, but still drinkable, I think. Tell me, Sister Winifred ever tell you where she came from... in Ireland, I mean?"

"Galway."

"She ever talk of Innisfree?"

"'I will rise and go now, and go to Innisfree.'"

"Yeats. Went there, you know. County Sligo. Visited his grave at Drumcliffe. Lovely, lonely country. His poems are not surprising when you see where he came from."

Her eyes danced with pleasure. "Did you really? She loved Yeats, Sister Mary Winifred. Taught me to love him too."

There was another awkard silence.

"I tried to visit Innisfree. S'not there you know. Doesn't exist."

"Made me learn by heart she did. Best way to learn English, says she."

The spoon rattled faintly in the saucer. He realised she was trembling.

"We leave today - this afternoon."

"Can you ever forgive me - us?" She watched the swirls spinning the spoon in her cup. "Poor Ny. My father forced him. I'm an embarrassment to him - my father."

"I don't understand," he said carefully: "I mean, the man at the airport. Your uncle. Your father's brother?"

She nodded.

The faraway whoop of the warship reached through the glass. He glanced out. The busy bay was blue, the far skyscrapers clear as if close - the calm before a storm

"A Professor of English Literature at Hong Kong University. Now in Tokyo, at the University of Tokyo, I think. He was sent to watch you."

Sent! The uncle was bloody sent! Sent to bloody watch them! No wonder he'd been familiar. The Hong Kong market.

"Explains the warning on the FAX."

She fiddled with the crucifix then asked again, hand venturing towards his arm: "Can you ever forgive us?"

He shrugged and looked away.

"He only wanted to help. Decided to watch out for you, without you knowing. Started in Japan but he missed you."

Daley whistled. "That far back! Not even *arrived* in China!"

"I know. Awful isn't it? He saw the message and realised *they* must have had sent it. Saw your friend pick it up so knew you'd left."

"We saw him in Hong Kong...*here*...in the market. Thought he might be following us."

She took a sip of coffee. "He had to warn you but daren't frighten you. You see, you *had to* come to China. He thought it was over when your passport was stolen. Phoned my father not to expect you, then saw you on the plane."

She returned her cup to the window-ledge. "He was puzzled. Then realised you must have had another passport. He didn't have time to warn Beijing, so you surprised 'em."

"You can say that again!"

She leaned forward.

"You're telling me we surprised 'em! That's when the cold started. We sat in it for two hours."

"I'm sorry."

He looked away. God, when she smiles...

"The *others* saw you too!"

"The Mercedes?"

She nodded.

"So both sides started 'even-steven.'"

He was appalled. The whole bloody visit, from time bloody zero. A setup! "And you knew nothing about it?"

Their eyes met for a moment. "Only that I was to go to Bojai as Ny's 'daughter' cos your party could travel freely, that's all. I thought it was silly. Didn't want to leave Beijing at all but I was an embarrassment, you see. He was vulnerable, my father. I was his Achille's heel."

Pompous prick. Bloody deserves it. Wish he'd got it!

"DHS?"

"My father's factotum."

"But he was attacking you on that river bank, wasn't he?"

She twined her fingers together so tight her knuckles went white. "No, he was warnin' me. About the woman."

"SHL."

She nodded.

"Do you mean to say you knew about her and him all the time and didn't tell us?"

"Awful, wasn't I?"

"And your pants?"

Her hands went to her mouth; she coloured and looked away. "You saw."

"Sure I saw. Anyone would."

"His idea. Said it'd look more real."

"God, you went to a lot of trouble!"

She looked at her nervous fingers. "How could I tell you? You'd never have helped me, would you?"

He stared at her bowed head, anger rising. She was right. That was the bloody trouble. He wouldn't have done it – any of it! God, why could women read him so easily? Was he so obvious?

"He told me I couldn't stay, that my only hope was to stay with you. T'was only a matter of time. Once you left, they'd have arrested me."

Her eyes were shining, close to tears.

He leaned forward and enveloped her hand. She turned with a small smile, looking the look he'd caught her looking sometimes. His throat filled and he sheepishly started to remove his fingers but hers followed, holding, gently pinching, touching his very finger ends.

"Can I ask you about the passport? How did it just turn up?"

"My uncle. Stole it back when I couldn't stay in Bojai. Gave it to DHS, who gave it to Ny, who gave it to you with the others at Xian airport."

That's why he missed the lecture that day - off in Xian to pick up the passport.

"And the man with the stick?"

"Dong Lin."

"That's his name. Think Choi mentioned him."

"My uncle's friend Choi?"

He squeezed so hard, she pulled her fingers away with a squeak. "Choi.Choi." he repeated like a child, refusing to accept.

"They went to the University of Minnesota together."

Choi. Choi. His laughing, roly-poly friend. Not possible. He really had been coming, had told him about it in spring, long before Tiananmen. Had warned him to stay away from things political.

Since the very beginning. Even before the very beginning!

She was staring at him, squeezing his fingers. "You all right? You look like you've seen a ghost."

"Okay, really. Just had a terrible thought is all."

He decided not to tell her and glanced away out the window. "The bureaucrat?"

"Dong Lin's son, Wong." She wrinkled her nose as if in a bad smell. "Used to like him, but now he's too smooth altogether. Joined the other side at Tiananmen." He felt her fingers tremble.

There was a silence Daley hesitated to break.

"Liked his sister though. The girl on the plane. She really was flying for the first time and was frightened."

He picked up the fork and drew spirals in the congealed bacon grease.

"Can I ask you something?"

She looked at him, eyes shining.

"Why? Why'd we do all this? Why was it so desperate you get out of China?"

"I told you on the bus."

"You told Ane."

"Did you see the statue?"

"The student's one?"

She nodded.

"Yes. Well, not close up, but I did see it."
"Did you see her smile?"
"No, not close."
"Well, if you had, you would see it was special. My friend...he said...well...I would be remembered...a thousand years."
"The smile?"
"Yes."
"So they *knew* and that's why – "
"That's why."

A knock.

Her mouth dropped. She glanced quickly at the door, at him, eyes wide, withdrawing her hand swiftly. "Your wife?"

He shook his head.

She picked up the paper bag and ran into the bedroom; vacated chair rocking.

The thunderheads had crept up behind the hills, greying the swells and shading the swinging warship. Yesterday's storm.

He straightened his robe. The spell was broken.

"Clear up, sir?" A voice in the dim of the door.

Room service. He nodded as the courteous boy slid past.

He felt cold, realised he was naked under the robe and damp to boot, so he clicked the door shut and turned into the bathroom to finish drying and get dressed.

Towelling, humming Judy Collins, he hit the yellow bruise on his calf. He smiled grimly, recalling the fracas. Seemed weeks ago, the day before yesterday! He towelled it gently.

A swish of cold air hit his bum.

He swung round, towel up.

She was standing, bag in hand, at the door to the bedroom. The bag dropped with a muffled squeak.

"Oh, glory be! I'm so sorry. F-f-forgive me," she flustered, knee-bending quickly for the bag.

"No, Yen. Wait. Please. Wait.." He tied the towel round. "Don't. Don't leave yet."

She hesitated.

Quickly picking up the piled robe and fighting into its sleeves, he walked behind her and gently cupped her elbow.

A sudden inhale.

"Please," he said in her ear. "Please, please don't leave yet. There's so much more."

He went to touch her hair but his courage failed. "Sorry," he mumbled, sitting down heavily on the toilet cover, head in hands. "I don' know. I just...I just wanted to talk."

Sudden wildflowers. Gentle towelling back and forthing his hair, head in her midriff. "Wisht now alanah. Wisht. T'is aw'right. T'is aw'right, so t'is."

She dropped the towel and covered his hands.

Leather, woman, soft. He leaned to her, relaxing, fevered heart pounding his ears.

He slid his hands from hers and she bent to him, supple as a sapling.

She stroked his damp hair, lifting strands, straightening them, making little sounds.

He felt her flex.

God, he was hard!

His knees tightened desperately.

She shivered.

Nose buried in tassels, eyes tight, timid fanning fingers following a long distant drummer, he shifted - *it* hurt.

She was swaying, humming puppy pules, fingers push-combing like purring cat paws.

Smother, suede, ears full of sea surf, close noises.

Sudden cold..Oh, God! Popped! He'd popped.

Free! Stretching the cool air.

She *knew*! Had to!

She pressed harder.

Gracefully, gently, she flowed onto him, hands tousling his hair. Wince...

Gently, easy.

Rough pain.

Don't care.

Cheeks in his hands as smooth as porcelain.

Sudden yield...wetness, warmness... yielding velvets. Push... stretch...stretch to forever, deep, deeper, so deep, spasms clamp. Stroking, sliding, breath shortening.

Something cold on his chest - the crucifix - keeping time, impotently forbidding.

Slow down. Easy. Stop! STOP.

Surprise...Oh.

From a long way, deep, delicious, gathering, luscious rushing, erupting, toe tingling.

Here love. Oh, love. Here, here's it all, all for you... forever!

She bit his tongue.

Silence.

Sounds. Sounds of faraway ships.

He raised his eyes, easing forward surreptitiously, gingerly testing his tongue. Salt.

She was sobbing softly.

"Quiet, little one. Quiet." He stroked her hair.

She trapped her curls, painting him on the nose with a giggle.

He stirred again.

A little squeak and she was gone.

Stunned. He sat.

She must have heard something.

He listened. Nothing.

A muffled siren.

He sat, head in hands, hearing her return: "Thank you. Thank you for everything."

He looked up but she wasn't there.

Up and after but his back kicked him double. He grabbed the sink, leaning, probing the ache.

A door closed.

Gone.

He strained straight, brittle as old china, and drew a deep breath.

'If God invented owt better, he kept it to his sen!' Mick Lister said from all those years ago.

Got that right, Mick. Bloody right!

The dress was on the bed. He rolled its tassels in his face... wildflowers.

He dropped it with a shrug and looked at his watch. 11.05. Jes.

He stood quickly, rolled it into a ball and started stuffing it into the case. Mustn't be seen, was all he could think, kneading at it.

Won't work.

He closed the case, tipped it over and reopened it, bottom-up. The pile of papers slid sideways. Page by page he carefully rebuilt the pile, then took the dress and, in one fluid motion, laid it on top, pulled the case body over, tucking in recalcitrant cuffs and whipped the zip part-way round. Then, with a heave, he returned it, opened the top and sat, finger-combing the hair from his eyes, panting.

He leaned backwards on his hands and a tight tube of a magazine rolled onto one.

Time. *The* Time.

He reverse-rolled it and idly riffled the pages.

Thought we'd lost this. Must've turned up when Ane emptied the bags.

Shit! Ane! He dropped the magazine and launched off the bed as if stung, grabbing his lower back as he did.

The door. Ane gave him a light kiss as he took her bags and lay them on the table, guiding her away from the bathroom as if the tryst still hung the air.

Out the wall-window, a barge, dray tugs worrying round like pups, ploughed past the lonely, black bird. Spooked, it rose slowly, end feathers rippling the choppy black wake, waving. Goodbye little one. He turned away, eyes filling.

"Got those shirts!" She announced triumphantly, fussing around the bed.

"Kids'll love 'em. Not sure 'bout Eddie's though. Might be too big. Still, it's done."

She folded it, went to lay it in the case and stopped dead. A loosely-rolled magazine was curled on the case top.

Time?

She'd been.

Returned the dress. Must be hung up.

She went to the closet. Empty.

A winter door opened.

She scanned the room, checked under the bed. Nothing.

Taking a deep breath, she insinuated her hand down the side of the case until she felt the stiff board of his 'stuff.' Not there! Delicious relief.

Liked it too much so kept it. Probably told him and he'll tell me when he remembers.

Couldn't wear it again anyway.

The rain arrived in large, thudding drops. Daley turned up his coat collar as they ran down the Regent prospect to a cab, followed, in spite of objections, by the Major Domo, huge black umbrella like a crow flapping above them, bellboy cart squeaking after.

She had not spoken since they checked out. He was worried she knew but didn't know how. Deep in his pocket, he found the Bojai stone. His breath caught. Would she *ever* leave?

He wondered should he tell her about Choi and decided not to. Didn't matter now.

The ANA aircraft was the same as had brought them two weeks ago; or at least it was the same crew. Daley recognised a demure Japanese stewardess.

"Penultimate passage," he announced as he sat and searched for his belt.

"Still have the loonie?"

He pinched his fob pocket. "Still worried about money," he joshed, poking her with his elbow.

She reached into the brown bag, emerged with the magazine, and rerolled it backwards.

"Time turned up," he observed. "Thought we'd lost it."

"Here." She held the open periodical upside down and pointed at a scene of milling students around tents. "Recognise her?" Her finger wavered round a white statue against a blue sky.

He put on his glasses and stared.

"Her!"

"She tried to tell you."

"That stuff about Liberty?"

She nodded.

"Christ! The Statue with the torch. What was she, the model?"

"Boyfriend was a sculptor, remember?"

"Told us that, too, didn't she?"

She nodded.

"Recognisable among billions. Explains the scarf."

"So now you know. You know why I couldn't tell you."

"No wonder she had to get out," he observed, grudgingly admitting he'd have run a bloody mile if he'd known.

He probed his cut tongue and looked out the far window. The sun was sitting in the apron pocket of a dark cloud.

He turned, smiled quickly at her, looked back to the page and frowned. The margin was smudged, as though fingered often. Depressed scribbled lines piled the bottom corner of the page betraying attempts to activate a ballpoint. He rotated the page and tipped it at the window. There was writing in the swirls but it was indecipherable. He turned on the reading light, canted the page and could make out some words.

His hand went to his shirt pocket, then he remembered. "You still got me pen?"

She searched her bag and passed it, tiny green nose showing. "Sorry, meant to give it back."

He pumped a lead and stroked the impressed lines. The lead broke, he pumped more. Words emerged.

"But one woman loved the pilgrim soul in you."

He rotated the page and adjusted his glasses.

"And loved the sorrows of your changing face."

Yeats, he sighed.

The pen had suddenly started to work, green, firm, line wandering in and out of the print, across the spine to bold writing.

"Just know *I* love you. Always have, always will."

The magazine slipped from his fingers.

She steepled her fingers through his arm and smiled.

Quebec, Canada
2001